A RIDE OF PERIL

A SHADE OF VAMPIRE, BOOK 46

BELLA FORREST

A Blaze of Sun (Book 5)

A Gate of Night (Book 6)

A Break of Day (Book 7)

Series 2: Rose & Caleb's story

A Shade of Novak (Book 8)

A Bond of Blood (Book 9)

A Spell of Time (Book 10)

A Chase of Prey (Book 11)

A Shade of Doubt (Book 12)

A Turn of Tides (Book 13)

A Dawn of Strength (Book 14)

A Fall of Secrets (Book 15)

An End of Night (Book 16)

Series 3: The Shade continues with a new hero...

A Wind of Change (Book 17)

A Trail of Echoes (Book 18)

A Soldier of Shadows (Book 19)

A Hero of Realms (Book 20)

A Vial of Life (Book 21)

A Fork of Paths (Book 22)

A Flight of Souls (Book 23)

A Bridge of Stars (Book 24)

Series 4: A Clan of Novaks

A Clan of Novaks (Book 25)

A World of New (Book 26)

A Web of Lies (Book 27)

A Touch of Truth (Book 28)

An Hour of Need (Book 29)

A Game of Risk (Book 30)

A Twist of Fates (Book 31)

A Day of Glory (Book 32)

Series 5: A Dawn of Guardians

A Dawn of Guardians (Book 33)

A Sword of Chance (Book 34)

A Race of Trials (Book 35)

A King of Shadow (Book 36)

An Empire of Stones (Book 37)

A Power of Old (Book 38)

A Rip of Realms (Book 39)

A Throne of Fire (Book 40)

A Tide of War (Book 41)

Series 6: A Gift of Three

A Gift of Three (Book 42)

A House of Mysteries (Book 43)

A Tangle of Hearts (Book 44)

A Meet of Tribes (Book 45)

A SHADE OF DRAGON TRILOGY

A Shade of Dragon 1

A Shade of Dragon 2

A Shade of Dragon 3

A SHADE OF KIEV TRILOGY

A Shade of Kiev 1

A Shade of Kiev 2

A Shade of Kiev 3

BEAUTIFUL MONSTER DUOLOGY

Beautiful Monster 1

Beautiful Monster 2

DETECTIVE ERIN BOND (Adult thriller/mystery)

Lights, Camera, GONE

Write, Edit, KILL

For an updated list of Bella's books, please visit her website:
www.bellaforrest.net

Join Bella's VIP email list and she'll personally send you an email
reminder as soon as her next book is out: www.forrestbooks.com

NEW GENERATION LIST

- **Aida:** daughter of Bastien and Victoria (half werewolf/half human)
- **Field:** biological son of River, adopted son of Benjamin (mix of Hawk and vampire-half-blood)
- **Jovi:** son of Bastien and Victoria (half werewolf/half human)
- **Phoenix:** son of Hazel and Tejus (sentry)
- **Serena:** daughter of Hazel and Tejus (sentry)
- **Vita:** daughter of Grace and Lawrence (part-fae/human)

1

SERENA

The Red Tribe camp site was the scene of absolute carnage, with succubi bodies scattered everywhere. Some had been consumed by the fires still crackling here and there. The smell of burnt flesh turned my stomach. Where it hadn't been charred, the once red grass that covered the ground at the base of the mountain was glazed in silver blood.

Thick pillars of smoke rose from the embers of what had once been tents. This site had been home to dozens of fierce, beautiful succubi who now lay lifeless before us, defeated by a horde of Azazel's Destroyers and traitorous Sluaghs. The Red Tribe was no more, and our strongest alliance was suddenly our weakest.

Hansa was on her knees, heaving and struggling to control herself. Tears streamed down her cheeks. I wanted to hold her and tell her that everything would be okay, but how could I? We all knew it would only get worse from here.

Azazel had wiped out her entire tribe, her family, in one organized attack.

The spell was always an optical illusion, so someone must have known where to look to find the succubi's camp. Someone had known where to come or who to follow to deliver the deadly strike.

"I will kill them all," Hansa growled.

Draven stood next to me, his brow furrowed and lips pursed, tension throbbing in his jaw. Bijarki was close, his eyes wandering around us, his hands balled into fists at his sides. The pain marring his otherwise beautiful features was undeniable.

"Each and every one of them... One worm after another... I will slice them up and feed them to the beasts!" Hansa roared. She stood.

Her leather garments were drenched in succubus blood, and her hands trembled. I saw in her face a tidal wave of pure, uncontrollable rage.

"Hansa, I am truly sorry for what has happened here," Draven said in a low voice. "Where do we start?"

"Don't trouble yourself with such details, Druid," she spat back. "This is my war to wage against the Sluaghs!"

"But who did this? Who betrayed you? Who will you go after?"

"All of them! All of those filthy parasites! I will destroy them until there are none left to feed off the bodies of my sisters!" she shouted, her eyes wide and glassy. "Krol," she growled in a lower, more menacing voice. She looked around like a vulture seeking prey.

"Aida saw him in a vision." I remembered her account of that encounter. It hadn't been easy to forget, the Sluaghs were creepy as hell.

"It was my generals that he met the other day. He's the traitor. He's the one I'm after."

"We'll get him. Together," I said, placing my hand on her trembling shoulder. "We'll do this together, Hansa. Your loss is our loss. Remember that." I was trembling too, not just from the devastation around us, but from the fear that Hansa instilled in me. She was terrifying with such rage coursing through her veins. I looked around, wary of asking the one question that I knew I had to ask. We had so little time left against Azazel.

"Hansa, we will get them," Bijarki added in a calm tone. "But you will not do it alone. You and Anjani may very well be the last of your tribe. You can't leave her alone to fight a battle you know you'll lose on your own. There are so many of them and only one of you."

"I will take as many of them as I can before I fall! My sisters deserve retribution!"

Bijarki raised his voice. "Damn it, Hansa! Snap out of it!"

She stilled, and from the way she stared at him, for a moment I feared for his safety.

Several moments passed before she took a deep breath, followed by another and a dozen more, until her shoulders dropped.

We all waited patiently for her to regain her composure.

She looked around, swallowing back the tears, and nodded slowly.

"Okay then, what's the plan?" she finally asked.

I could hear a sigh of relief leaving Bijarki's lungs. He waved an arm around at the camp. "We need to find the book, first," he said. "Then, we need to burn everything down. We leave nothing behind, not a sliver of meat for the Sluaghs to occupy. Some must be lurking in the waters nearby, since they know where the Red Tribe is now...was."

We made our way to the remains of her tent, a jumble of burned animal skins and lumps of charred wood beams. Black smoke still rose from the middle, unraveling upward in trembling rolls. She frowned as she took the details in.

"The passage stone," she said.

We all froze as soon as we realized what she was talking about.

"It's gone," Draven said.

I gasped. "Oh no. What...what do we do?"

Hansa and Bijarki started digging through the remains.

"The passage stone is a peculiar instrument," Draven explained. "If one travels through a passage stone without a specific destination, one may pop out anywhere in Eritopia. There are thousands of these scattered throughout Eritopia, most of them lost—dumped in lakes or at the bottom of the seas or forgotten inside a volcano or in the darkness of a pit. It's extremely risky to take the way of a passage stone without knowing where you'll come out on the other end. No one is foolish enough to try it."

"But if you do know where you're going," I added, "it requires your blood."

"Exactly. Nobody besides you, Anjani, Hansa, Bijarki, Jovi, and myself know of the passage stone at the mansion. Even if they have Hansa's stone, the chances of them landing in my house are minimal."

"It's still a risk though, isn't it?" I asked, unable to shake the feeling that we were still open to an attack from the inside.

"It is, but even Azazel won't venture through a passage stone without knowing where he's headed. Even if he does find out where the mansion is, unless he knows there's a passage stone beneath it, he won't get in." Draven lowered his voice.

I watched as Hansa pulled pieces of wood, smoky strips of fabric, and animal furs from the mess that had once been her home. As soon as she reached the warm ground beneath, she dug her fingers into it and scooped out as much as she could. Bijarki found a wide piece of metal that was sturdy enough to be used as a shovel blade and joined her.

"We need to dig down a few feet," Hansa said between breaths. "I buried the book at the bottom of the central pillar that held my tent together. No one ever dared to go in, and no one knew about the book besides Almus."

I looked around, a feeling of uneasiness prickling the back of my neck.

"Are you sure all the Sluaghs are gone?" I asked.

"I don't think so," Bijarki replied. "Some are probably still lurking nearby, waiting for us to leave so they can find new bodies."

"They won't get that chance," Hansa spat. "They might as well shrivel up and die! I won't let them take any of my sisters!"

"We need to do a body count," Draven said. "Maybe not all your sisters were here at the time of the attack."

Hansa looked up at Draven, a glimmer of hope twinkling in her emerald gold eyes. She kept digging. "You might be right!" she replied.

"I'm of no use to anyone right now," I said. "I can help with the...counting."

She gazed at me for a second and nodded. Then, she refocused her attention on the soft, black dirt. I took it as her approval and went to the north side of the camp. I started counting from there, clockwise, making a mental note of each memorable detail—every scarlet feather, finely crafted medallion, or sword hilt, anything that would later remind me of that specific succubus. I recognized the one who had marked Draven as hers during our first night at the camp. She'd died cuddling a young succubus, both their bodies pierced with Destroyer arrows.

I couldn't help but cry at the sight of them. My eyes stung, and hot tears rolled down my cheeks.

Fifty-seven... Fifty-seven... Fifty-seven... I repeated the same number in my head in an effort to keep a semblance of composure.

Draven came behind me and wrapped me in his arms. The warmth of his body seeped into my back and relaxed my stiff muscles. I surrendered to his embrace and cried. His chin rested on my right shoulder, and his temple leaned into mine. We both looked down. He held me tightly as I let it all out.

"She was the first to see the truth," he said after a few minutes.

I sniffed and gave him a sideways glance. My vision was blurry from the tears but still good enough to make out his gray eyes, the blade of his nose, and his soft lips. He was my rock and my refuge, and I still marveled that he was mine.

"What truth?" I asked.

He looked at me, his gaze softening and a faint smile tugging the corner of his mouth.

"That I belong to you and you alone," he replied. "She was the first to see it. And that's how I will always remember her, no matter what happens next."

I felt the heavy weight on my heart lifting at Draven's words, if only for a moment. Despite the death and darkness, he pointed to the little glimmers of light, giving me strength when doubt found a way to trickle into the back of my mind. How had we come to this? How had he become so important to me?

We walked together for a while, as I counted the rest of the fallen members of the Red Tribe.

Soon afterward, Hansa's voice broke through the silence with a thundering echo.

"Found it!"

We rushed back to the center of the camp, where her tent had once stood tall and proud. She rose, holding up the second book of the swamp witches for us to see. She removed it from its protective covering, what looked like a triple layer of fabric and thick brown animal hide.

"Can I see it?" Draven asked.

Hansa nodded and handed him the book. I watched his fingers pass over the front side of the leather cover before they untangled the strings and revealed the multitude of pages inside. I recognized the markings from the first book I'd retrieved at Mount Inon—the same swirls and lines that formed the handwritten language, the geometric symbols and partial pentagrams that would help us perform powerful spells in our war against Azazel.

"It is yours, now," she told Draven. "Your father would have wanted you to have it, given the circumstances. Keep it safe."

Draven nodded and closed the book again, stuffing it in the duffel bag that Bijarki had brought with him, where we also kept the first book. We all looked at each other, our expressions lighter than before. Despite the death surrounding us, we were still closer to destroying Azazel than we had been before. There was a faint idea of hope lingering in the air among us.

"So, what now?" I asked.

"We give my sisters a proper burial, and we leave nothing behind," Hansa replied.

2

SERENA

We spent a couple of hours gathering all the bodies in the middle of the camp, stacking them on top of pieces of wood. Several corpses had once belonged to the attacking Sluaghs, paler than the rest and lacking their heads, oozing black blood. According to Bijarki, silver blood turned black when the body was occupied by a Sluagh. We counted ten of them in total. I figured the succubi had put up quite the fight, to be able to decapitate ten of these so-hard-to-kill monsters. It was an impressive death toll, given that they'd been taken by surprise.

Hansa and Bijarki piled on all the dragon tears they could find, then set the funeral pyre alight.

The task had been a daunting one, and my arms and back were sore, but it was nothing compared to what Hansa must have felt at the sight of her sisters burning. Black smoke rose in heavy plumes, a sad contrast against the violent pinks and purples of dusk. Crickets chirped in the woods around us, while night birds began their melodious exchange of trills in the branches above.

Hansa stood before the pyre, torch in hand. She turned around to face us, and I could see tears streaming down her dirty cheeks, revealing thin lines of smooth, silvery skin. The pain in her eyes tore me apart. I decided to offer my help.

"Hansa," I said. "If you want, I can syphon some of the pain off."

She gave me a warm smile and shook her head.

"Thank you, Serena, but I need this pain. It fuels me," she replied.

A moment passed before she spoke again.

"How many, in total?" she asked.

"Ninety-three," I answered, my voice barely a whisper.

"That leaves us with twelve unaccounted for. Twelve of my sisters who might still be alive somewhere."

She looked over her shoulder, frowning at the sight of the bright orange blaze that consumed the flesh of her dead sisters. There hadn't been enough time for us to wrap them all in burial cloaks. There weren't enough of those anyway. The Red Tribe had never anticipated its own sudden extinction.

"My sisters were brave and strong," Hansa said, her voice trembling. "Some were older than me and carried with them millennia of traditions and tales of succubi virtue. Most, however, I nursed myself from the day they were born. Sweet little bundles of joy and curiosity, with bright eyes and millions of questions about the world, about our nature, and about our freedom. I raised them all with the elders, trained them, fed them, and prepared them for everything that awaited them outside the boundaries of our camp. Eritopia is beautiful and wild, intense and unforgiving, cruel and fascinating. I remember each and every one of these girls, from their first steps to their first kills."

Bijarki took a few steps forward, holding a large bunch of wild pink and yellow flowers. He walked along the length of the pyre and threw the blossoms into the fire, one for each succubus lost. Sadness darkened his face, and I could see tears glazing his eyes. These were creatures of his own kind, after all. Despite their separate lifestyles and the frequent animosity, the succubi and incubi only had each other in this world. Loss was painful in any universe.

"In many ways, I grew up with them, over and over again, rediscovering the wonders and terrors of Eritopia," Hansa continued hoarsely. "I laughed with them, and I lost sleep whenever one of them didn't come home. Seven of them were my own daughters..." She choked up.

My heart twisted in my chest. I could only imagine what it must feel like for a mother to lose her children like that.

"Six are here now, burning. One is missing. I am hopeful she is still alive, somewhere," Hansa continued, swallowing back more tears. "We are all mothers at some point in our lives. We all carry life in our wombs. We all feel the unbreakable bond that comes with giving birth. But the Red Tribe was even stronger. The bond was greater, stronger than the blood ties. Today, I am parting not just with my blood daughters, but with all my daughters, all my sisters...my friends...my mothers."

Hansa stepped back, wiping the tears from her face with the backs of her hands.

"Nevertheless, Druid, rest assured, for as long as I'm still standing, there is a Red Tribe. Anjani is still standing. Twelve more succubi might still be alive. Azazel may have killed most of us, but he hasn't defeated us."

Her resolve was truly phenomenal. The emotional rollercoaster of the entire day had ended on a note of determination. Hansa was an exceptional creature. As she watched her entire family turn to ashes, she still had enough strength to stand tall and tell us that there was still hope—that this was not defeat.

Hansa walked over to a large black stone several feet away from the pyre. She took out a knife and carved a few words into its smooth surface, words I did not understand. She noticed my confusion and smirked as she etched her message.

"We invented a code language a long time ago. Only the Red Tribe knows it. We use it for safety and to communicate when no one else can be trusted. If there are any of my sisters out there, they will come back here to see if there are any survivors. They will find nothing but ashes and this message. It will guide them back to the mansion, back to safety."

"The Red Tribe is welcome in my home anytime," Draven replied.

"You're more like your father than you think, Druid." Hansa smiled at him, a familiar warmth glimmering in her eyes. "Ever the gentleman, even when he had to deal with wildlings such as myself. It's what drew me to him in the first place. Unlike the rest of his elitist kind, Almus saw past the leathers and sharp blades and sought to communicate, to get to know us better. I cared for him deeply, more than you might think, in fact."

"You were close to my father, then?"

She nodded. "I have met all kinds of creatures in Eritopia. Some I liked. Others I loathed. A few I simply tolerated. But your father was something else entirely. I must be honest, Druid, I loved your father...deeply."

Her candor surprised me, and judging by how Draven's eyebrows arched up, it surprised him as well. We knew there had been something between Hansa and Almus, but she hadn't told us anything about it. We'd only had Phoenix's vision.

"I didn't know," Draven replied.

"You couldn't have known. I asked him to keep it a secret, especially after the swamp witches gave us the books. We couldn't risk people outside the Red Tribe knowing we'd ever met. Ultimately, things changed between us when he rescued Elissa." Hansa's voice dropped, enough for me to understand that her separation from Almus had not been her idea. "I don't think your father ever truly reciprocated my feelings. Sure, there was affection...attraction...but the moment he met Elissa everything between me and him faded, except for our friendship and loyalty. Both we take to our graves."

The dynamic between Almus and Hansa became much clearer, as I understood what they had meant to each other beyond what Phoenix's vision had shown us. Draven's past ran deep into Eritopia, rooted in his father's relationships with creatures who were now key players in his present and in our entire strategy against Azazel. Hansa's loyalty was just one of the many treasures that Almus had left his son with, even if Draven hadn't known anything about her up until a few nights ago.

I maintained hope that we might stumble upon more of these lost friends of his father's along the way. We needed all the help we could get, now more than ever.

As night gathered above us in shades of ultramarine and dark purple, we collected as many weapons and other unburned items as our horses could carry and galloped back to the mansion.

The woods hissed with discontent. A myriad of stars and a fat, pearly moon guided us down the beaten path of the jungle on our way home. The rumble of hooves was the only sound to come out of us until we reached the safety of the mansion's protective shield.

3

AIDA

A few days had passed since Serena, Draven, Hansa, and Bijarki had left for Mount Inon. Despite the passage of time, I was stuck in a most delicious loop, constantly replaying Field's kiss in my mind. Whenever I wasn't giddy and whistling happy tunes around the mansion and remembering every detail of our moment together, I was shut in the attic, honing my Oracle skills.

Despite the dangers that awaited outside the mansion's protective shield, and despite the predicament I'd found myself in as an Oracle, Field was my beacon of hope, the root of everything that was still good and sweet in my life. His promise to be with me even if I went blind and barren didn't make the potential outcome any better, but it gave me enough strength to face the possibility with my chin up.

Shortly after we'd kissed that day, Field had taken me inside for a cup of coffee in the banquet hall. We'd laughed and talked for a while.

Then he'd excused himself and gone out for a bit. I couldn't blame him for wanting to be outside. Hawks weren't made for life indoors. They needed freedom, the air brushing against their wings, the sky open and all theirs.

This morning had started out nicely, with colorful droplets of glee in my soul. The sun shone brightly outside. I could see it smiling down at me in warm rays peeking through the rich pink magnolia trees by the windows.

Soon enough, however, that old part of myself that I disliked started rearing its ugly head, spoiling the memory of Field's lips on mine and our bodies melting against each other. I'd hoped it wasn't our last kiss. Doubt started seeping through the cracks of my happy bubble like dirty water, determined to soil the pristine image of Field's soft gaze warming my face before his mouth captured mine.

The little voice in my head, the one that had once judged my wolf hair and my curves, was back. In need of the attic's silence I went upstairs. Maybe I could lose myself in a vision instead of paying attention to the doubtful part of me that, until that moment, had been relatively quiet since our arrival in Eritopia.

I sat down beneath one of the large windows, letting the sunlight wash over my face in shades of white and gold. I closed my eyes and tried to channel the present. But I had trouble focusing. That little voice kept yammering about Field.

Was he really into me? Were his feelings genuine? Or was I

the rebound girl he needed to get over Maura? Maybe she'd been the real love of his life, but, due to lifestyle incompatibilities, they'd lost each other, and here I was, the fool ready to give him enough affection to help him deal with the loss.

I shook the thought away and took a few deep breaths, once again focused on tapping into a vision.

But the thought came back, pounding in my temples like a migraine, eager to ruin everything.

What if he didn't feel anything? What if I was just handy? Would he really be that selfish? Or did he not even realize he was doing it? Maybe he was fooling himself into thinking he liked me—some sort of subconscious defense mechanism to help him bounce back from his life with Maura.

I mean, she was pretty and smart and a woman with years of wisdom and experience. I was still in my teenage years, still grateful for the spell that had helped me shed all that extra body hair. I'd been stuck between human and wolf for most of my life, and that was how Field had known me. How could he see past it, even with it gone now?

I kept spiraling down that dark hole, deeper and deeper into my insecurities, while Field's kiss stayed at the top of the hole, shrinking in the distance.

"Are you okay?" Field's voice startled me out my thoughts.

I looked over to my right and found him at the far end of the attic, standing and watching me with concern etched on his face. His turquoise eyes found mine, and my heart tumbled and fluttered at the same time, torn between the memory of our kiss and the subsequent doubts of his intentions toward me. After all, he hadn't been specific in how he felt about me. He'd just kissed me.

The floor seemed to vanish from underneath me as he took a few steps forward.

"Yeah. All is good," I said, barely hearing myself.

I decided to raise that barrier between us again, just until I could understand how he really felt about me. I straightened my back and gave him a polite smile. How could I get him to tell me what I needed to know? Asking was the only straightforward solution, but the closer he got to me, the faster I felt my courage slip away.

"Why am I having a hard time believing that?" he asked, his head cocked.

"I don't know. I told you, I'm fine. Just working on my visions. Nothing to see here," I mumbled and looked away, bringing my knees to my chest defensively.

Field wasn't one to quit so easily. He sat in front of me, crossing his legs while his gaze searched mine. There was a playful flicker in the tropical blue-green of his eyes. Clearly, he didn't understand my struggle.

Why should he, anyway? These are my demons, not his.

"Seriously, Aida, what's going on?"

I tried to be brave, but doubt had chipped away at my self-confidence, leaving me naked and vulnerable and fearful in front of a man who had the power to crush my heart with a handful of words. The swing in my mood from one hour to the next had taken its toll on my resolve.

"I'm fine, Field."

"I haven't seen you at all today."

His voice was low and smooth, making nerve endings in my entire body tingle.

"Well, you've been out a lot," I replied, unyielding.

"And you've closed yourself off in the attic. Have I done something wrong?"

I sighed and shook my head. Why punish him for my insecurities? It wasn't fair.

"I've just... It's hard to explain," I said, my voice barely a whisper.

He bent forward, leaving just a couple of inches between our faces. He kept watching me, his eyes looking for something in mine. His gaze shifted to my lips.

I bit the inside of my cheek.

"Try me." He smiled gently.

I stilled as he drew his face even closer, our lips nearly touching. I wanted to feel him again. I needed the courage he unknowingly gave me. I needed the hope he instilled in me. I needed him to kiss me and hold me again, enough to smother that stupid doubtful voice in my head that had ruined my morning.

"They're back!" Vita's voice made both of us jump. She popped her head into the attic, enough to notice how close Field and I were to each other and to realize that she'd interrupted an intimate moment. "Sorry, just wanted to tell you that Serena and Draven are back."

"It's okay," I mumbled and stood up.

It clearly wasn't the right time for me and Field. It would

have to wait until later, until I'd gathered the courage to ask him how he really felt about me. As I walked over to Vita, I heard Field's footsteps behind me. I wasn't even brave enough to face him.

Damn my insecurities.

4

JOVI

We all gathered downstairs as the sun moved closer to noon above us. Field, Aida, and Vita descended from the attic, while Phoenix and the Daughter came from the banquet hall. Anjani was already standing outside by the porch steps. I joined her quietly as we watched Serena, Draven, Bijarki, and Hansa come in through the protective shield from the northern jungle path.

Their expressions were dark and solemn, and a bunch of swords, shields, crossbows, and various other weapons clanged from the horses' saddles—far too many items for a group of four people. Something was wrong.

Draven was the first to get off his horse.

"What happened?" I asked, not just for myself but for Anjani as well.

Her frown said more than she ever would in words and, judging by the way she looked at her sister, she seemed to understand more than I did.

"They're dead," Hansa replied in a low, husky voice.

"What...what do you mean?" Anjani took a step forward.

"The Sluaghs betrayed us," Draven answered when Hansa wavered. "They brought Destroyers with them and raided the Red Tribe. None of the succubi there survived. They didn't stand a chance."

"I am so sorry, Anjani," Serena added as she got off her horse.

It took a few moments for the information to sink in. I heard Vita and Aida gasp somewhere behind me, but my attention was focused on Anjani. I couldn't see her face from that angle, but I could tell from the way her shoulders dropped that she was about to react to the news of her sisters' deaths.

"Twelve of our sisters might still be out there," Hansa said, avoiding Anjani's gaze. "The rest are dead."

A long moment passed before Anjani collapsed. She fell to her knees, bending forward in a heart-wrenching wail that pierced through the silence and echoed all around us. My stomach burned at the sight of her crying. I couldn't stand it.

I dropped next to her and pulled her into my arms. To my relief, she didn't object. She just cried as I held her tight, her face nestled in my chest. Her sobs were a muffled wave of hot tears. I brushed my fingers through her rich black hair, and looked up at Hansa.

She wore a look of silent approval. She seemed thankful to see me there comforting her sister. Hansa was a fierce warrior. I figured that their customs didn't leave room for much compassion and grieving—at least not where she was concerned, as the tribe chief. Someone had to hold onto the reigns, despite the grief and devastation, and Anjani was too young and probably not seasoned enough to process everything the way Hansa did.

Nevertheless, I saw tears welling up in Hansa's eyes, and I knew it was harder for her than she'd ever let on. I could only imagine what losing dozens of sisters felt like. My heart broke for Anjani. I did my best to keep her close to me while she cried uncontrollably in my arms.

"What do we do now?" Field asked.

Draven took a deep breath and looked at the mansion. Behind him, Serena and Bijarki started unloading the saddles. Aida and Vita joined them, taking some of the weapons and placing them on the front porch. I could see the blades smeared with silver blood. The sight of it made the hairs on the back of my neck rise.

"Hansa left a cryptic message for any survivors. They'll know where to find us," he said. "We burned the bodies, as we didn't want any rogue Sluaghs taking over a Red Tribe body."

"The time will come when I will avenge our sisters' deaths, Anjani." Hansa took off her red cape and tossed it on the grass. "I will personally drive my sword through Krol's shriveled little head, I promise you."

Anjani looked up between sobs and nodded. She hid her face in my chest and cried some more. I figured it was as close as she would get to being consoled by her big sister and, somehow, it made sense.

"For now, however, we need to find the third book of the swamp witches," Draven added. "Serena went through quite the trial at Mount Inon to retrieve the first book, and Hansa was kind enough to give us the second one. The third is hidden somewhere on this property."

Serena and Draven exchanged looks, and I could see something that wasn't there before. They'd been through horrible things over the past few days. I could tell from the dark shadows under their eyes. But there wasn't just understanding flowing between the two; there was also affection—the kind derived from deeper feelings, much like the ones that compelled me to hold Anjani so close to me in that moment.

"Where do we look?" Aida asked, one foot resting on the porch step.

"Everywhere," Draven replied. "I suggest we split into groups and take different parts of the house. Search through every nook and cranny until you find something like this."

He pulled out one of the books from the duffel bag at his feet. It was a large piece, hundreds of pages wrapped in dark brown leather. I knew it was one of the most important weapons we had in our fight against Azazel. I committed the image of it to memory.

"Jovi and Vita, you take the eastern wing," he continued. "Serena and I will take the north. Phoenix and the Daughter can search the west wing. Hansa and Anjani can look in the south wing, and Field, Aida, and Bijarki, please search the grottos underneath the house. Let's take our time and do this properly. Leave no stone unturned. My father wouldn't have taken the book outside the protective shield, so it must be in here somewhere."

It took me a few minutes to part from Anjani. She swallowed back more tears, stood, and gave me a weak but thankful smile. I didn't want to leave her side, but at the same time I understood that spending some time with her sister would do her good. It would do both of them a lot more good than crying in my arms. They were warriors. They had to grieve like warriors. I'd read that about the succubi tribes, and I deeply respected that.

The Red Tribe was a key component of Anjani's identity. It fueled the fire that delighted me about her in the first place. Whatever I could do to help her stoke those flames, I would do. In this instance, it involved leaving my beautiful succubus with her sister. I took a deep breath and stepped away from her.

I followed Vita inside the mansion but not before looking over my shoulder to see Anjani watching me, her emerald and gold eyes flickering with a peculiar warmth, a shade I'd never seen before. Something had changed between us.

5

AIDA

We started out in the basement. Bijarki led us through one of the three doors that we had yet to explore in that part of the house. These doors were always locked, but Bijarki had a spare set of keys from Draven.

We followed him through the narrow corridor, carved directly into the limestone, each of us carrying a torch. Bijarki walked in front of me, and Field was right behind. I could almost feel his breath brushing against the back of my neck, sending shivers down my spine.

"There's an entire network of these tunnels and chambers beneath the mansion. About ten rooms in total, interconnected. The passage stone is kept in a separate grotto, for good reason though. Wouldn't want anyone to just stumble upon it," Bijarki explained.

We searched the first chamber, which we found on the left side of the corridor, behind a set of heavy black iron bars. It had once been used as a prison cell, from what we could tell. There was a makeshift bed against the eastern wall consisting of several hay bales and a couple of wool blankets. Charcoal lines had been crossed off in a repetitive pattern on the limestone above. I counted at least thirty small lines at first glance.

There were a few wooden crates in there, along with a pair of broken shackles abandoned in a corner. We started searching through the chamber, opening each crate, turning each stone, checking every drawer and obscured space.

I finally broke the silence. "Someone was held captive in here." Maybe Bijarki would know more about it.

"Almus had a few run-ins with incubi and other friends of Azazel during his campaign to weaken Azazel's advances on Eritopia," the incubus replied. "He used these chambers to keep them from running but also to protect them from Azazel. Azazel doesn't take kindly to traitors."

He lifted the shackles from the ground and brought them closer for both Field and me to see the symbols etched into the dark metal.

"What are these?" I asked, squinting in the dim torchlight.

"Binding spells, proprietary Druid formulas. Only a Druid can unbind them. Once they're on, you can't speak or act against the Druid who bound them," he explained. "I'll hold on to these. Draven might find them useful."

"There's nothing here," Field said, looking at me.

I turned away and headed straight for the door.

"Let's try another room then," I replied as I made my way further up the corridor.

Three chambers later, Field and I had yet to exchange another word. I watched him when he wasn't looking, and as soon as his gaze would find mine, I'd look away, making myself busy with various boxes and crates.

I could feel the tension building between us, but I couldn't address it with Bijarki around. But even if Bijarki were to leave us alone, I wasn't sure I'd be able to clarify anything. I mentally chastised myself as I found another crate to rummage through.

Bijarki stood up from one corner and let a heavy sigh roll out of his chest. Both Field and I looked at him curiously.

"You two clearly have something to sort out between yourselves," he said.

I froze and gave Field a sideways glance, noticing his straight face and the sudden flush in his cheeks. Bijarki had seen that there was something off between us, making me marvel at both the incubus's impressive attention to detail and the intensity with which my dynamic with Field seemed to function.

My face was on fire as I realized just how transparent I was despite my attempts to seem cool and composed. Who was I kidding? Field rattled my senses. Why play that down?

"So, I'll make myself scarce and look in another room. You two take the next chamber, and I'll meet you somewhere later," Bijarki added.

He then left me alone with Field, closing the door behind him with a loud screech. The hinges were rusty, probably as old as the mansion above.

A few moments passed with Field and me looking at each other before we both laughed nervously. He took a few steps in my direction, and I felt my heart racing the closer he got. There was nowhere for me to run or hide. I had to face my insecurities.

His expression hardened as he towered above me, measuring me from head to toe. I wasn't sure what to make of the thin line of his mouth or the darkness in his eyes.

"What's going on with you, Aida? Talk to me, please," his voice sounded softer than the look on his face.

"I...I don't know how to explain it." I had a hard time finding the right words. My fingers fumbled behind my back as if I was the nervous little wolf-girl he'd once caught staring at him during GASP training.

"I'm in no rush," he replied.

I sighed, finally accepting that I only had two choices: tell him about my doubts and get the truth out of him, or walk away and forever ruin whatever this was between us. The mere thought of the latter made me feel miserable, so I braced myself.

"I'm nervous, Field! I don't understand this sudden interest you have in me. What happened? How come we kissed? What changed?"

He looked at me for a while, turquoise flames bursting in his eyes as he licked his lower lip, then bit into it.

My temperature spiked at the sight of his tongue. The memory of its taste teased me.

"Aida, it's only now that I can see you for who you really are," his voice was low and deep, sending heatwaves through my core. "I am sorry I didn't see you sooner, as the woman you are, as the extraordinary creature you've become. It's like I've been blind over the last few years, and it took this unexpected trip into the

In-Between for me to realize how utterly stunning you are, both inside and out."

He'd said something similar before, and it wasn't enough for me. It didn't feel like a good enough reason, not when I could still sense Maura's shadow chilling my spine. I almost choked up, but I decided to let it all out.

"I don't know what this means, Field," I replied. "I feel like I'm your post-break-up crutch. I feel like I'm the rebound chick, the one you're suddenly noticing because you need to get over Maura. I don't know how you feel about me, and I don't really get why you'd ever be into me in the first place. I mean, look at me! I'm not your average girl for sure. You've known me since I was covered in wolf hair, I've got too many curves on my body, and I'm the tomboy of The Shade. I fight and kick my way through almost anything, and—"

Field's mouth crashed over mine and shut me up instantly. His lips were soft, and his tongue demanded access. I gave it to him. I opened my mouth and welcomed his hunger. His breath was hot, as was his body against mine. He held me, his hands finding their place on my hips as he pulled me deeper into the kiss.

This felt different. He emanated desire, and my knees weakened as he gently pushed me against the cold wall behind me. His lips refused to part from mine. His hands, however, moved up and down my sides, kneading the flesh as they slipped upward, high enough for his thumbs to brush against the sides of my breasts.

I gasped as we tasted each other, as he told me more with his touch than he possibly could with his words. I suddenly felt foolish and lightheaded as his musky smell invaded my lungs, and I couldn't stop a heartfelt moan from leaving my throat.

Field raised his head to look at me, his eyes burning straight through my soul. His lips were raw, red, and slightly swollen, and I couldn't help but lick mine in response, yearning to taste him again.

"Aida, I'm sorry," he breathed. "I should have been clearer the other day, but I promise I won't make that same mistake again."

The pessimist in me tried to brace for the worst, expecting this sublime moment to end on a sour note, with Field probably telling me that yes, I was his rebound chick.

"I never looked at you for more than a minute because I *was* with Maura...and deep down, maybe I knew I wouldn't have been able to stop thinking about you afterward if I did look at you," he said. "I watched you grow before my eyes, and I didn't fully realize what you meant to me until my scuffle with the shape-shifters. I could have died then. But I didn't. I got to live another day, long enough for me to notice how you bite into your lower lip every time I get close to you..."

I felt myself slowly sliding down against the wall, but Field pushed his thigh between my legs to keep me standing. It also sent ripples of electric jolts through my core, tearing ragged breaths from my chest.

I was speechless, a prisoner under his fiery gaze. His fingers were busy digging into my waist, thumbs brushing over my ribs. I could feel everything through the thin linen fabric of my shirt.

"I'm sorry I didn't tell you from the moment I realized it, Aida. You set my soul on fire, which is something Maura never did. I know you better than most, but seeing you like this now makes me feel like I'm barely scratching the surface with you," he whispered. His teeth grazed my earlobe gently, making me quiver in his arms. "Please, don't compare yourself to any other woman."

His lips traveled slowly down the line of my neck, and I let my head lean backward against the stone wall, abandoning my senses completely. He kissed my collarbone before he raised his head to lean his forehead against mine.

I was hot against his hard thigh as he wrapped his arms around me and tightened his hold. I could feel his heart thundering. I whimpered in his embrace.

He watched me carefully, analyzing every line, every movement, every ragged breath I took.

"Field, I...I'm sorry I doubted—"

Once more, he didn't let me talk. Not that it bothered me. He swept me off my feet, taking my lips hostage in a sweet kiss. He gently bit into my lower lip. His tongue worked in passionate strokes, caressing my lips and the inside of my mouth, making me feel consumed with desire for him.

Any doubt I'd had about him was instantly obliterated. The way his hands held on to my body, the way he enjoyed tasting me, the way he reacted every time I softened under his touch— they were all signs that further confirmed everything he'd just said to me.

I let the heat of his being burn into my soul, as I opened

myself up to him. There was more to this, more to discover about each other. Field was a new experience altogether for me, rattling me on a subatomic level, and I needed to take it all the way. I was his, and he was mine, despite everything else that happened around us.

After years of pining over him, he was there, holding me, setting me on fire, and making my heart twist with a single touch. Our mouths fused, our tongues met, and our souls demanded more of each other. I was safe, I was desired, and I was truly cherished in the arms of the only man I'd ever loved.

As much as I'd tried to deny it, that's what this was. Love.

I am in so much trouble.

I mentally chuckled, wishing to never see the end of this incredible moment.

6

VITA

We started our search from the top floor of the eastern wing, which was mostly comprised of bedrooms and a small library. Jovi and I turned each chamber upside down, looking through every box, every dresser, drawer, and shelf, for anything resembling the swamp witches' third book.

I noticed the frown on his face, but I didn't mention it straight away. I guessed it had to do with Anjani, but I wasn't sure he would be willing to talk about it. We rummaged through two bedrooms in absolute silence, occasionally dropping a "Nothing here!" before moving the search to another corner.

"Jovi," I eventually said once we made it into the third bedroom. "I've noticed there's something going on between you and Anjani, and I just want you to know that if you ever want to talk about it, I'm here. No judgment!"

Jovi looked up from one of the dresser drawers and gave me a weak smile. He was searching one of the two massive mahogany dressers.

He sighed. "Is it that obvious?"

"It wasn't at first, just minor details that otherwise would slip through the cracks," I replied, my gaze focused on several shoe boxes at the bottom, hidden beneath layers of moldy clothes. "It's getting serious, isn't it? I mean, there's definitely chemistry between the two of you. It doesn't take a chemist to see that."

"You're right, Vita. There is something going on between Anjani and me, but I'm not sure exactly what it is, if that makes sense."

"More than you might think." I smirked as I opened one of the boxes, thinking of Bijarki.

My relationship with the incubus wasn't exactly clear either. There was something, but it was difficult to pin it down beyond the point of attraction. It went further than lust but was still undefined. I understood Jovi perfectly. I crinkled my nose at the sight of an old pair of men's shoes, worn down by the passage of time.

"Whatever it is," Jovi said, "it has the potential to be the most extraordinary thing that I could possibly experience. Anjani is fierce and always on the defensive. It's a cultural thing, mostly. But I want to get through her defenses. I swear I have never felt like this before, and I'm positive that the feeling is mutual. Her body, her reactions, don't lie, no matter how cool she tries to play it."

I nodded slowly, moving to the second dresser.

"I'm surprised by your courage," I replied. "I mean, the

incubi, the succubi, their nature is designed to be seductive, to attract. How do you know for sure that these are genuine feelings that you're experiencing for Anjani and not the effects of the succubus influence?"

I had asked myself the same question about Bijarki before, so it was interesting to get insights from one of my own about this peculiar race of Eritopians. I was hoping that it would help shed some light on my own situation, to get some kind of confirmation that feeling like this could genuinely be just me, and not the incubus influence.

"It's all me, Vita," Jovi replied, moving to look under the bed.

"Aren't you afraid you'll get hurt?"

"You mean, get my heart broken?"

He looked up at me for a moment, amused, before he resumed his search.

"Well, yes. You're not made of stone."

"I'm positive that I'm not under her succubus influence," he replied.

"How do you know for sure?"

"At first, she wasn't really aware of her succubus effect being on all the time, and yes, I was under her spell. But the moment she realized that she was affecting me, she tried hard to reign it in. She was quite frustrated about it, actually. Slowly but surely, she got the hang of it. Anjani's a young succubus. Even her sister says there's so much that she still has to learn," Jovi explained.

I found nothing in the second dresser either and moved to the vanity table, while he looked through the bedside tables, which were beautifully carved in red mahogany with gold inlays.

"I can definitely tell whether I'm under her influence or not by now. She's given me her word that she doesn't want me under her succubus spell," he added, the shadow of a smile flickering over his face as he seemed to remember something. "She said that if I was ever to come to her, it would be of my own volition."

I stood up, processing all the information he'd given me. A lot of it made sense and resonated with what Bijarki had already told me. But I still found myself in awe of Jovi. He was much braver than I was when it came to his feelings. Personally, I worried about getting my heart broken in the end.

"How can you tell?" I asked, ready to check potential symptoms off my list.

"First of all, the one thing I've learned so far, with absolute certainty about both succubi and incubi, is that their word is their bond," Jovi smiled. "If they tell you they're not using their ability on you, or that they're trying their best not to, it is the absolute truth. They're genuine. Well, at least the succubi and one incubus I've met so far." He pulled the bed covers aside, checking under the pillows and the mattress.

I was finished with my search, so I stood at the foot of the bed, waiting for him to finish.

"Second, Anjani used her succubus nature intentionally once, and believe me when I tell you, I felt the difference. Your head gets light, you're off balance, your body tingles, and your heart beats at an alarming rate. You can feel it, Vita. It's something so intense, it's impossible to ignore or mistake for something else. Your mind stops listening, and all you can think of is touching, kissing, and feeling everything."

"So, it's basically more intense than pure physical attraction?"

"It's like hugging the sun, Vita. You burn and you can't do anything about it. Putty in their silvery hands." He chuckled. "Anjani used her nature on me once at full power, just to prove a point. Trust me, you can tell if Bijarki ever uses it on you. No doubt about it."

I nodded, feeling a wave of relief washing over me. At the same time, my heart twisted into knots, as I got the confirmation I needed—I had feelings for Bijarki, all of them mine, not a single thread fabricated by the incubus, not even a smidge to sway me in his direction. And Jovi had noticed. The realization smacked me over the head, making me gawk at him.

"You know about Bijarki?" I managed to ask.

"It doesn't take a scientist, Vita." He smirked. "There's clearly something going on between the two of you."

The way he took my words and used them against me merited a round of applause. I nodded my appreciation with a faint smile.

"That being said...yes, of course I'm afraid I'll get my heart broken, Vita."

He looked at me. His gaze softened, and his lips stretched into a faint smile.

"I'm falling for a warrior succubus, after all," he added. "But that won't stop me from trying for what I want. And I want her. Life is way too short and, in our case, far too dangerous to worry about a broken heart. I'd rather regret something I've done than look back with my last breath and hate myself for not having acted on my feelings."

His words sank into me like cement bricks in a lake. I mulled over his reasoning as we went back out into the corridor. We had two rooms left on the top floor before we moved our search downstairs.

"Don't get me wrong, Vita, I really enjoy your company, but I get the feeling we'd cover more ground if we each take one room. What do you think?" he asked, smiling sheepishly.

I laughed lightly and patted him on the back.

"Of course. I can't stand you anymore, either." I grinned, then pointed at the bedroom on our right. "You take the bedroom. I'll take the study, and we'll meet up downstairs, okay?"

"Sounds like a genius plan." He smiled and pecked me on the cheek. "Thank you for listening. I've not spoken to anyone about this. I really appreciate it."

"Anytime, Jovi." I sighed. "We are family, after all. And here, we're closer than ever."

He grinned and disappeared into the bedroom, while I made my way into the east wing study. It looked far more spacious than it actually was, mainly because the bookshelves that covered the walls from ceiling to floor were carved inward rather than mounted. There were hundreds of books on them, most of them leather-bound.

I sighed, taking it all in, and leaned against the writing table set in the middle. It was a beautiful room, with a comfortable chaise-lounge under one of the three large windows facing east. There was plenty of natural light coming in, and the wood floor flaunted a handcrafted herringbone detail beneath the smooth lacquer. This room had been cleaned recently, and I couldn't help but wonder which one of our group had taken an interest in it.

I had my work cut out for me, so I started from the left, flipping through pages and checking every book for the swamp witches' symbols. I lost track of time. When I reached the other side of the wall, I'd had no luck in retrieving the third book.

The silence was blissful, as I continued processing everything that Jovi had told me about his budding relationship with Anjani. No matter how I flipped my own situation from one side to another, the conclusion was the same. Life was short and dangerous for an Oracle like myself, I clearly had feelings for Bijarki, and all I had to do was gather the courage to do something about it.

A creak to my left startled me. I jumped back a couple of steps when the library wall split open. One of the shelf segments was pushed forward like a secret door.

I felt the cool breeze blow over me and froze when Bijarki emerged from the darkness. The torch in his hand had died out.

He stilled in the bookshelf doorway, clearly surprised to find me there. The look of confusion on his face as he quickly scanned the room made me realize he didn't know where he was.

"I'm sorry, Vita. I didn't mean to disturb you," he said.

"It's... It's fine. I was just looking for the book," I managed to reply, my voice high pitched.

"Where am I, exactly?"

A moment passed, and I blinked several times before I could process a response.

"The study in the east wing, top floor."

"Ah," he nodded and smiled. "I followed one of the underground tunnels. It brought me all the way up here. Someone actually took the time to carve out all the stairs, if you can believe it."

I started wondering where else those tunnels would lead, but before I could think of anything else to say, Bijarki measured me from head to toe, a familiar twinkle in his eyes.

"I won't keep you any longer. I'm sure you have a lot of areas to cover," he said politely. He bowed respectfully and turned to go back down through the secret tunnel.

This is it. This is my moment. Be brave! Be Jovi!

"Wait!" I said and walked over to him.

Bijarki turned around just in time for my lips to find his. I pushed myself up on my toes and kissed him, thrilled by my boldness, then instantly melted by how good he tasted. I didn't move, but Bijarki opened his mouth, and his tongue demanded to taste mine. I welcomed him, and he instantly devoured me.

He set aside the torch and drew me into his arms, holding me against his solid chest, and I softened into the kiss. He groaned softly, and my core ignited as he took me deeper into our moment. We consumed each other, and I felt the intensity between us grow to the point where I thought we would eventually explode and tear the clothes off each other.

I reveled in his embrace while he explored every corner of my mouth. I felt it. Jovi was right; I could tell the difference.

My head felt light, my mind barely a feather. Arousal roared like crackling lava through my veins, setting me on fire. My whole body tingled, and I could almost feel jolts of electrical currents rippling through me. I felt weightless as I welcomed the reckless abandon and wrapped my arms around his narrow waist.

My fingers clutched the hard muscle ridges along his spine, my chest incandesced by the feeling of his body so perfectly molded against mine. Billions of colors swirled before my eyes. I couldn't stop. I didn't want to stop. I wanted more.

I heard Bijarki groan before he pulled himself away, clutching my shoulders as my arms fell to my sides.

I was breathless and unable to formulate a single coherent thought. I felt my eyes droop as his steely gaze found mine, his lips swollen and glistening from our kiss. His skin glowed peculiarly, and I wasn't sure whether it was the sunlight or something else. He seemed to light up from the inside.

His breath was ragged as he looked at me. "I'm... I'm sorry, Vita... I can't control my nature when you go and do crazy things like that." His voice was husky and incredibly seductive.

I felt the tingle dissipate from my limbs, but nothing else changed. I was hot and in serious need of him. He tasted like heaven, and I felt the absence of his lips profoundly. That was all me. I knew it.

He seemed to struggle to keep himself under control. I could feel the power emanating from him in scattered pulses as he took deep breaths and closed his eyes for a moment, trying to regain his composure.

"Crazy things like what? Like this?" I said and kissed him again.

I hadn't exhausted my courage. Clearly there was more where the first round had come from.

He groaned and responded, his tongue touching mine as we dissolved into each other.

And I felt it again, enveloping me like sheer bliss, this mind-less need for him buzzing through my veins.

He cupped my face with his hands and forced himself to a halt, breaking our kiss to take another look at me. His eyes were two pools of dark silver, hooded and laced with desire. He breathed heavily and stifled his incubus nature once more.

"Yes," he gasped. "You are shaking me to the core, Vita. I'm forgetting who I am and what I'm doing here."

We stared at each other, until I realized that it didn't matter whether his incubus nature was on or off. All it did was amplify what I already felt to a ridiculously superb level, rocking every inch of flesh and every flicker of soul that made me who I was.

The touch of his skin was my cure for everything. I smiled and leaned into his right hand.

He looked at me, his gaze settling on my lips before it found my eyes. My heart ached for more of him, and I welcomed the feeling. The freedom it offered me was priceless, as opposed to the doubts I'd been struggling with over the past few days.

I placed my palm on his chest, feeling the muscle beneath his shirt as it flexed and hardened even more under my touch.

"I've stopped fighting this," I replied, my voice barely audible. "Maybe it's time for you to stop fighting it as well. Maybe you should stop worrying and simply be yourself. I like it."

He stilled, his breath stuck somewhere in his throat. His eyes were wide, watching me as I threw him a lazy smile and left the room. I closed the door behind me and nearly collapsed, shocked and exhilarated by my decision to take our relationship to another level.

My heart throbbed, violent butterflies wrestled in my stomach, and my lips were tender. I could still taste him, and I smiled as I realized it had all been worth it. I would do it again. He would crumble, and I would melt into him. We would forget about the world for a minute.

7

SERENA

After searching through a couple of bedrooms with no luck, Draven and I started looking through his study. The fire was out, and I was thankful to not be boiling while rummaging through shelves and drawers of Draven's most precious belongings. This was his safe space, his haven when everything else was dark or dismal around him.

On many levels, my presence there felt as intimate as being in his bedroom, in his bed, sleeping in each other's arms. I found myself treating each object I touched with absolute reverence, out of respect for him and his Druid craft. Draven sifted through one bookshelf, while I took the other one, our backs to each other.

We'd been at it for a couple of hours.

Talking through things with Draven had yielded results in the past, and it often gave me the resolve I needed to keep fighting the possible future described in Vita's visions. While he wasn't exactly the most optimistic creature I'd ever met, talking to him did help me find solutions to problems that were critical for our survival in Eritopia that I would have missed otherwise.

"So, once we find the third book, what do we do next?" I asked.

"We put the three together and decrypt their pages. They're broken in three, hence there's a high probability that we'll have to do a little mix and match between them," he replied, moving his attention to another shelf.

"Do you think that will be enough?"

"I don't, actually, but it's a good place to start. The swamp witches were known to walk through fire without ever getting burned, along with other equally stunning accomplishments. Finding that spell and figuring out how it works is the only way for us to reach Mount Zur, the volcano closest to Azazel's dungeon. You know, since we're not made of lava and limestone like the Dearghs."

I found his sarcasm endearing. I looked over my shoulder to find him smirking at me and gave him a brief eye-roll in response before I resumed my search. We had a way of saying more to each other without words, sometimes.

"And once we make it that far, what next?"

"There's approximately one mile of jungle and hills up to Azazel's castle from there," Draven replied. "We'll have to sneak through and infiltrate the dungeon. But there are spies and hostile elements all over that stretch of land. It will be extremely dangerous."

I had a feeling he'd oppose me coming with him on this mission, so I decided to stomp that flame before it turned into a full-blown argument. "Yeah, not the first time or the last," I shot back. "You'll need me there, and you know it."

He said nothing for a while, and I didn't challenge him further. I'd made my point. Persistence would have dismantled my stance, making it seem like I was trying to convince him to let me come along instead of stating it as a fact.

I could feel his gaze drilling into the back of my head, but I didn't look at him. I focused my attention on another shelf stacked with leather-bound books.

"Why are all your books leather-bound, Draven?" I asked sarcastically, changing the subject before he could ponder it too long. "Do you not realize how difficult it's making this task of finding a specific leather-bound book if they all look the same? Hm?"

"Unfortunately, I was not responsible for the printing and binding process," he replied, his voice tinged with amusement.

"Of course you're not responsible," I sighed, continuing the ruse and flipping through another book, this one a brief history of Lamias.

I'll read this one later. I put it back and moved on to another shelf.

Draven changed the subject. "We need to get Sverik out of that dungeon in one piece, alive and motivated to cooperate with us. It's not just his intel that I'm after. He's known well enough in these lands to rally the few remaining incubi and succubi who have yet to swear fealty to Azazel. He's essential to our cause, especially now with the Red Tribe decimated to a bare dozen."

I sighed, remembering the harrowing scene we'd witnessed the day before. A thought occurred to me, given that Sverik's father was still a traitor to Eritopia.

"Are you sure Sverik can be trusted, since Arid is under Azazel's command now?" I asked.

"I don't trust him at all, but he's a risk we have to take, given how little support we've managed to gather so far from the remaining peoples of Eritopia. If we're to make any progress against Azazel, we must take a leap of faith," he said, then turned to look at me. "After all, I'm already risking everything by opening my soul to you, Serena."

I stilled, and my gaze found his. For a moment, I lost myself in his gray eyes, feeling the absence of the wall between us and relieved to be able to sense him entirely. Warmth emanated from him in ribbons of gold that twined around my heart.

"I've never allowed myself to get so close to anyone," he added. "And mind you, we're in the middle of a war. I'm no longer merely taking risks with you; I'm downright reckless."

I couldn't think of anything to say. All I wanted was for him to not push me away again. I wasn't sure I'd make it without him, and it scared the hell out of me. *Yet I wouldn't have it any other way.*

"Though I wouldn't have it any other way." He smiled, and my heart fluttered.

I nodded, delighted by how our minds worked in perfect

unison, and resumed my search. I flipped through another book and found three graphite portraits on loose pieces of paper. They all depicted the same woman, a beautiful creature with familiar features. The cupid's bow mouth, the light-colored hair flowing loosely over one shoulder, the slim nose and soft lines—I'd seen her before, perhaps, but I couldn't put my finger on it.

"Draven, who is this?" I showed him one of the portraits.

His expression changed, a shadow passing over his face as he recognized the figure. His brow furrowed as he looked up at me.

"My mother, Genevieve," he replied.

I was surprised, but, a few seconds later, it began to make sense. I looked at the drawing, then at Draven, then back at her. I noticed the similarities. The softness in his cheekbone lines, the shape of his lips, even a little around the eyes. Yes, she was definitely his mother. I admired her beautiful face and couldn't help but wonder about her. There was something there in her eyes, a certain gravitas that the artist had captured perfectly, a flicker I'd noticed in Draven when he spoke about Azazel and the Druids.

He noticed my curiosity and came up to me, taking one of the portraits in his hand to get a better look. I noticed affection lighting his face up, and I instantly fought back the urge to hold him. I could only imagine what growing up without her must have been like for him.

"She was a Druid of great skill, a mistress of natural sciences," Draven said, his voice low. "She died giving birth to me. It was a great loss to Eritopia and the beginning of the end, in a way."

I could feel his pain freely pouring into me. Whether it was my sentry nature or just perception, it didn't matter. I placed my hand on his chest, and looked up at him, the question floating in my mind. He understood somehow and nodded slowly. With deep breaths I syphoned the grief, a deep shade of ice blue. Sharing his feelings felt more intimate than anything else that had happened between us.

"Tell me more." I beckoned him to open up, so I could syphon more and ease his suffering as best I could.

"She was one of the leaders of our kind. She controlled one of the richest parts of Eritopia, a vast land ripe with valuable resources, one of twenty planets, or kingdoms, as they were officially referred to. Most of her kingdom's income came from trade, and her revolutionary advances in science made production processes easier and more cost-effective. Azazel ruled over another region which, funnily enough, subsisted mostly from the imports from my mother's land. Her influence reached across all of Eritopia's planets, and she held great power over Azazel at the time. He didn't dare make a move against her or anyone else, for that matter, since she supplied all of Eritopia with precious metals and ore, not to mention grains and other goods."

"And your father?"

"He held control over the neighboring planet. It's how they met, actually." A smile passed over his face. "It was love at first sight, he once told me. By then, there were already rumors that Azazel was getting too ambitious for his own good. He went after the swamp witches first, killing them off one by one, using paid assassins that were never traced back to him. He'd been constantly reprimanded for his territorially aggressive actions, but my mother was held back by the council. She would have done more to punish him for the way in which he annexed strategically important strips of land, using his armed forces, but the Druids persisted in their peaceful, diplomatic ways, unwilling to accept that the world as they knew it was coming to an end. And there could be no reasoning with the likes of Azazel."

I stopped syphoning, fearing that I might deplete his energy levels and weaken him. He frowned slightly and leaned against his desk, and I took a step forward, closing the distance between us. I brushed my fingers over his cheek, and he leaned into my touch. I spread my palm out for him to rest his face against as he looked down at the drawing.

"And after you were born, Azazel was unhinged," I concluded in a low voice.

"My father had already smelled the danger. There had been a few assassination attempts against her, but he could never prove it was Azazel. After my mother died, my father told everyone that I had died with her. He knew that I'd grow up to be a powerful Druid, with both his and my mother's blood coursing through my veins. He knew Azazel would try to kill me before I'd even reached my first birthday.

"Soon afterward, Azazel became more brazen and started eliminating his opponents, amassing armies and sending them out for hostile takeovers of neighboring sectors. The Druid alliance grew weak, and my father knew that he wouldn't be able to defeat him on his own. A year later, he was forced off his own planet, out of the kingdom. He smuggled me out and retreated farther to the south, where the new breed of Destroyers had not yet advanced. It was then that he started looking for Oracles and found Elissa. That's how we got this mansion. That's how I wound up here, isolated from everyone."

My soul ached, and all I could think of were ways of making him happy, of bringing some kind of joy back into his life—the kind he'd felt with Elissa, the closest person Draven had had to a mother as a child.

"My father kept a secret from everyone," he added, looking at me in a way that made me want to curl up in his arms and never let him go. "I'm surprised that the Nevertide Oracle hasn't told Azazel about me yet. Although he's bound to find out sooner or later. I'm out now. Someone will see me. He'll put two and two together."

"There's a reason why you've been alone and hidden here for so long," I said. "You are the most powerful weapon against Azazel. My brother, my friends, they're here to help. But I know, deep in my heart, that you'll be the one to vanquish him."

He pulled me closer, placing the drawing behind him. I left the book on the desk along with the other two sketches, bending forward enough for my hair to brush over his jaw and for me to hear him take a deep breath against the line of my neck. His nose touched my skin, and the sheer contact sent shivers down my spine.

I straightened my back and cupped his face in my hands. I could feel his golden energy flowing through me again, and it surprised me, as I wasn't syphoning. Yet somehow Draven was feeding me without me having to use my sentry ability. I stared at him in shock, and he responded with a warm smile, while his life force washed over me.

"I didn't know I could do this either," he said.

"This is amazing."

He wrapped his arms around me, pulling me close enough for my body to mold against his, my softness surrendering to his hard, massive frame. I felt tiny in his embrace but sheltered from everything. His steely eyes were hooded, ready to change the direction our conversation was headed.

"I reckon we were somehow made for each other, Serena," he quipped, a smirk twisting his lips.

I was speechless, unable to express how blissful it felt to be so close to him. How I dreaded the possibility of never seeing him again. I shook the thought away and kissed him.

His lips parted, welcoming me home. It was soft and hot and tender. I tasted him slowly, enjoying every second of him. I opened myself up, projecting my own emotions onto him. It took him a while to realize what was happening. As our souls became connected, I understood that my sentry nature clicked differently with his Druid abilities.

It wasn't just that he was making me syphon off him. I was somehow feeding him with my energy as well, in a bond that we had never experienced before. Judging by what we felt, the array of golds and soft pinks and dashes of yellow, neither of us had expected this to happen. We were basically syphoning off each other, and it felt extraordinary.

He deepened our kiss and tightened his grip on me, his fingers reaching under my shirt and clutching my hips. I moaned against his mouth and ran my hands through his tousled hair before I found his broad, muscular shoulders and arms.

Draven's groan echoed in my chest as our kiss grew more and more intense. His hands reached further up under my shirt, slowly moving toward the front of my ribcage. His thumb and index fingers pressed gently into my flesh, and I squirmed against him.

"How did we come to this?" he whispered against my mouth.

My lips throbbed, demanding more.

"I don't know, Draven, but I don't want it to stop," I gasped.

My body trembled against his, and he stilled for a moment, looking me in the eyes as I tried to catch my breath. My mind was switched off.

"Are you cold?" he asked, concerned.

I shook my head, losing myself in his steely gaze.

"I think it's all because of you," I managed to say before he smiled and captured my mouth in another brain-smashing kiss. I let go completely, as his thumbs moved higher still, setting my soul on fire.

A knock on the door crashed into us like thunder. It startled me, and I took a step back, remembering where I was and what I was supposed to be doing.

Books. I'm looking for books.

We stared at each other. He was gorgeous, his hair

disheveled and his lips almost begging for my return. I felt flushed and unable to focus.

The second knock tore a sigh out of his chest as he turned his head toward it.

"What is it?" he called out, irritation dripping from his voice.

I couldn't help but grin.

8

PHOENIX

The Daughter and I had been searching through the top floor of the west wing for several hours. We started from the banquet hall, where several cabinets and drawers seemed like reasonable hiding places for the swamp witches' third book.

She wore a white linen dress that accentuated her alabaster skin, reddish pink hair, and cherry lips. The way she crinkled her nose every time she had to blow dust off a surface was endearing, tearing a smile from me without exception.

I made myself busy with one of the cabinets while she rummaged through the cutlery drawers. I'd spent the last hour trying to explain what grief felt like, getting nothing but confused frowns from her. No matter how prosaic I got with my descriptions, it didn't seem to faze her much.

"Phoenix, I had a dream last night," she changed the subject. "Or at least I think it was a dream."

"Oh? Tell me about it."

She stood up straight, hands in a drawer. I could hear the silverware clinking beneath her fingers.

"I saw my sisters."

I stilled, a wave of dread instantly crashing into me. I tried hard to keep a straight face.

"They came to see me, all seven of them. Well, I think it was them. It was dark and misty, and I could only see their shadows. Seven shadows."

I nodded and waited for her to continue. White heat sizzled in my throat. I carefully counted my breaths, struggling to not show her how terrified the prospect of her sisters made me, particularly after they'd swayed me into stabbing myself.

"Did they say anything?" I asked and heard my voice tremble.

"They whispered. They said I am the only one who can save Eritopia. But that salvation will come with a cost. They said I must be willing to sacrifice myself for this."

I nearly lost my balance as I gripped the side of the cabinet.

This can't be real.

"It was just a bad dream." I put on a reassuring smile. "A bad dream. That's all."

I wasn't fooling anyone, not even the Daughter. She walked across the hall until she stood inches away from me. I took a step back, as if fearing that if she got any closer, she could smell the fear on me. If she'd been a sentry, she would have seen the acid yellow cloud brewing a storm in my chest.

"What sacrifice did they mean, though?" the Daughter asked.

She'd become an expert in asking the most difficult questions. I wondered whether I'd made life that difficult for my parents. They must have put up with a lot like this from me when I was a kid and they told me that I was going to live much longer than most people. The first time I'd come across the concept of death, I'd had so many questions about it.

Finding myself on the receiving end this time was no walk in the park.

How do I explain death to her?

"It's death. Giving up your own life to save countless others. That's the kind of sacrifice your sisters would mean. I'm surprised they'd bother to intervene in anything related to Eritopia. The last time we asked for their help, they told us to get lost and took the Druid's eyesight." I figured blunt clarity was the best way to go. The Daughter had yet to distinguish nuances.

"What is death, really? What does it involve?" she asked.

I cringed a little, dreading the answer. I'd hated the answer my parents had given me. I had rejected it altogether, unwilling to accept that some of my friends would be gone before my first century. The grief was unbearable, even for a young sentry like me, a creature much more aware of the way the world worked. The Daughter was even more innocent.

Her brow furrowed as she looked at me. I remembered then that she was finely tuned to what I was feeling, so there was no way for me to really hide anything from her.

Let's see you talk your way out of this one, you charmer.

I took a deep breath as my chest decompressed from a heavy sigh. I took her hand and pulled her closer to me. Barely an inch was left between us as I lifted her palm up to my face, her fingers gently grazing the stubble along my jawline. I leaned my face into her touch and welcomed the warmth it generated deep in my chest.

A smile tugged at the corners of her mouth as she tilted her head. Her violet eyes sizzled with a dizzying array of emotions. I recognized affection, joy, pleasure...and a tint of desire emanating from her.

"How are you doing this?" I croaked, unable to stop myself from taking it all in.

The Daughter shrugged, her innocent expression further driving me off the edge. "I don't know. I just feel like I can make you feel what I feel. Can you feel me?"

"Yes," I smiled. "All of you. Bliss."

I bent forward and took her in my arms and nuzzled the delicate curve between her long neck and shoulder. I breathed her in, drunk on her scent, a delightful mixture of lilies and the sea. She sighed, her palm resting on my face.

"Can you feel this?" I asked, my voice low and raspy.

As much as I tried to keep my desire under control, I couldn't. The chain reactions shook me to my core. But I had to explain death to her. I had to teach her. I had to make her understand the concept of loss. I couldn't let her give in to her sisters. They were cruel and unforgiving. She had to know.

"Yes," she sighed, trembling.

I raised my head to see her expression. Her eyes were half-closed, her lips parted, begging to be kissed.

"Imagine that you wouldn't be able to feel any of this ever again," I said gently.

I ran my fingers down her face, tracing the contour of her jaw until I reached her lower lip. Her breath hitched as she softened against me, arching her back.

Keep it together.

"Imagine that you can never touch or be touched again. That you can never see me—or any of this world—again."

Her eyes widened, a small crease forming between her eyebrows. Her nostrils flared, and I watched as tears welled up and rolled down her cheeks. With each minute that passed, her devastation became more evident, and I could feel her grief.

It poured through me, rippling within my chest until I felt a tear leave my eye. Whatever she felt, I felt.

I did it.

I got my point across, and the Daughter was now faced with the prospect of an end to all of this. She hated it. She rejected it. Just like little Phoenix when his parents told him he'd outlive his human friends.

The Daughter was unable to stop the wave of emotions washing over her. I took it all in. The grief. The pain. The sadness. She sobbed as I held her, her head resting against my chest.

"I don't want to die. I don't want you to die. I don't want to feel like this ever, not even hypothetically!" she cried, and I tightened my grip on her, running my fingers through her silky hair.

"Nice use of the word 'hypothetically.'" I smiled, and she

broke down even further, shuddering against my body and tearing me apart.

"It's okay, it was probably just a bad dream," I whispered.

I didn't want her gone either. The invisible string that tied our hearts to one another would be severed, and I'd end as well. I'd only just found her.

"I don't like death," she whimpered between hiccups.

Her suffering was raw and genuine, and it broke me down. I had to stop it.

"You're a Daughter of Eritopia. Death is not for you."

"But why would my sisters want me dead?"

"It was just a bad dream. You said so yourself." My gaze found hers. "Listen to me. It was just a bad dream."

"Don't leave me."

Why would I ever leave you?

"I won't."

Why would I ever part from the one creature who brings a purpose into my life without me even asking?

"Don't die," she pleaded.

"I won't."

Why would I ever die, when every fiber in my body only draws me closer to you, pushing me to live?

"It was just a bad dream," she finally conceded.

9

PHOENIX

We stood like that for a while longer, long enough for her tears to subside.

I felt her relax in my arms and relished every second I got to be so close to her.

Eventually she took a step back, wiped her tears, and took a deep breath. I smiled at her and looked around, realizing we'd pretty much finished searching the banquet hall.

The solution to our problem, as interconnected beings in this world, was to eliminate Azazel's threat. Finding the third book and retrieving Sverik was part of the process.

I was ready to do anything to keep the Daughter here, with me.

"Do you think the ancient wards might know something about the book?" I wondered out loud.

Her face lit up, and she beamed at me.

"That is a great idea! Why didn't I think of it?" She closed her eyes.

A moment passed before she gasped and looked at the double doors leading outside. "Let's go," she said, then took my hand and pulled me out of the banquet hall.

We ran up the stairs, then turned left and reached the far end of the corridor, where the ladder leading to the attic extended to the open hatch above. She climbed up, and I followed. She walked toward the middle of the attic room, looking left and right until she found what she was looking for.

She pulled an old chest from underneath a pile of dusty carpets. It was an old traveler's chest, made of wood with a metal frame, the sides covered in snakeskin. The lock on it was massive but rusty.

"I don't think there's a key," I said.

"We need to open it. The wards have spoken," she replied.

I nodded, then searched for something with which to break the lock. I found a hammer, forgotten in a tool box by the wall and swung it down with all my strength. It rattled the lock, but it didn't open. I hit it again and again and again, but still it didn't budge.

"It should've opened by now," I said, out of breath.

"This is strange," the Daughter said. She got down on her knees.

I joined her, and we both got a better look at the lock. I wiped some of the dust and dry dirt off to reveal the fine filigree details in elegant swirls and floral motifs. This was no ordinary lock.

The Daughter sighed and closed her eyes again. I figured she was reaching out to the wards again.

"It's been sealed with magic," she said, then looked at me.

"Whose magic? Draven's father, maybe?"

"No, the wards." She pursed her lips.

"And they couldn't say so before I started pounding on it with a hammer?"

"Well, they're not very good at communicating." She smiled sheepishly. "For centuries, no one has spoken to them, so they're still getting used to me being able to see and talk to them. There are many secrets in this mansion, many of which the wards have also forgotten, including this chest."

"What does that mean?"

"It means there's a key to this lock made with ancient magic, but they can't find it. They don't remember where they put it."

"You've got to be kidding me," I said. I looked around, hoping there were some wards around to hear me. "You've got to be kidding me!" I shouted at them.

"It's... It's all right," the Daughter said.

She bent forward to get a closer look at the lock again.

"It's a shame you can't see them now. They're shuffling around, apologizing profusely." She giggled. "They're old, Phoenix. They're old souls who never left this world and were repurposed by ancient magic to serve as wards for my sisters' spells. They don't remember everything anymore. They've been around for so long."

"Great. So they're basically everybody's great-grandmother!" I quipped.

The Daughter passed her fingers over the lock, her head cocked to one side, as if listening for something.

"It's okay, Phoenix. I think I can open it."

"How do you know?"

"I don't know. But I can try." She shrugged.

I sighed and nodded. It was the best she could do. Not knowing her limits was a setback, but I had faith in her ability to surprise me and herself. So, I waited patiently as she passed her fingers over the keyhole, over and over again.

Minutes passed, and she repeated the motion, but nothing happened. At one point, we heard a small click, but when she pulled the lock, it didn't open.

"I think it's reacting to me, somehow, but I don't know how to convince it to open," she said.

"Convince it to open?"

"Well, yes. I'm basically stroking it and asking it nicely to open."

I stifled a laugh and pressed my lips together, keeping a straight face as I watched her repeat the caress for a few more minutes.

"Oh, come on! Open already!" She slapped the lock hard.

Sparks flew from the hit, and an invisible pulse threw us backward, followed by a loud click. We sat up and saw the lock drop open, the keyhole glowing an incandescent red.

"Wow," I said. "All it needed was a good spanking, then."

The Daughter laughed and shuffled back to the chest, pulling the lock away and lifting the lid. The interior was draped in soft red velvet. We found the third book dressed in several layers of black fabric with fine golden embroidery.

I pulled the cover away and revealed the swamp witches' third book, identical to her sister volumes, bound in leather with off-white pages and incomplete scribbles and pentagrams.

Warmth enveloped me as I looked at the Daughter and found her smiling, lit up with joy and excitement. She'd helped us. I knew it made her happy that she was able to help me, to help us. I felt her glee in my heart, and I swore I'd do everything I could to always help her feel like that.

10

SERENA

Later that night we all gathered in the banquet hall for dinner. The table was rich in delicious smelling food, from grilled dishes and vegetable stew to baked breads and sumptuous fruit platters. Crystal pitchers of water infused with different berries and leaves glistened under the candelabra, and I was surprised to see a fine set of silverware and porcelain with gold filigree designs.

The candles from both chandeliers above were lit, along with every other wall sconce in the hall, bathing everything in pleasant amber light. It looked like a celebration.

Vita, Aida, and Phoenix sat next to each other, while the Daughter, Field, and Bijarki faced them on the other side of the table. Jovi and Anjani had taken their seats closer to the grilled platters, and Draven sat at the head of the table with Hansa to his right.

I sat to his left.

I couldn't help marveling at how beautiful it all was.

"This looks like quite the feast. What happened?" I asked, smiling and eager to enjoy a bit of everything on display.

"I asked the wards to prepare for a celebration," the Daughter said, helping herself to a spoonful of vegetable stew.

"I cannot express how grateful I am to have you here with us," Jovi quipped, already stuffing his face.

I nodded my appreciation to the Daughter, and she responded with a smile. I looked at Draven and found him already watching me, candlelight reflections flickering in his gray eyes. I filled my plate and ate quietly.

The rest of the group talked about the books, the swamp witches, and what we could do next.

Draven stood and took the lead in the conversation. "First, let's see how the books come together." He fetched the books from a cabinet nearby and placed them on the dinner table next to each other.

We were all silent, watching as he flipped them open, one by one, and frowned.

"Something's not right," he mumbled.

"What do you mean?" I asked, gazing at the first pages.

They didn't seem connected at all. The symbols from one book didn't match any of the other two. He shuffled them around, changing their position, trying a horizontal and vertical order, but still, they didn't say anything.

"They're not making sense," Draven groaned. His jaw muscle tightened.

Hansa stood up and came to his side, looking at the pages with identical befuddlement. She turned several pages and moved the books around again.

"He's right. They're not linked in any way. The half-symbols and sketches in one book don't match any of the other two. It's not supposed to be like this," she muttered.

One by one, we all stood up and inched closer to get a better look.

"This can't be happening," Draven hissed and sat down with a defeated expression.

"Why don't we just finish dinner, go to sleep, and look at them again tomorrow with fresh eyes?" I said.

I took my seat and ate a bite.

Draven nodded, then put the books one on top of the other and poured himself another glass of water. Once again, his plate was empty.

"Out of curiosity, when is it that you actually eat?" I grinned, hoping to steer the conversation away from the books for a while.

"Once a day, but I don't like to be seen when I feed," he replied, staring absently at his plate.

"Why not?"

"Druids are, in many ways, like snakes," Hansa interjected as she sat back down. "They don't eat cooked food. They only tolerate raw meat."

Draven cut her off. "She really doesn't need the full graphic description."

"She's a big girl. She can take it, especially after everything she's seen so far!" Hansa shot back with a smirk, then looked at me. "They eat like snakes, basically. Swallowing large pieces of flesh, which they gradually digest over the course of the day. In the old days, they used to gobble up entire animals, spitting the bones out after a couple of hours, but they've come a long way since then."

A moment of silence passed as I looked at him and noticed he was avoiding eye contact. I couldn't help but wonder whether he was embarrassed. Judging by the flush in his cheeks, I guessed he was.

Hansa seemed to notice as well. "He's ashamed," she chuckled.

"What's there to be ashamed of? He eats raw meat. I literally suck the life out of people. We're all weirdos here," I quipped.

I didn't want him to feel like a misfit, not in my presence, not with my family or friends—particularly when we were all hybrids of sorts, crosses between sentries, vampires, witches, Hawks, werewolves, and fae. He looked at me, and his gaze softened, a faint smile animating his features.

"I find your Druid abilities to be quite fascinating," I added and gave him a sideways glance. My spine tingled as I felt desire emanating from him like a heatwave. His gaze locked on my lips.

A strange shuffling sound drew my attention to the books next to my elbow. I dropped my fork on the plate with a clang, my mouth gaping and eyes nearly popping out of my head. Draven looked down and immediately shot up from his chair.

The books, placed neatly one on top of the other, trembled. The layers of leather rubbed against each other. The covers began to ripple, and over the course of a minute, their texture changed as they merged into one large and very thick book. The leather turned black, and we stared as we realized that the three books had become one.

"What the heck," I managed to croak as I stood.

The others joined us on our side of the table, each gawking at the book.

"What happened?" Aida asked.

"What's that?" Phoenix asked.

"I have no idea," Draven replied, equally baffled. "They seem to have morphed into one. I think it was part of the spell."

With slightly trembling fingers, I reached out and turned the first pages. The writing was clear and linear, the sketches and pentagrams complete. The swamp witches had used a spell to protect their knowledge by splitting it into three separate books. They were useless on their own, and, even when they were put next to each other, they still made no sense. One had to put them together, literally stacking them, for the knowledge to emerge in the form of one large compendium.

"This is still wrong," Draven added, once again frustrated. "I don't recognize the language."

"Oh, come on!" Hansa groaned and flipped through the book. "Figures! They used their cryptic code to write it all down."

"If they were the only ones who knew this language, and they were obviously going extinct, why write it all down in a code that would die with them?" I asked.

"Don't expect much sense out of the swamp witches," Draven

sighed. "They were brilliant but never easy to work with. It seems like even beyond the grave they're still experts at making everything unnecessarily difficult."

"What do we do now?" Phoenix asked, his brow furrowed.

The Daughter seemed pensive as she slowly moved closer to the book, one step at a time.

"Unfortunately, we have no swamp witch translators lying around," Draven replied, his tone laced with sarcasm. "We're stuck with a book that we cannot decipher and the spell that we need somewhere in it."

"Are you sure there's no other way to get to Mount Zur, then?" I started going over options.

"Not unless you want to get captured, tortured, and killed along the way," Hansa said. "It's a very long way from here, and the closer you get to the castle the more spies and traitors roam the dark woods. It's nearly impossible to get there in one piece, given how paranoid Azazel's gotten over the past few decades."

"Why can't the Dearghs from Mount Zur help with getting Sverik out?" I asked, aware that it sounded like a long shot.

"A massive stone giant can't infiltrate Azazel's dungeons without getting noticed," Draven answered. "I'm not even sure they would fit through those corridors. You've seen them yourself. They're gigantic."

It made sense. Based on Aida's descriptions, the dungeons were relatively small, with narrow corridors and not enough room for a Deargh the size of a plane to move around and pluck Sverik out of captivity.

The Daughter stood next to Draven, her fingers running over

the first line of writing on the first page. She read aloud: "*To the one reading this, you are most fortunate. The swamp witches bestow this gift upon you.*"

"You can read this?" Draven asked, his voice barely a whisper.

She nodded and looked at the text.

"*For this is the knowledge of the Aelias, the all-powerful mistresses of dark waters, the coven of witches blessed by the Daughters of Eritopia.*"

A wave of relief washed over the room.

The Daughter looked up at us, slightly confused.

"I'm sorry. I didn't know I could read this. I don't know how I can, to be honest," she said.

"There is no need to apologize," Draven replied with a brilliant smile. "You couldn't have known. The important thing is that you can!"

"Can you read it all?" I asked.

She looked through the book, pursing her lips and squinting, then nodded.

"Yes. It will take a little while. There's a lot of text here. But they look like instructions with clear measures and diagrams."

"Like a manual," I added.

"Indeed. These are all spells, for sure, and they all seem to have spoken formulas, invoking the power of the word," the Daughter explained, glancing over snippets of texts.

Hansa cocked her head, as if analyzing the Daughter. "I wonder," she mumbled, then spoke in a different language.

I didn't understand it.

The Daughter looked up.

"The answer is violet," she replied.

Hansa nodded, then looked at Draven and me.

"I spoke in my tribe's code. Only my sisters and I know it. Yet the Daughter understands it perfectly. I asked her a simple question about the color of her eyes, and she answered."

"So, she understands an ancient succubi tongue as well," I concluded.

All eyes were on the Daughter, who seemed a bit overwhelmed by the attention. Phoenix swiftly joined her and wrapped an arm around her shoulder, keeping her close. I watched her relax under his touch.

"She's a Daughter of Eritopia," Draven reasoned. "She most likely understands every word of every language, every code ever invented in this world."

"It makes sense, if you think about it," Hansa replied.

"Indeed, it does." He nodded, then looked at the Daughter. "Would you be so kind as to help us translate this book? The sooner we find the spell we need, the quicker we can rescue Sverik and make progress against Azazel."

The Daughter took the large compendium in her arms, smiled at Draven, then headed for the door.

"Phoenix, she can use one of the study rooms upstairs," I said to my brother as he joined the Daughter on her way out.

He waved in response, without turning his head.

We all sat down. A collective sigh of relief fell over us as we finished our meals.

"We're one step closer to getting Sverik out of there." Draven looked at me and smiled.

His hand covered mine on the table, his grip tightening gently, enough to send sparks up my arm and fill me with his familiar warmth.

11

PHOENIX

We'd been at it for hours. Midnight had come and gone as the Daughter and I worked on translating the swamp witches' book. She read passages out loud, and I took notes, using old pencils and several journals I'd found in one of the drawers.

A few candles gave enough light for our eyes to handle the reading and writing process without struggling. Owls hooted outside. A giant moon spared a few milky white rays for the study room.

"This one's a concealing spell," the Daughter said as she read a couple of passages from another chapter. "It's supposed to be like a paste of sorts, a mixture of ingredients that one spreads over any surface they wish to conceal. The incantation is short. We should write this down. Draven and Serena might need it."

I couldn't help but gaze at her, unable to wipe the smile off my face. She was so innocent, yet capable of the strangest things. And here she was in the middle of the night thinking of ways to help my sister and the Druid. Despite her ingenuity, the Daughter had developed this sense of urgency that we'd all been facing for days. She looked at me questioningly.

"What is it, Phoenix?"

"Nothing. I'm just amazed at how selfless you can be. Others would be moaning about how tired they are, yet you're fishing for more spells to help Draven and Serena," I replied, my fingers playing with a lock of her hair.

"Well, I haven't found the protection spell that they need against fire yet, so we might as well write the useful ones down in the meantime."

I nodded and proceeded to jot down the ingredients for the concealment paste. Most of the herbs and powders she mentioned sounded familiar, giving me the impression that I'd seen some of them downstairs in the greenhouse and in the basement. Vita had put labels on everything.

However, as the minutes went by, I started to acknowledge the heaviness in my limbs and head. I hadn't syphoned in a while, and I was hungry for energy. I tried to concentrate as I wrote down the quantities in the order in which she dictated them, but eventually I started to lose track and blanked out for a few moments, unable to get my brain back in motion.

"Phoenix, are you okay?" the Daughter asked, furrowing her brow.

"Yes, I'm fine. I'm just a little hungry."

"But we had dinner."

"I'm a sentry. I need energy," I reminded her, and she

nodded. "Don't worry. I'll ask Field or Jovi tomorrow. I can syphon from them."

I'd told her about my abilities before but without much detail. She shook her head and took my hand.

"Why not me?"

I blinked, then blushed, remembering the times I'd secretly tried to mind-meld and syphon off her during our first couple of days together. I scratched the back of my head and decided to tell her the truth.

"Well, to be honest, I tried before, but I couldn't. I mean, you're blocked off from me somehow. I can't touch your mind. I can't draw energy from you."

She thought about it for a while, then smirked.

"What about earlier?" she asked.

"What...what about earlier?"

My mind raced to our moment in the banquet hall, before we found the third book. She'd opened up to me, and I'd been able to feel her emotions in ways I'd never thought possible. The memory of her scent inundated my consciousness, and I felt that invisible string between us tugging my heart. Then it hit me.

"Earlier in the banquet hall, when we talked about death," I said.

"Yes."

"You opened up to me. I felt what you felt."

"Yes."

A heartbeat later, I conceded. "I'm confused. I'm sorry. I don't think straight when the sentry side of me is hungry."

"I don't know myself well enough, but I think that it has to do with *me* whether you can or cannot syphon off me. Why don't we try? I give you my permission. I will open up the way I did earlier, and you can try."

My gaze found hers, and a delicious heat spread through my chest, making my arms tingle. I shifted in the chair to face her. I cupped her face with my hands and took a deep breath.

"Are you sure?"

She nodded and let a sigh roll out of her chest. I felt her then, like earlier in the banquet hall, as she relaxed and let her walls down. A flurry of emotions flowed through me, and I closed my eyes, looking for the source of energy inside of her.

First, there was darkness. Then, there were thousands of thin ribbons of pink, white, and orange—her emotions, all aimed at me, different but delightful shades of yearning and affection. I let it all in as I swam through the darkness searching for the center of her being.

A thick pillar of electric violet energy towered in front of me with no apparent beginning or end. It pulsated and buzzed and beckoned me to come closer. I reached out for it.

A tremendous life force crashed into me. Wave after wave filled me up and rushed through my veins like a river during a storm.

The world began to unravel through the darkness, the galaxy exploding outward as I watched Eritopia come to life. I traveled through time and space as I syphoned this primordial energy from the Daughter, and I watched it all evolve. The planets, the sun, the moon, the trillions of stars. The mountains, the rivers, the endless plains, and the angry seas. I saw incubi and Druids and countless other species. I could see everything inside of her, layer upon layer of creation. She was Eritopia.

I felt my strength recover, and I opened my eyes to find the Daughter looking at me. Her energy continued to flow through me, unstoppable and powerful. It was more than I could take, and the idea of an overdose started shaping in the back of my head. It was something I had never felt before.

Whatever she was made of, it was of godlike proportions. The energy stored inside of her, that endless stream of liquid violet lightning, was insanely intense. The destructive potential chilled me, as I realized that she could probably wipe out an entire galaxy if she released all that force at once.

I pulled back and took a few deep breaths to recover. My whole body sang, and my limbs vibrated from the extraordinary nourishment. I felt like a titan, ready to move mountains if need be. The Daughter's energy hadn't just sated me, it had given me an extra kick I'd never felt before.

I couldn't find the words to thank her. At the same time, I worried. What if all that energy inside of her would one day destroy her and everything around her?

The Daughter sensed my concern, our emotions still intertwined. She shook her head and leaned forward.

And then she kissed me. Our lips touched for the first time. I felt my brain melt and dissipate into billions of sparks. My muscles tensed, as I pulled her closer to me, wrapping my arms around her delicate waist. I deepened the kiss.

She tasted like summer sunshine, and her energy buzzed through me, igniting every atom in my body. Heat coursed through my veins. My tongue found hers. I could've stayed there forever, our bodies fused together.

But as sheer arousal began to cloud my judgment, I pulled back to look at her. Violet sparks flickered in her eyes, and her wet pink lips quietly asked for more. I saw the shadow of fear pass over her face as her fingers clasped the collar of my shirt.

"I don't want you to be afraid of me," she gasped, leaning in again.

"Is that what this is? You think I'm afraid of you?" I asked, gradually recovering my breath.

She nodded, biting into her lower lip. Her doe eyes tore me apart. I couldn't bear to see her like this. I kissed her, opening myself up and projecting everything she made me feel. I had to make her understand that it wasn't fear that I felt. Not of her. I tasted her once more, reveling in the sensations she triggered from my very core.

"You don't understand," I whispered in her ear. "I'm not afraid. I am in awe of you."

The Daughter blinked several times. Her lips stretched into a smile, and I felt her relax further into me, colorful ribbons once again flowing through both of us.

"I can tell there's something in me," she mumbled. "Something even I don't understand. I know you felt it too. I just don't want you to fear me. I would never hurt you. I would never hurt the ones you love. I've been around you and your family and friends for long enough to tell that you are all kind, wonderful creatures. You've made me feel at home. You've looked after me and taught me the ways of the world. I may not know much, but the one thing I do know is that I would never hurt you, Phoenix. I can't."

I needed a moment to take it all in. I caressed her face and dropped a few kisses on her forehead, her cheeks, and the tip of her nose. I knew in my heart that I would never let her out of my sight. She was everything to me, and more.

"You're an extraordinary being," I said to her. "It isn't fear you saw in me. It's something else. I am amazed, I am entranced, I am weightless when I'm around you. And the energy inside of you...it's colossal...like nothing I've seen before."

"I feel it too, every day. I know it's there. I just don't know what to do with it. It's scary, but if you're near me I feel brave enough to face it, to face anything."

I held her close, running my fingers through her hair. She rested her head on my shoulder for a moment. Then, she pulled herself back and resumed her search through the swamp witches' book. I watched her.

What had my life been like before her? I couldn't tell anymore. It was as if I hadn't existed before we fell out of that shell together.

Her face straightened as she flipped through another page. She straightened her back and looked at me.

"I found it," she said.

12

SERENA

I slept in our room that night, sharing the bed with Vita and Aida. We hadn't spoken much since I'd returned from Mount Inon, and we'd spent a couple of hours catching up. I was thrilled to find out that Aida and Field were becoming an item. She deserved all the happiness she could get, and I knew, deep in my heart, that Field was perfect for her. The wolf-girl needed the Hawk.

I was equally delighted to learn that Vita had also found the courage to take the first step toward Bijarki. I figured the incubus was probably still reeling from that kiss, but I couldn't help but applaud Vita for handling it the way she did.

We fell asleep while talking, eager to catch up as much as possible but unable to keep our eyes open.

I woke up at dawn, the sun peeking through the window. Vita and Aida were still far away in dreamland. Their expressions were soft and serene, and their muscles were relaxed. I hadn't seen them like that in forever, or at least that's how it felt. Time seemed to flow differently in Eritopia, each day bearing the intensity of a month from end to end.

I got up and showered quickly. The cold water energized me. I found another bar of soap in a cabinet beneath the sink. I sniffed it and was delighted to discover a mixture of lavender and lemongrass in its fragrance. I washed my hair with it and used a towel to dry it as much as possible.

The thought of Draven sleeping alone in his room quickly surfaced, drawing me out into the open corridor. I didn't want him waking up alone—that was, if he was still sleeping. I reached his door and opened it slowly, poking my head in to get a quick look.

My breath stopped in my throat. Draven was sprawled on his back wearing nothing but a pair of dark green velvet pants. The morning sun poured through his window, bathing his bare chest in a warm, golden light. His eyes were closed, his arms stretched out.

I bit my lower lip and went inside, closing the door behind me. I tiptoed all the way to his bed and slowly sank into the mattress, lying next to him, close enough to rest my neck against his forearm. I sighed and relaxed, watching his chest move up and down with each breath. I couldn't get enough of him.

He took a deep breath and turned his head to face me, peeling his eyes open. His gaze found mine, and his lips stretched into a lazy smile. He turned to his side and instantly wrapped his arms around me, pulling me close.

"It took you forever to get here," he muttered, then showered me with short, delicious kisses.

I melted into him, my fingers running along the valley between his pectorals.

"Had to make myself presentable," I mumbled beneath his lips.

"You're irresistible by default, Serena, and I don't like it when you're not near me."

His hand reached up to caress my face, his fingers tracing the contours of my jaw and setting me alight once more. His other hand gripped my lower back, holding me against his body. I felt my muscles relax while tension built up in my abdomen.

He pulled his head back to look at me, and I felt his fingers slowly lifting the hem of my shirt, leaving my lower back exposed. His other hand followed the line of my neck and shoulder in a series of small circular moves.

"I must apologize, Serena, but I'm having a hard time keeping my hands off you," Draven whispered and kissed the tip of my nose.

"If it makes you feel any better, I'm faced with the same problem," I replied as my fingers followed the deep line down his stomach, delighted to discover his abs, firm beneath his soft skin.

His bedroom eyes made me lose my breath. I pushed my hips forward, enough to feel him hard against me. I belonged there, with him.

"I'd like to see where this will take us," he said, his voice low and husky. "With everything else that's going on around me, with all the dangers waiting beyond the shield, you're the only thing that keeps me afloat, the only one to give me the strength I need to keep fighting."

His gaze softened, and my heart thudded, struggling against my ribcage. I felt my cheeks burn as I lifted a hand to his face, tracing an invisible line from his temple to his chin.

"I feel the same way, Draven. I don't know when and how, but you've burrowed inside my soul."

He glanced at my lips, bent forward, and captured my mouth in a long and tender kiss. I surrendered completely as his tongue brushed mine.

The taste of him set me aflame.

My fingers splayed across his chest, groping into the flesh, ripping a guttural moan from him. His hands traveled down my back, pressing into my muscles and pulling me on top of him. I found myself straddling him. He lay there, hot and tense beneath me, his nails gently scratching my skin as they reached my shoulder blades.

He deepened our kiss, and I felt him open up, sending ribbons of his heady energy my way. I took it all in, slowly moving my hips to relieve the tension budding inside of me. I was soft on top of him, my chest molded against his. He groaned and sank one hand into my hair, grasping the back of my head and pulling it to one side. He left my mouth, dropping burning kisses down my neck.

"My mind stops functioning every time I touch you," he whispered, his teeth gently nipping my skin.

I squirmed, unwittingly bringing my knees up. Despite the two pairs of pants between us, I could still feel him, and I knew I'd set something off inside of him.

"You've become essential to my existence, Serena," Draven said, then flipped me on my back.

Heat built up as his body weighed heavy on top of mine. He found my neck again, dropping kisses between soft bites, making me gasp and arch my back. His thumbs traced my bra-line as his mouth caressed my collar bone, then moved lower, bringing me closer to an edge I'd never experienced before.

I'd barely scratched the surface with Draven, but each moment of discovery brought me closer to what I was beginning to define as heaven. I wanted everything he had to give. I was hopeless in his arms, irreparably addicted and head over heels for the Druid. I projected all of it outward, hoping I'd make him feel what I felt, since my words had already abandoned me.

Draven stilled, his lips hot over my collarbone. He lifted his head, his darkened gaze finding mine. His breathing was ragged, his breath like liquid fire brushing against my skin.

"I've realized I'm more terrified of losing you, Serena, than I am of losing this war against Azazel," he said, resting on his elbows while his hair fell on both sides of his face, tickling my cheeks. "I feel you, I feel everything you want me to feel, and the more you give me, the more I need."

He lowered himself into a long, heartfelt embrace. I felt the air leave my lungs as our bodies fused into one, and he rolled us over to the side. He gave me a warm smile, his expression gentle and loving, like I'd never seen before. This was a new side of him, and it made my heart twist in knots. I felt the synergy between us.

I could see it in his gray eyes. He could feel it in my heart-beat. I could sense it in the ribbons of gold energy he offered me, and he could taste it in my kiss.

We stayed like that for a long time, lying next to each other, our bodies close, and our souls pouring into each other. The fire burned between us, but as the minutes passed, the cold reality settled back in.

"We have to get moving," I whispered.

"I know. Azazel needs to go," he mumbled, then tightened his hold on me again.

"We have to get Sverik," I added.

"We'll get him. We'll destroy Azazel. There's nothing I can't do with you by my side, Serena."

I let out a tortuous sigh, struggling with the notion of leaving that bed. I wanted to stay there forever and take everything to another level with Draven.

But I also wanted to see Azazel burn.

"We need to get up," I moaned.

He kissed me again, setting off another chain reaction in my core. I quivered in his arms. He lifted his head and put on a playful smile to match the twinkle in his steely eyes.

"We'll continue this later. I promise," he said, then got up.

I stretched my whole body to relieve some of the tension. Draven stood by the bed and watched, before taking a deep breath and disappearing into the bathroom.

"I need a cold shower," I heard him say before he closed the door behind him.

13

VITA

We all met in the banquet hall for breakfast, one of the few occasions we were all in the same room. I enjoyed these meetings, as it gave me the opportunity to observe how the relationships were evolving between all of us.

After the conversation I'd had with Serena and Aida before we fell asleep the night before, I was delighted to notice the subtle differences. Serena sat next to Draven, as he poured her coffee and quietly watched her eat. The tender look on his face said it all. The Druid had fallen for Serena and was unable to take his eyes off her. He stole glances whenever Hansa wasn't talking to him about the swamp witches and the journey to Mount Zur.

On the other side of the table, Field was seated next to Aida. His gaze softened every time their eyes met, and he made sure that our wolf-girl ate well, filling her plate with proteins. They were still getting used to each other being so close. I could tell from the way Aida hesitated before she offered him another cup of coffee or the way in which Field took what felt like forever to place his hand over hers on the table. The moment they touched, however, it all seemed to fall into place. Aida blushed like a rose, and Field whispered something in her ear, making her smile and press her lips together.

Next to them, Phoenix sat quietly, watching the Daughter go through several pancakes. He occasionally added another drizzle of syrup to his plate without bothering to eat anything. Sitting next to me, Jovi and Anjani seemed as awkward as ever. Jovi appeared to be focused on his plate, while the succubus kept poking a large piece of fruit with her fork, occasionally giving him a sideways glance.

In all fairness, we'd all been through enough, and there was more waiting for us down the line as the showdown with Azazel drew closer. Each of us deserved to at least feel something, to find refuge in the arms of those we wanted. There was no telling what tomorrow would bring, so why waste today?

As far as I was concerned, I was still processing my first kiss. I poured myself a second cup of coffee and glanced at Bijarki sitting on the other side of the table. His silvery eyes were hooded, his gaze fixed on me. His nostrils flared as I tucked a lock of hair behind my ear.

I replayed the scene in my mind, and heat expanded through my body. I remembered the intensity of our kiss and the speed with which we'd turned a simple peck on the lips into a merger of flesh and souls. His incubus nature was truly extraordinary, taking everything I was already feeling and amplifying it to the point where I was close to touching ecstasy in his arms.

I took a sip from my coffee and popped a small red berry in my mouth, chewing slowly. I felt lightheaded. I relaxed in my chair while my heart fluttered and my limbs tingled. I looked up and saw Bijarki watching me, a peculiar glimmer in his eyes. His skin was a lighter shade, shimmering more than usual. I realized then that he was channeling his incubus nature in my direction, opening up to me and intensifying my feelings.

I wanted to reach out and touch him. I wanted to jump over the table and lose myself in his kiss. My body trembled. My core tightened. But the only intimacy we could have in that moment was an exchange of glances. Still, I told myself that I would experience that bliss all over again, and more, as soon as I got the chance. He nodded once, then cocked his head to one side, as if reading my mind.

Draven's voice broke me out of my reverie. "We now have a plan going forward."

Bijarki sat up straight, shifting his attention to the Druid, who stood up, hands in his pockets. We all listened, while digging into our breakfast.

"The Daughter was kind enough to find the fire protection spell we needed to reach Mount Zur through Mount Inon," Draven continued. "She also deciphered a couple more useful tricks, including a concealment spell, which will come in handy when we get to Mount Zur. We can now go and get Sverik out, hopefully without getting ourselves killed in the process."

"I have to say, I love your optimism," Phoenix interjected with a sarcastic grin.

Draven nodded and gave him a friendly smirk.

"That being said, there is absolutely no point in all of us being focused on the same thing. Due to the high-risk nature of this mission, we will split into three groups to gain maximum efficiency and cover more ground. Serena, Hansa, and I will go to Mount Zur and retrieve Sverik," Draven said.

"What about us? Me?" Jovi asked, his mouth full.

"You, Anjani, and Bijarki will reach out to the Lamias on the western bank of the River Pyros, where a large settlement of these creatures is rumored to exist," Draven replied. "Lamias are solitary by nature, and the Pyros settlement is considered to be the only organized group since they were first banished from the Druid society thousands of years ago."

"What shall we do once we get there?" Bijarki replied.

"I'm convinced their leaders can be reasoned with, given the circumstances. The Lamias have quite the bone to pick with Azazel since he's killed off the Druids —leaving them with no mates and on the brink of extinction."

Bijarki nodded in agreement and exchanged glances with Jovi and Anjani, while Draven looked at me, Aida, and Phoenix.

"I need the Oracles to stay here, beneath the safety of the shield. You must keep working on your visions, as you've made impeccable progress so far," he said.

I couldn't help but feel a tinge of pride.

"You can conjure your visions without any herbal or physical aids, and you've also extended their length. You can now focus on specific topics. We need all the information that you can gather regarding Azazel and his Destroyers. Once we bring Sverik back, we'll be able to rally more rogue forces against the former Druid. We cannot walk blindly into battle."

"How do we get visions of specific topics, though?" Aida asked. "I've barely managed to hold a vision for more than five minutes. How do I pick what I want to see?"

"Think of the world as a library," Draven replied. "Space, time, and matter compressed into moments. Little books on shelves. This is what I learned from Elissa, years ago. Once an Oracle can control the way in which the vision occurs and its length, it's only a matter of practice and focus before specific timelines can be tapped into. She used to tell me that all she had to do was close her eyes, imagine herself inside a massive library, and think of a specific topic as if it were a book on a shelf belonging to a certain person or a certain year."

It didn't sound difficult, but given the efforts we'd made to have visions in the first place, the three of us knew we were in for quite the ride.

"Field will stay with you," Draven added. "His wings and fighting skills will come in handy, especially if the Daughter decides to go beyond the protective shield."

"I'm not leaving Phoenix's side again," the Daughter shot back.

A smile lifted the corner of Draven's mouth, but he responded with a simple nod and looked over the translated spells, written down in a pocket journal with pale brown pages and black ink. He flipped through the pages and looked up.

"We can gather most of the ingredients for these spells ourselves," he said to Serena. "But there's one specific item that the Dearghs will provide."

"I have to ask," Serena replied. "In our world, witches are born with the ability to conjure magic and to control the elements. It's hereditary. How can we use the swamp witches' magic without their abilities?"

"This isn't your world." Draven smiled. "There are spells in Eritopia that can be achieved with the power of the word. There are formulas, there are ingredients, and, if performed correctly, there is magic. Eritopian magic isn't genetic, at least not as far as the swamp witches are concerned. Druids are different. We are born with it, indeed. But the swamp witches tapped into something ancient of Eritopia, and it took them millennia to develop the craft they needed to use it. They weren't born witches, which is why they preserved their knowledge in that book in the first place. They hoped someday someone would pick it up and start over."

"The power of the word," Serena repeated absently, her eyes fixated on the notebook.

"Yes. Formulas and chemical reactions combined with the right words can create powerful magic. Eritopia listens if you know what to say."

14

AIDA

I had made notes of my visions over the past couple of days. I'd written them down along with rough sketches of the dungeons and halls I had seen in Azazel's castle in a small journal I'd found in the attic. I took it out of my pocket and walked over to Serena to hand it over.

"I've been writing down everything I remember from my visions," I told her, then looked at the Druid. "Given that you don't know what you're walking into, I figured you'd have more use for these than I will."

"Where are these from?" Draven asked, glancing over the notes.

"Mostly from Azazel's dungeons and the other halls inside his castle. I've made some rough sketches as well to give you an idea of the layout I've been able to decipher so far."

"These are incredibly useful. Thank you, Aida." Serena smiled and stood up to hug me.

I welcomed her embrace. I worried for her safety, and I needed her back in one piece, so I was doing my best to help her on this mission to retrieve Sverik. Serena was the rock in our group, the one both Vita and I had admired over the years, the light that pulled us from our insecurities. She meant everything to me.

"It's the least I can do to help make sure you come back in one piece," I whispered.

"I can't tell you how much this means to me," she replied.

"You'd better keep her safe, Druid, or I will tear you to pieces. You hear me?" I said to Draven, only half-jokingly.

"I can take care of myself, thank you very much!" Serena exclaimed.

"Don't worry, Aida," Draven replied. "I won't let anything happen to her."

His gaze softened when it found Serena's, and I instantly understood what they'd come to mean to each other. There was something deep and warm flowing between them, an energy I'd never felt before. She wasn't kidding when she'd said they were taking things to the next level.

Despite his solemn reassurance, I couldn't help but worry.

I caught movement at the corner of my eye and turned to see Bijarki get up from his chair and walk out, his eyebrows drawn into a frown.

Vita got up and left the banquet hall as well.

I smiled, mostly to myself, able to guess where she was going.

15

VITA

I'd seen the expression on Bijarki's face as soon as Lamias were included in the conversation. His mood changed, shadows settling beneath his eyebrows. He was concerned about something, so I decided to find out what was troubling him.

I found him in the greenhouse, cutting yellow leaves off a small potted tree and stuffing them in a leather pouch.

He looked up at the sound of the glass door closing behind me.

"Is everything okay?" I asked, my voice barely audible.

I kept my hands behind my back. My fingers fidgeted nervously. My heart was already racing at the thought of us alone in the same room. It spelled the most wonderful kind of trouble.

He nodded and resumed his collection of leaves and herbs from a group of strange-looking plants with vibrant yellow and violet foliage.

"Yes," he replied. "Just collecting some poisons for our trip. The River Pyros, and its lush banks, is home to some dangerous creatures."

"Does that include the Lamias?"

"Especially the Lamias," he said.

"What's the plan once you get there?" I asked, unable to stop the avalanche of concerns from tumbling around in my head.

"The Lamias are vicious and cunning. They love a good trade. We'll offer some rare gifts, including some of these poisons I'm collecting. You can't find these along the river. They're endemic to other regions and nearly extinct. The Druid's greenhouse is a treasure trove of such rarities."

"So," I replied, stepping toward him as my eyes scanned the flowers around me. "You're planning to offer them deadly poisons as gifts. And?"

He stood up straight, watching me intently.

"We'll propose a trade. They have plenty of reasons to want Azazel dead. We just need to motivate them to actually do something about it," he said, his voice low.

"And what will you offer in trade?"

"That will be up to them to tell us. They already hate Azazel, and that alone is the start of a fruitful negotiation."

I nodded and took a deep breath, my eyes locked on his.

"Promise me you'll be safe, Bijarki. Come back in one piece."

He smiled, and my heart melted. It was always a beautiful sight with his perfect white teeth framed by his firm lips. He scratched the back of his head, his gaze wandering up and down my figure.

"I must apologize, Vita. I've not been myself since yesterday," he sighed. "I'm still...recovering from your kiss."

"Oh?" I stilled and felt my cheeks catch fire.

"I never expected you to do that."

"Oh." My brows gathered into a frown, and I felt an inkling of concern clouding my judgment. Had I done something wrong? Had I been too forward?

"It's just that..." He sighed again, struggling to express himself. "How do I say this? You surprised me. I wanted you to come forward. I wanted you to come to me. I still want you to come to me, but I didn't expect you'd be so brave. You stunned me, Vita, and that is not an easy feat to accomplish."

Bijarki noticed my pause and moved toward me.

My breath hitched.

"Don't do that," he said.

"Do what?"

"Don't close yourself off, Vita. I find you incredibly attractive as you are, but when you take the lead the way you did yesterday, you blow me away completely."

He closed the distance between us, and I felt my temperature spike, heatwaves rippling through me as he stood in front of me. I looked up, taking in all his features, my gaze lingering on his lips.

"Take control again, Vita," he urged me.

I blinked several times before I decided to do just that. I pulled him down by the collar of his shirt and caught his lips in mine.

A familiar lightheadedness instantly took over, along with

electric tingling in my extremities. He unleashed his incubus nature, drawing me in and setting me on fire. Everything I felt was amplified to infinity, and I feared I would die from all the bliss he poured into me. My knees weakened, and my legs nearly gave out, as I lost myself in his kiss.

He sensed my physical weakness and wrapped his arms around my waist, pulling me tight against his hard body and deeper into the kiss. I moaned softly, welcoming the feel of his muscles engulfing me. He tightened his grip, and I felt his fingers stroking my sides.

Bijarki pulled his head back long enough to look at me. Lust swirled in his eyes, and he whispered in my ear. "The only reason why I'm not holding myself back anymore is because I want you to feel everything that I feel, everything that I am." He caressed my earlobe with his lips. "If you can handle me without my restraints, Vita, I can give you pure, unadulterated happiness."

I felt his heart thundering against mine. His hands found the hem of my linen shirt. As he kissed me again, sparks ignited my entire body. My skin rippled as he traced imaginary lines up my back. He pressed his fingertips into my skin and gently kneaded his way down.

I arched my back. I could hardly take it anymore. I gripped his shirt so hard it almost tore. He held me close and gazed deeply into my eyes, visibly delighted by my reaction. He smiled, his eyes dark and filled with silver fire.

"Your reaction to me is perfectly natural, Vita, and utterly delicious," he whispered and covered my mouth with his again, taking me on another trip around the galaxy.

When he finally pulled himself back again, putting a few inches of hot, humid air between our incandescent bodies, we stared at each other. My lips pulsed from the memory of our kiss. Our breath came ragged as we slowly regained our senses.

A smile formed on his lips, and his eyes flickered with desire.

"I promise I will come back in one piece, Vita," he said, his husky voice sending more shivers down my spine. "With you in my life, I have every reason to stay alive and destroy anyone or anything that stands between us."

He tucked a strand of hair behind my ear, his fingers brushing my jaw before his hand retreated to his side.

I took a deep breath and gave him a weak smile, nearly shattered by the amount of energy I'd burned in his arms. I loved every minute of it, and I needed more of him. It was the only certainty I had in that moment.

"You'll have to excuse me now. I must pack a bag for the trip." He nodded curtly, took his pouches of poisonous herbs, and left the greenhouse.

I just stood there, leaning against the table. It took me several minutes to recover. I was unable to wipe off the smile that had settled on my face. I bit my lower lip, and I could still taste Bijarki.

16

SERENA

After lunch we gathered in the reception area downstairs. Bijarki, Anjani, and Jovi were ready to leave for the River Pyros, each with a satchel and a minimum of two weapons, including the large hunting knives we'd found in the attic. Draven and Hansa were waiting for me, along with the rest of our group.

Phoenix stepped forward.

The Daughter watched quietly while we all said our goodbyes.

My heart felt like a rock. I was all too aware that it was possible we'd never see each other again.

Hansa walked up to Anjani, who stood tall and proud, visibly focused on keeping a straight face despite the sad look in her eyes. Hansa grasped her sister's shoulders firmly, wearing her signature confident smirk.

"You be good, little sister," she said. "Be sharp, be ready for anything, be ruthless."

Anjani nodded, but I could tell she was wary of leaving her sister in these circumstances. The loss of the Red Tribe had taken its toll on both of them.

"What do we say when we go on quests like these, Anjani?" Hansa asked.

"May the sun guide your way."

"May the moon light your path," Hansa added.

"May the wind be your wings," Anjani continued.

"May the earth serve your feet."

"And may your blade keep you safe," they said together.

"That's right, sister," Hansa said. "Be fierce, darling. You've got everything it takes to represent our tribe. You are one of the most promising warriors I've been blessed to raise. I know you will not let me down. You show those Lamias that we're not to be played with."

Anjani laughed, swallowing back tears as her sister hugged her tight.

"Come back in one piece, Hansa," she whispered. "I still need you."

"You only need the sun, the moon, the wind, the earth, and that beautiful blade of yours, little sister. But I will see you again soon. If not in this life, I will find you in the next. That I can promise."

I felt my eyes sting as I watched the exchange between the two succubi. One by one, Vita, Aida, and Jovi hugged me goodbye, wishing me well. Phoenix waited his turn patiently, occasionally glancing over his shoulder at the Daughter.

"You stay alive, you hear me?" Aida mumbled, her lips trembling as she tried hard not to cry.

"It'll take more than a crazy snake dude to take me down, Aida. You know that. I'm like a cockroach, nuclear disaster and all," I joked, even as I squeezed my eyes shut to jam my tears.

She nodded, then took a step back, leaving Vita in front of me. I hugged my little fire fae, taking a moment to sniff her hair, wondering if that's what sunshine would smell like if it had a scent of its own.

"Take care of these kids for me, Vita. You're the only reasonable adult in this house now," I quipped, and she grinned.

"Have you fed?" She asked.

"We just had lunch," I mumbled back, and Vita rolled her eyes at me. "Ah, sentry-wise. Yes, I'm well-fed." I nodded toward Draven, who was engaged in conversation with Bijarki, leaving him some last-minute instructions for his trip.

"My two-legged lunchbox," I smirked.

"You feed off the Druid now?" Vita seemed surprised, knowing he'd pushed me away in the early days whenever I'd tried to syphon off him.

"Yes, and his energy is extraordinary and seemingly inexhaustible."

She nodded and gave me a weak smile instead of a goodbye. I then walked up to Jovi and playfully poked him in the stomach. When I nearly strained my finger, I instantly regretted it. The guy was pretty much made out of rocks.

"You'd better come back with all your limbs intact, wolf-boy," I said.

"I know you'd be devastated without me," he grinned.

"Not really, but I really enjoy kicking your ass once in a while."

He wrapped me in a bear hug, lifting me off the ground in the process. Then I made my way to Phoenix, who took me in his arms and held me for a good minute in absolute silence.

"I'll be okay, Phoenix," I said.

"I know you will. There's no way we're not getting out of this alive. Do you hear me?"

We looked at each other and smiled, but I couldn't shake that ominous feeling lurking in the back of my head. I had to let it out.

"But in case we don't, in case I don't, I want you to—"

"Serena, don't." He cut me off, his voice low. "Don't even go there."

"But, Phoenix, I need to say—"

"No, Serena, you don't. Let me be perfectly clear. You're going to sneak into Azazel's dungeon, you're going to get Sverik out of there, and then you'll come back here in one piece. I need you. I need you now more than ever. Don't even think about not making it back. No."

I took a deep breath, swallowing hard as Phoenix gripped my shoulders and put on a reassuring smile.

"You are the strongest, most resilient creature I have ever had the fortune to meet," he added. "On top of that, you are the best sister anyone could ever wish for. I have all the faith in you, Serena. This is nothing for us. Just a crazy snake dude with an army of equally crazy snake dudes. Think of it as real life GASP training."

I chuckled and cupped his face with my hands.

"Take care of yourself, big brother, and look after them as well. I'll see you soon."

He winked in response.

I pulled my satchel over my shoulder, waved goodbye to them all, and walked over to Draven.

"Ready?" he asked, his voice as smooth and calm as ever.

"Ready as I'll ever be."

17

SERENA

We took three horses to Mount Inon, as time wasn't on our side. The stallions were purebred athletes, strong and fast, shooting through the jungle like arrows. We reached the volcano just as night unraveled around us in shades of indigo.

Inon welcomed us with limestone arms wide open. He guided us to another plateau on the western side of the mountain, where the other Dearghs had been kind enough to prepare dinner for us. It awaited us on large wooden platters.

After we ate, we followed Inon inside the volcano, into one of the chambers closest to the lava core. Draven took out the translated notes from the swamp witches' books, while Hansa and I sat in front of him, quietly watching as he prepared for the fire protection spell.

He laid out all the ingredients we'd brought from the mansion, a variety of herbs, seeds, and dried roots. He used a wooden bowl to mix them all together. He looked up at Inon, towering behind us with a curious expression.

"This is the fire protection spell we talked about, courtesy of the swamp witches," Draven explained. "Do you have the powder I mentioned earlier?"

The Deargh nodded and reached out, revealing a small black leather pouch in his hand. Draven took it and poured its content into the bowl. The dust scattered over the herb mixture like bits of glimmering charcoal.

"What's that?" I asked.

"Remains of a fallen Deargh." Draven looked at me. "The volcano only accepts Dearghs. The spell is meant to fool the fire into thinking we are Dearghs, basically."

He then placed his hands above the bowl, palms facing down, and recited the words that would bring the spell to life. "We are not what we seem. We are spirits in stone bodies. We do not burn, for fire is our crown."

He clapped his hands twice, and the mixture instantly caught fire, a vibrant green flame that died out almost immediately. It left behind a dark green paste with limestone and crystal particles, reminding me of the mineral cleansing masks that Aida had once brought back from the American mainland.

The more I learned about this spell, the more I appreciated the swamp witches. In the absence of magic flowing through their veins, they'd learned to trick the elements with formulas and chemical combinations, fueled by the power of the word. The concept was extremely fascinating, and I was eager to understand it better.

I made a mental note to figure out a way to read through the swamp witches' book once we got back.

"I must say, Druid," Inon said, "you're either extremely brave or extremely crazy to do this."

"Do what, exactly? Swim through hot lava or sneak into Azazel's dungeons?"

A moment passed as the Deargh carefully measured his answer.

Hansa and I glanced at each other.

"Both," he replied.

"I've never been one to shy away from a challenge, especially not when we're so close to defeating Azazel once and for all," Draven said.

"I know you're young and motivated now that you have the swamp witches' spells, but don't let that go to your head, Druid," Inon said. "Azazel has seen many centuries come and go before you. He knows how this world works. He knows Eritopia's weaknesses and strengths, and he knows how to use them against anyone looking to undermine him."

Draven nodded, his eyes focused on the bowl.

"I'm not looking to discourage you in any way, Druid. I am merely trying to prepare you."

"I understand that, Inon, and I greatly appreciate it."

"That being said, do not underestimate the snake. It slithers, and it spreads its poison with great skill," Inon continued.

"So, what do you suggest we do, then?" Hansa rolled her eyes and looked up at him.

"It takes a snake to fool a snake. Be quiet. Be one with the darkness and one with the walls."

"We have a trick up our sleeve. Worry not, Inon," Draven replied.

"Be timely. The snakes sleep as the moon begins to set. Leave tonight, as the best time to infiltrate Azazel's dungeons is at dawn. My brother, Zur, is waiting for us on the other side."

"Us?"

"I am coming with you, Druid. You cannot swim through the fire alone. You wouldn't know where to go. The fire only listens to the Dearghs."

"That makes sense," Draven replied, then stood up with the wooden bowl. "We need to eat this."

Hansa was the first to take a fistful of the mixture and swallow it. The look on her face told me it tasted somewhere between horrible and repulsive, so I scooped up a serving of my own and tried to eat it as quickly as possible. The pasty combination of foul-smelling herbs, crystals, and limestone dust didn't exactly go down easy. Draven was quick enough to hand us both some water to wash it down. He did the same, and then we all stood there, watching each other.

"What now?" I asked.

"Now we wait for the spell to kick in," he said.

We each took our satchels and tied our weapons to our backs and belts. We followed Inon through a series of narrow tunnels with incandescent lava veins that served as ambient light guiding our path.

We reached the core of the volcano, a massive circular area

that shrank its diameter upward. Liquid fire bubbled up in what resembled an amber-colored pond that hissed and gurgled. It was bright and unbearably hot in the chamber. I broke out in an instant sweat, and my throat felt like it was closing. I was ready to tear everything off me.

"Hang tight, Serena. This will be over soon," Draven whispered and held my hand.

As if listening to his words of comfort, the spell started to kick in just as my face felt like it was melting off. A cool wave washed over me, and I suddenly felt like I was at a very normal room temperature. A little chill ran down my back as my fingers tingled and my skin rippled. I could breathe again.

I first looked up at Draven, and my jaw nearly dropped. A warm golden light emanated from inside of him, spreading outward like an aura. My heart skipped a beat, as I realized how the spell worked. It had to be ingested before it could manifest as a protective layer. Everything we wore and touched, including our satchels and weapons, was covered in that golden light.

The nuance reminded me of his energy, and it created a beautiful impression in my mind, as if I was seeing him for the first time, a creature made of golden light who smiled down at me with such warmth that my soul ached.

I then looked at Hansa and was surprised by her appearance. She too was bathed in the same golden light, giving her a different look. Her otherwise silvery skin glistened in shades of amber, amplifying the colors in her eyes—two beacons of emerald and gold.

I looked at my hands, my arms, and down at the rest of my

body. I wore the same spell effects. I marveled at the way in which light emanated from my skin, making my insides feel cool and energized.

"I take it the spell kicked in?" I asked.

"Could be, although I'd give it some more time, just in case." Draven smiled, seemingly unable to take his eyes off me. "I must admit, you look incredible, Serena. Like a goddess of Eritopian legends."

I felt my cheeks catch fire, and my lips pulled into a smile.

"You're not too bad looking yourself, Druid," I quipped.

"By the Daughters, you two need to spend some time alone. It's clearly long overdue!" Hansa chipped in.

I automatically let go of Draven's hand and looked away— the instincts of a girl caught doing something she wasn't supposed to. I wasn't sure whether Draven was okay with people knowing about us, about what was blossoming between us. Given the way his gaze jumped from me to Hansa and back, I had a feeling he didn't know either. It made sense to me. Draven had spent his whole life living in isolation and certainly had no idea how new couples behaved. He looked awkwardly adorable to me.

"Oh, please, stop fidgeting like two little kids! I've known from the moment I laid my eyes on you that you were made for each other." Hansa rolled her eyes at us. "Wear it with pride!"

A moment passed before Draven looked at me again. My heart was filled with warmth as I saw his gaze soften and settle on my face, a smile tugging at the corners of his mouth. Something flowed between us then—something I'd never felt before but resembled millions of diamond threads gently caressing my skin, my lips, and my very soul. The sentry in me had picked up on something that Draven was sending my way, but I couldn't figure out what it was.

Inon cleared his limestone throat, kindly reminding us that he was still standing there, waiting for us to get on with this mission.

"Okay, let's see if this works!" I said, a little too loudly.

I stepped forward and dropped to my knees, left hand grasping the black stone edge while I lowered my other hand toward the lava.

"Serena," Draven called out. "Be careful, please."

"It's okay. I can't feel the heat at all," I replied, surprised by how close my skin was to the searing liquid.

I couldn't feel a thing as I dipped a finger, then submerged my whole hand.

I felt nothing other than a tickle, as if I'd just put my hand in burbling water.

I pulled it out and gasped at the sight of my perfectly intact hand.

The spell had worked.

"How long is it supposed to last?" I asked.

"The notes say for about an hour," Draven replied. "There's enough for us to use on the way back as well, including Sverik."

"All three of you must climb on my back," the gentle stone giant said as he descended to one knee, leaning forward to make it easier for us.

One by one, we climbed onto Inon's back. I took the left

shoulder, Draven took the right, and Hansa pulled herself between us, grasping the back of the Deargh's neck. Inon then stood.

"Close your eyes and hold your breath. It will be a very short trip as I jump into the liquid fire and emerge on the other side at Mount Zur, but you shouldn't witness any of it, as you have never done it before and might experience panic," he said.

None of us said anything, and Inon took it as a silent agreement. He jumped into the lava, and I followed his instructions, closing my eyes and grabbing a lungful of air right before he submerged us. I felt the liquid fire the same way I felt water, moving against my skin as the Deargh made his way through it.

It was over in less than a minute, as Inon breached the surface on the other side. Traveling through lava had nothing to do with distance, I realized. The volcanic cores were magical, like portals across space—a rudimentary form of teleportation, taking us from point A to point B in seconds, with no regard for the miles between them.

I opened my eyes and noticed the inside of the volcano, different from Mount Inon, as it proudly displayed deep reflections of indigo, obsidian, and yellow striations streaking from the top. Several Dearghs waited for us on the edge. They wore the same stone colors as the mountain.

Draven and Hansa still held on tightly, gradually opening their eyes. Inon swam toward the Dearghs and pulled himself out of the lava. We jumped off his back, and I felt relief at finding the ground beneath my feet again.

"Welcome, Brother Inon," the Deargh in the middle said.

"Welcome, fellow travelers. I am Zur, guardian of this mountain."

Draven and Hansa bowed politely, and I followed suit. Customs seemed to be precious among these creatures.

"Thank you for having us, Zur. I am Draven. This is Hansa, and this is Serena. We are honored to be in your company."

Zur looked at us, measuring me from head to toe before he tilted his giant stone head to one side.

"You are different," he murmured.

I wasn't sure what to respond with, so I just smiled awkwardly.

"I see a Druid, and I must admit, I am pleased to see one still standing while the rest of the species has been swallowed by darkness and poison," Zur continued, nodding at Draven. "I see a succubus, as tall and proud as I remember her mother to be."

Hansa's eyes grew large.

"You knew my mother?" she asked.

"All the people north of the River Pyros knew Dorna of the Red Tribe. Her beauty was passed on to you, and, I hope, so was her bravery and determination."

Hansa smiled and bowed once more with reverence.

"But you, young lady," Zur turned to look at me again. "You are not of this world, are you?"

I shook my head.

"No, I am not. But my brother and my friends are inexplicably tied to it. And so, I am too," I replied, hoping to leave the inquiry there.

"I understand. Then your brother and friends must be the Oracles that everyone has been talking about," Zur replied.

"You know about the Oracles?" Draven asked, his voice low and cold.

"We've all heard of the Oracles," Inon said. "Word travels fast around the mountains from here. Azazel is desperately looking for them, burning and torturing his way through the land to get to them."

"Our mountain is the closest to his castle. We hear more than others," Zur added.

The thought made me nervous, but I took comfort in the fact that the Daughters' protective shield made my brother and friends impossible to find.

"You should get ready to leave soon," Zur said. "There is about a mile to Azazel's castle, and nightfall will keep you safer than daylight. If you leave within the hour, you will reach your destination before dawn, when the monsters sleep."

We followed Zur through the mountain corridors. He led us to the western edge, where the ridge opened up to a grassy plateau, where a small camp fire burned, with water and pieces of seed bread waiting for us.

Draven opened his satchel and started taking out more ingredients from their small leather pouches, along with the Daughter's notes. I watched as he followed instructions and mixed everything into another bowl.

"This is the invisibility spell," Draven said. "It will keep us cloaked throughout this mission. We should ingest it, to be safe."

"Oh good, another delicious midnight snack," I replied, and Hansa chuckled at my side.

"Whatever it takes for us not to get killed, I will gladly eat," she said, a shadow passing over her face beneath the giant moon above. "I have a score to settle with the Sluaghs, and I'll be damned if I'll die before I get to crush their wormy heads with my bare hands."

Zur and Inon nodded.

"We heard the Destroyers as they returned from the northern mountains. They were quick to boast about how they had wiped out the entire Red Tribe," Zur said to Hansa. "Little did they know then that the Red Tribe survived, for here you are, standing before us."

She looked up at the stone giant and grinned.

"It'll take more than a handful of snakes and worms to kill this succubus, Deargh. Don't you forget that!"

HALF AN HOUR LATER, the invisibility spell was ready. Hansa was checking our supplies and weapons, stocking up on poisoned arrows by dipping their tips in the purple toxin she'd brought from the mansion. I was filling up the water bladders for the road while Draven was busy sharpening his knives, when he looked up, his gaze finding mine. He stood up, took my hand and pulled me away from the center of the grassy plateau, leading me to the edge.

We were slightly obscured by darkness, as the camp fire's light faded with the distance. Before I could open my mouth to ask what this was about, Draven wrapped his arms around me and pulled me close to him, his expression firm.

I felt his heart thudding in his chest as he tightened his grip on my body.

"What's going on?" I asked.

"Absolutely nothing," was his reply.

"Then why did we stop?"

"Because I might not get to tell you what I want to tell you later." His voice was low and raspy in my ear.

My breathing accelerated as I felt his lips on my neck. His mouth moved upward along my jawline, until it found my lips and ravished me with a hungry and unapologetic kiss. I lost myself in the moment, grateful for a few minutes in his arms. Draven's hands gripped my hips and pulled me closer, beckoning me to feel every hard line of his body.

"I need you to be careful, Serena," he said hoarsely, breaking the kiss for a moment. "I simply can't fathom the thought of you getting hurt on this mission, and I need you. I desperately need you to make sure you come out of this alive and unharmed. Do you hear me?"

"I hear you, Draven," I whispered, my breath ragged, and my lips tingling for more.

I raised my hands to his face, cupping it firmly. His words plucked invisible strings in my chest, and I wrapped my arms around his neck, our bodies melting in a long embrace. I realized I'd started having a hard time picturing my life without him in it. The thought was frightening, because I'd never been so close to someone before. But, at the same time, my whole being was exhilarated by him.

"It's becoming increasingly difficult for me to keep myself away from you, and I can feel you going through the same thing. Your body and your soul talk to me in ways I'd never thought possible, and I..." He drew in a breath. "I want to hear the whole story," he whispered. His lips moved down my neck until they reached my collarbone.

"I'm still trying to figure out the whole story, Draven," I replied.

My heart pounded, and I wanted to tell him everything that was weighing on me in that moment, especially the idea of never seeing him again. He belonged in Eritopia. He was fighting Azazel so he could free his home, restore order, and lead it back to prosperity.

Where did I fit in? What would happen if we defeated Azazel? Did we mean enough to each other for one of us to follow the other into a foreign world, or would it end here? And if the answer to whether we meant enough to each other was yes, which of us would be the one to leave their world for the other? These questions had started to eat away at me since Mount Inon.

"Tell me," his voice trickled into my ear, his breathing heavy.

"I don't belong here in Eritopia. I'm from a different world," I sighed. "But, at the same time, every time I see you, everything makes sense, and I don't feel like a stranger anymore, like there could be something here for me other than death and cruelty."

I was telling the truth. My body and my heart were pulling me closer to him. I loved our debates and even our arguments, and I looked forward to peeling back another layer of who he truly was on a daily basis. I enjoyed the discovery, and he surprised me every time.

Each time he looked at me, and I lost myself in his gray eyes, it all disappeared, leaving just the two of us standing in front of each other. There was an invisible line connecting us, ribbons of our souls intertwined and tugging, yearning for more. All the contradictions went away, leaving only Draven and me together.

He took me in his arms and held me tight, breathing against my neck. I could feel his heart beating frantically, resonating with what was going on inside my own chest.

I was beginning to consider the idea of a different life from what I'd been accustomed to. Even a different home. In another world. Draven had changed me in ways I'd never thought possible, and I was starting to think that what I felt for him was too deep to relinquish when this war was done.

"What are we doing here, Draven? What am I doing here, with you?"

As giddy as I'd been at the concept of nobody seeing us so close to one another, I disliked being unable to see the look in his eyes. All I had to go on was his labored breathing, the thudding in his chest, and whatever I sensed in him with my sentry abilities. It all spoke of something similar, if not identical, to what I was feeling.

And it all pointed to a four-letter word I was afraid to pronounce. I'd only read about it in books and seen it in my parents. I'd never considered feeling it myself. I'd had other ambitions to focus on—a career in journalism being my priority. Still, Draven had managed to stomp into my life and change my perception entirely, to the point where all my previous plans seemed superficial.

What was the plan after we defeated Azazel? We'd go back to The Shade, and I'd go on to study journalism? It all seemed so far away. I'd found more meaning in freeing the people of Eritopia, in saving my friends and destroying the evil that had corrupted a beautiful world. My whole ethos of being was gradually maturing as life revealed itself as much more complex than I'd initially believed.

"I don't know yet, but I think we're close to figuring this out," Draven replied gently.

He made me smile, and I pulled his head closer so I could feel his lips on mine again.

"Either way, I'm so addicted to you that you'll most likely be the end of me," Draven chuckled lightly, while his hand gripped the back of my neck and pulled me upward for another delicious kiss.

This time, he kept it short and sweet, holding me close and filling me with ribbons of his golden energy.

"Do you feel this, Serena?" he asked, his lips against mine.

My heart vibrated in my chest. I gradually regained my senses and walked away from the edge where he'd taken me. I was buzzing with warmth, but I could feel something cold and sharp poking the back of my mind. I closed my eyes and tried to identify that emotion. I had sensed it before, just seconds before we'd kissed.

I breathed him in, a heady scent of musk and deep birch forests invading my nostrils and filling my lungs. It was fear that I was feeling.

"I feel a lot of things coming from you right now, Draven."

"I'm aware," he replied. "But I've yet to identify them all myself, even though they're all aimed at you. What is it you recognize, from what you can feel?"

I took a deep breath, as he leaned his forehead into mine. His fingers caressed my face and ran through my hair.

"A bit of fear."

"Indeed, Serena. It's fear I'm feeling. The fear of losing you. The fear of never seeing you again...the fear of being unable to save you."

"Don't—"

"You can't tell me to not feel this, Serena. I've tried. Believe me. It only gets worse, unless I embrace it. Which is why I'm here now, standing before you, nearly begging you to be careful and not get hurt or killed once we reach the dungeons. Do you hear me?"

I held him, nestling my head against his chest, enjoying his strong arms around me.

"I promise, I'll do my best to not get hurt or killed," I mumbled against his shirt.

He groaned, but before he could respond, Hansa's voice shattered our bubble.

"Are you two okay?" She was standing merely five feet away.

Draven cleared his throat, and we stepped apart. His hand found mine and clasped it firmly.

"Yeah, I'm good," I said, a little too loud and high-pitched.

"Good," she replied. "Let's move. We're losing moonlight."

18

JOVI

We traveled south on foot for several miles before we reached a nomad marketplace. Bijarki told me that merchants often settled in the riverbank areas in those parts, as many travelers crossed the region over the year.

"We'll find some good horses there," Anjani said, clutching her crossbow.

Bijarki led the group, while Anjani walked behind me. The jungle was green and lush in these parts, slightly more open, and had fewer marshes in between. We'd shot at some hungry shape-shifters along the way, but the road ahead seemed clear.

"The further south you go, the fewer shape-shifters you'll find," Bijarki explained. "The south is less feral, with more settlements. The wildlings fear the southern nations."

"Why's that?" I asked.

"It's not just the incubi and succubi who carry these shifter-killing poisons. The Lamias are just as ruthless, and so are the imps, the Bajangs, and the Maras. They have very little patience for such perils in their woods, so they have decimated the shape-shifter population over the centuries, forcing them further north."

"You've named some creatures there that I know nothing about," I replied, suddenly chastising myself for not reading much during the couple days' downtime I'd had back at the mansion. There must have been books there about these Eritopian species too.

"Don't worry, Jovi. You'll get to see them live once we reach the Sarang Marketplace," Anjani said from behind.

I looked over my shoulder to find her grinning, as if she knew the ending to a good joke that she hadn't shared with me. It made me feel uneasy wondering what creatures I'd run into at that marketplace.

"Eritopia is home to many different creatures," Bijarki said. "The incubi and succubi are the predominant species, but there are also imps, Bajangs, Maras, and other subspecies in the far east. Then there are... Well, *were* the Druids, and the Lamias deriving from that species. The Dearghs are standalone, as are the Sluaghs. There were once storm hounds and gorgons, too, but Azazel killed them off."

"Some of these names sound familiar," I said. "But mostly the stuff of legends. Gods, monsters, heaven, hell, angels, demons."

"From what I understand, our universes are connected, so I wouldn't be surprised if a handful of our creatures found ways to infiltrate your world. You should tell us more about your home, Jovi, when this is all over," Bijarki replied.

"Provided we all live to hear the tales," Anjani muttered under her breath and shot an arrow through the trees.

I had a crush on her crossbow, custom built for long range shots. Mine and Bijarki's had an effective range of 200 feet, while Anjani's was able to kill from 500 feet. She'd spotted another shape-shifter deep in the woods to our right.

We stilled and listened. I let my inner-wolf sniff the air, and I caught the scent of blood, but the creature was still moving.

"I really need to practice these long shots more," Anjani grumbled and loaded another arrow.

I saw the creature running toward us with a limp, jumping over gnarly tree roots as it reached the road. It shifted right before my eyes into a creepy version of me, sending instant shivers down my back.

We all aimed our crossbows at it and shot at the same time. The arrows pierced through the beast's head, throat, and chest. It fell backward, writhing in agony for a minute before it died.

"I must say, Anjani, you seemed to enjoy killing that shifter a little too much," Bijarki quipped.

I knew what he meant. The beast looked like me. I looked at her, and she wore a sheepish smile that both irritated and enchanted me. The dynamic between us was constantly filled with such contradictions. I was learning to take it all in stride.

"It wasn't as handsome as me," I shot back. "She obviously disliked the copy's cheap quality."

Bijarki chuckled as we continued walking down the road. The sun set in shades of violet and orange.

Soon enough, the Sarang Marketplace emerged ahead, as the woods thinned out. It was large, covering at least half a square mile, with small paths between dozens of stalls and wooden constructions resembling boutique stores.

It was loud and colorful. An abundance of red paper lanterns hung above on a network of strings tied to outer pillars. It was a sight to behold, given that I'd grown accustomed to the lonely mansion beneath a protective shield. There must have been a thousand creatures, all selling and buying everything and anything, from trinkets and fabrics to weapons, tools, animals, and foods.

"Stay close, Jovi," Bijarki said. "You're an outsider to these folks, and they don't always take kindly to strangers."

I nodded and walked ahead, reaching his side and tucking the crossbow in the leather holster mounted on my back. We entered the marketplace, and Anjani headed toward the stables on the far eastern end.

"I'll start looking for horses. You boys get some food and supplies for the rest of the journey," she said, disappearing into the crowd.

I looked around and was surprised by the diversity. Short creatures with thick, wrinkled skin wobbled from one stall to another with large pointed ears and crooked noses. I assumed that those were the imps Bijarki had told me about. They talked quickly and cursed a lot, forcing people into buying things rather than actually selling their merchandise.

There were plenty of incubi moving around, many of them putting distance between us and themselves at the sight of Bijarki's military attire.

"They think I'm from an incubus army, and most of them are defectors and rogues," the incubus said. "I make them wary, which is good. We don't want them asking any questions anyway."

We moved through the stalls, and I watched quietly as Bijarki purchased a variety of nuts and breads for the rest of our trip to the River Pyros. He haggled with the imp in charge until we got an extra bag of nuts on account of the incubus's uniform.

"Those are Bajangs." Bijarki pointed at a group of three males and one female.

They were similar to the incubi and succubi, beautiful by default with pale skin that shimmered golden in the fading sunlight. They didn't have horns, and their eyes were a vibrant yellow with wide black pupils, reminding me of a cat. The males' hair was rich and black, while the female wore hers in ginger and white braids.

"I can see some small differences between your kind and theirs," I mumbled, careful not to be heard as they walked past us.

They wore leather garments and sharp blades hung on their belts. They gave me and Bijarki a sideways glance that was anything but friendly. The female hissed at me, and I stilled as I watched her shift into a large, orange feline with white stripes. She darted through the crowd as one of the males cursed under his breath and picked her clothes and sword up off the ground where she'd left them.

The same male frowned at me and ran after her, followed by his two companions.

"I guess we made her nervous," Bijarki replied, amused.

"Okay, scratch what I said earlier. There are obviously some major differences between your kind and theirs," I added. "They turn into cats? Seriously?"

He shrugged. "They've been like that since before we've had a recorded history. They're usually solitary creatures, and they live in our cities, sleeping wherever they can and eating whatever they catch. Sometimes, they befriend incubi clans and live with them. They can be very useful in feline form."

I could only imagine what useful meant to Bijarki. All I could think of was that the rodent problem was taken care of and fur balls would permeate the house. The female's antipathy suddenly made sense, though. She had most likely sensed my wolf blood. Cats and dogs and all that.

We found a jewelry stall further down the aisle. I recognized the old woman as a fae. Her dress was large with glimmering purple ruffles. She sat back in her rocking chair and played with a violet flame between her fingers. The moment she heard us she sprang to her feet, putting the flame away, and smiled.

"Welcome, fine travelers," she greeted us with arms open. She stood behind a large table loaded with precious gems and metals. There were earrings, bangles, necklaces, collars, bracelets, pearls, rings, and pendants. "What a pleasure to have you here!"

Bijarki nodded politely while scanning the table.

"You're a fae, aren't you?" I couldn't help asking.

"Indeed, I am, young man. And you're not from around here, are you?" She grinned, revealing two rows of perfect white teeth.

She'd aged very well, with just a few fine lines and a cascade of white hair pouring down her back. From what I knew about the fae, she was most likely several thousand years old. I shook my head in response.

"Neither are you, for that matter," I replied.

"No, I am not, young man. I take it you know my kind?"

"I do. I was a guest of Sherus," I said and immediately watched her smile drop. "You know him?"

"Oh, I do indeed. You might not believe it, but he was once my protégé." The old fae sighed. She ran her fingers over the precious gems on the table, absentmindedly moving them around.

"What happened, if you don't mind me asking? How did you end up here?" Bijarki interjected, suddenly interested in our conversation.

"I was here on a diplomatic mission, many centuries ago. I was betrayed by someone close to me and found guilty of a crime I did not commit. They left me behind as punishment. Sherus, unfortunately, believed others instead of me. I've been here ever since, before Azazel even began his bloody conquest," the fae replied.

I wondered what the crime was, and what would have made Sherus do that. There was sadness in her voice, but she quickly reverted to her bright smile.

"Anyhow, that is in the past, and it doesn't matter anymore," she continued. "What matters is that you are here, and I have so many wonderful jewels for you to buy. There must be a special lady in your life."

Bijarki picked out a small turquoise pendant, sculpted in the form of a flame and hung on a delicate silver chain. A faint smile passed over his face as he lifted it between his fingers.

"How much for this one?" he asked.

She looked at the pendant and squinted.

"Just two pieces of gold, soldier. The turquoise flame protects and nourishes the spirit," she replied. "Well chosen!"

"Thank you," Bijarki said and handed her two gold coins from his coat pocket. Draven had given us gold from his father's inheritance for occasions such as this. Almus had gathered a healthy fortune during his service to Eritopia, leaving plenty of gold for his son.

She stashed the money in a small leather pouch on her belt, then picked up a pendant to show me. It was a silver wolf's head, its jaws wide open and fangs holding on to a tear-shaped diamond. She held it up for me to see up close.

"This is a special trinket. It should only be given to the one you love unconditionally."

There was a small flame burning white inside the diamond, the result of some kind of spell, for sure. I took it in my hand and found myself entranced by how it burned on the inside.

"How will I know if I'm giving it to the right person?" I asked.

"Worry not. The diamond will know."

It was a beautifully crafted piece, and I felt compelled to get it. I instinctively thought of Anjani as I reached for the few gold pieces I had in my pocket, courtesy of the incubus. The old fae shook her head as she looked at me.

"This pendant will not cost you gold, young man."

"But I must pay you for it."

"One day, I will seek you out and ask for your help," she smiled. "Repay me with a favor then."

"How will you know where to find me? I'm not from this world."

I felt a sting on the back of my head, something akin to a mosquito bite. I touched the skin and noticed a tiny speckle of blood on my fingertips.

"Worry not. I have my way of finding people when I need them," the fae replied and bowed before me.

I couldn't help but wonder whether the sting had anything to do with what she'd just said, or if it was from some bug that had coincidentally landed on me. My attention was drawn back to the wolf pendant. She gave me a velvet pouch for it, and I stuffed it in my pocket, feeling slightly creeped out.

"Uh, okay." I wondered what I might have just gotten myself into but didn't want to be rude and reject the pendant. "Thanks, I guess."

"We should head for the stalls," Bijarki said to me. "It will be night soon, and we need to move."

I waved goodbye to the old fae and followed the incubus through the crowd. I had a feeling she was watching me as I walked away, but when I looked over my shoulder she was gone, her stall unattended. I checked the sting on the back of my neck once more, and the blood had stopped flowing. It must have just been an insect bite.

We reached the stalls, where Anjani waited next to three beautiful horses, tall white steeds with short red manes.

"These three are perfect for what we need," she explained and patted one of them on the neck.

It nuzzled her face in response, and she smiled. As I watched her interact with the animal, I felt myself soften inside. My fingers felt the jewel through the velvet. The old fae's words still rang in my head, and I was starting to see Anjani in a different light. Was she the one truly worthy of the wolf's head pendant?

"I trust your judgment," Bijarki said, breaking me out of my thoughts.

The salesman came out. He was a crooked old imp with tufts of white hair and long, curved horns poking out from behind his large pointed ears. He measured us from head to toe with a frown.

"What do you want?" he asked, as if we'd disturbed him.

"These three horses." Bijarki took the lead, pulling his money pouch out. "How much for them?"

The imp hesitated, his gaze fixed on the pouch.

"Fifty pieces of gold. At least that's how heavy that bag of yours looks," he replied with a smirk, revealing his yellow, crooked teeth.

"That's too much, you old imp. There's no way anyone will ever pay that much for three horses," Bijarki shot back, irritated. "Don't try to rip us off."

"What, you think I'm afraid of your uniform?" The imp got

loud and snappy. "I'm not afraid of you! It's fifty pieces of gold, or you walk wherever you need to go!"

"This is robbery, old imp! These may be good horses, but I wouldn't give you more than twenty pieces for them. And that's if I'm feeling generous," Bijarki held his ground.

"Then walk!" the old imp snapped and moved to go back inside his little cabin.

"Please be kind, sir," I heard Anjani purr from my side. "We're just trying to get to the River Pyros in time."

My head felt light, and my whole body tingled as a heatwave poured through me. She'd turned on her succubus nature and aimed it at the old imp.

I was downright collateral damage, based on how badly I suddenly wanted to kiss her and lose myself in her.

I felt Bijarki's arm grab mine and squeeze tight, enough to help me focus. Judging by the smirk on his face, he knew exactly what Anjani was doing. I then looked at the imp and under-stood. The creature looked smitten. His eyes had softened and a goofy smile slit his face from pointy ear to pointy ear. He was certainly responsive to Anjani's charms.

"You're heading down to the river, you say?" he asked, his gaze devouring her.

I couldn't stifle the tension rising in my chest. My hands balled into fists at my side. I was ready to knock the old imp out if he so much as moved a finger toward Anjani. Bijarki's fingers dug harder into my flesh, keeping me tethered, and I was grateful.

"Yes, good sir, and my feet are tired. I just want to get to the river before sunrise," Anjani replied. "Can't we settle at twenty pieces of gold, please? We still need some money for food and shelter where we're going. Surely a handsome imp such as yourself doesn't have the heart to leave a creature like me stranded."

Her voice was honey, and it did all sorts of things to my brain. I stilled, my mind imagining her engulfed in my arms, that sweet voice beckoning me to let our bodies and souls merge into one. I needed a few deep breaths to return to reality.

"Twenty pieces of gold it'll be then," he told Bijarki. "But only because you've got this gorgeous creature here with you! I don't want her feet to suffer!"

Bijarki nodded and gave him the money, while Anjani dropped a kiss on the old imp's forehead. She put the reins on the horses.

The imp seemed to melt, smiling like a lovesick puppy and watching as she took the horses out and put the saddles on them one by one. He didn't even bother to put his money away. His fistful of gold hung by his side.

"I think we should travel with her more often," Bijarki muttered next to me, then addressed the imp. "Thank you, sir. You've been too kind! May the Daughters smile upon you!"

We got on our newly acquired horses and moved toward the exit. I felt Anjani's succubus nature shut itself down, leaving me with my usual longing for her in its wake. The emptiness was just as unbearable but somehow more manageable. She was truly a force of seduction. I was putty in her hands. I couldn't blame the old imp for giving in so easily.

My mind froze as we passed a group of creatures—tall and

slim with pale white skin and black eyes, wearing long gray robes and hoods.

"Don't look at them," I heard Bijarki say too late.

I made eye contact with one of the creatures and blanked out completely.

Next thing I knew, we were out of the market, our horses trotting farther south toward the River Pyros. The jungle was dark and silent around us. I looked over my shoulder to see the marketplace we left behind, several yards back.

"What just happened?" I asked, realizing that I'd lost a few good minutes since I'd seen those hooded creatures.

"Those were Maras you made eye contact with," Anjani replied with a smirk.

"They looked rather strange," I said, remembering the paleness and full black eyes.

"They're very dangerous if you cross them in any way. They have impressive mental abilities. They do not read minds, but they can sneak into your head and play tricks on your thoughts. What did you see while you were out?" Bijarki asked.

"What do you mean I was out?"

"Your mind pretty much shut down. You were stunned and quiet with eyes wide open, as if paralyzed. It's what happens when a Mara enters your mind. Most of the time, they implant the nastiest of visions and bad dreams, so you might be in for a rough night," he replied.

"I didn't see anything. I just lost some time from the moment I made eye contact to the moment I asked you what happened," I mumbled, looking over my shoulder.

"We'll have to keep an eye on you tonight, just in case."

"Just in case?" I asked with an increasing sense of alarm.

"Don't worry, the effect doesn't last for long. You only looked at them for a second or two. You'll be fine!" Anjani interjected.

I nodded weakly, trying to push the worry aside, and focused on the road for the next minute.

Then, on an impulse, I looked behind me again. My nerves resurfaced as I noticed more and more creatures gathered at the gates of the marketplace, more than two hundred feet away.

I engaged my inner-wolf to get a better look. They were all looking at us suspiciously, and some of the incubi in the crowd gripped the hilts of their swords. Shadows darted from the marketplace into the jungle on both sides, and my instinct put me on high alert.

I heard whispers and shuffles through the trees as our horses picked up the pace. The hairs on the back of my neck rose, and I took my crossbow out, loading it with a poisoned arrow and gripping it firmly.

I couldn't shake the feeling that something was going to follow us.

19

AIDA

I was having a vision. I'd managed to bring myself to a state of focus that allowed me to browse through the present with a little bit more precision than usual. I'd homed in on Azazel and his Destroyers, and I was making progress.

As the darkness dissipated to the outer edges of my visual field, I realized I was standing in Azazel's personal chamber. It was built entirely from obsidian blocks, beautifully polished and stacked to impressive heights, allowing a massive black iron chandelier to dangle from the ceiling. Its white candles burned red.

It was a spacious room. Crimson flames reflected in the smooth black walls. A massive bed was mounted against the wall, covered in red silk sheets. A sturdy round ebony table stood in the middle, its legs sculpted to resemble snakes, their jaws open and fangs ready to pierce flesh.

Azazel was looking at a large map sprawled on the shiny

surface. The map was riddled with ink marks defining conquered areas of Eritopia. Joining him were two other Destroyers, one bulky and rough, the other also large but athletic, with carved muscles and softer features. They were engaged in a heavy conversation, constantly pointing at various points on the map.

"Patrik, I do not have the patience to deal with Roderick's clan anymore," Azazel said, running his fingers through his long black hair.

The infinity snake medallion glistened in the semi-darkness, its ruby eyes reflecting the crimson flames from the overhead chandelier. It creeped me out, as if it were sentient and able to see me, so I did my best to avoid looking at it.

"I'm very close to convincing him to join us, my liege," the athletic Destroyer, identified as Patrik, said. "I just need another day or two. That is all. There is no point in spilling the blood of potential new soldiers when I can persuade Roderick to swear fealty to you."

"I'm giving you another day before I send Goren to take care of things the old-fashioned way," Azazel replied, stroking his medallion.

The bulky Destroyer named Goren wore a self-satisfied grin, and his thick arms crossed as he looked over the map.

"I'm happy to fly in and teach that self-righteous incubus what obedience means," he hissed, while Azazel rolled his eyes.

"My biggest concern isn't with Roderick," Patrik insisted. "He can be persuaded eventually. I just need to point out the repercussions of rebellion for his entire clan, including his seven sons and his wife, and he will bend."

"He's had it too good, if you ask me. Seven sons, and he got to keep the mother, unlike most incubus clans. Perhaps you are right. A reminder of how fortunate he is might help him see things more clearly," Azazel smirked. "Like I said, you have one day, Patrik, before we send in the brute force."

Patrik nodded and pointed at another district further north on the map.

"What about Marchosi, my liege?" he asked.

His snake-like tongue flickered between his lips, and his yellow eyes scanned the territories beneath his large palm.

"What about him?"

"Can he be trusted? You may have finally conquered his district, but his people might still put up a good fight. He might have said yes just to live another day, while his troops prepare to defend the city."

"Do not worry about Marchosi, Patrik. He is under my spell now. The darkness is slowly eating away at him, and soon enough, he'll be forever under my control, whether he likes it or not. The City of White Stone will be mine by the end of this month," Azazel replied, then dipped a quill in black ink and crossed out the entire district on the map. "The last Druid-owned city fell the moment Marchosi said yes. The rest is purely administrative clutter, as far as I'm concerned."

"It's true, though," Goren interjected with the same obnoxious grin, his sharp fangs bared and menacing. "Once Azazel's darkness takes over, it's not just your body that caves in. Forget control over your snake form altogether. It's your will that gets corrupted. The more you fight it, the harder it gets, and the more you suffer. You've seen the bastard hissing and wailing, barely holding on to the walls while he struggles to maintain his Druid form, Patrik. He's almost gone!"

The words sounded strange coming from a Destroyer who had also lost his mind and body to Azazel. It was as if Goren didn't recognize his own corruption.

Patrik nodded slowly, looking away. A muscle tensed in his jaw, and a frown drew his brows close, casting shadows under his eyes. I couldn't help but wonder whether Patrik was content with his status, as one of Azazel's most trusted lieutenants.

Goren's statement provided me with some crucial information. Azazel's corruption spell went deeper than Draven had originally told us. It wasn't just physical. It was able to bend the will of its victim. Destroyers were once Druids, but we'd been under the impression that they'd all willingly joined Azazel. It turned out they hadn't really had a choice.

"Remember your first days, boy?" Goren cackled and slapped Patrik on the back, causing him to hiss with irritation. "You were crying and punching walls, crying after Almus like a little girl, swearing that you would rather die than lead any of Azazel's armies. Now look at you. A fine lieutenant, racking up territories and bodies like trophies!"

Clear displeasure imprinted itself on Patrik's face. His hands clutched the edge of the table, his knuckles white.

"Give it a rest, Goren," he shot back. "We weren't all spineless traitors like yourself!"

"Traitor?!" Goren growled. His pupils dilated, his nostrils flared, and his tail rattled furiously. "I saw where the true power is! It's with Azazel! I chose to be here, and I do my best to please our lord! Besides, I do a very good job of it too! Better than you, if you ask me! I didn't waste a minute trying to persuade those succubi in the Red Tribe to join us. I rained down on them with spears and arrows laced with poison. I burned and killed everything that dared to stand against us! Isn't that right, Sir?"

Goren addressed Azazel, who was rolling his eyes so deeply that I could only see the whites.

"If you're looking for praise and flattery, Goren, you've picked the wrong Druid," Azazel smirked. "You all caved in, whether you liked it or not. Your wills are mine, and it makes no difference to me whether you came in willingly or kicking and screaming. I give the orders. You execute. That's all there is to it. No awards, no medals, just the honor of still breathing."

Goren's grin faded.

A smile tugged at the corner of Patrik's mouth. Clearly, he'd been forced to become a Destroyer, while Goren had willingly joined the Destroyer ranks. Patrik was still struggling, but Azazel's spell ran so deep, he had no way of fighting it. His will was no longer his own. I couldn't help but feel sorry for him, wondering how many lives he'd taken, how loaded his conscience must be. How many tears had he shed for the innocent creatures he'd been forced to kill?

"If you expect me to congratulate you for killing a bunch of succubi, Goren, you've got another thing coming. They're succubi, not Dearghs. You snap them like twigs, you oaf," Azazel added, then turned to give Patrik a surprisingly sympathetic look. "My dear Patrik, I have always kept you in the highest of regard, even when you were commanding Almus's troops. Your skill in battle and flawless strategy have brought me this far, after all. It's the only reason why I tolerate your whims and blatant displeasure regarding your role as my Destroyer. Do not worry about Marchosi. He'll be fully under my control very soon. He is much weaker than you ever were."

Patrik nodded again and pointed elsewhere on the map.

"When do we move south, then?"

"We'll start very soon. I've set up a fine strategy for this campaign, Patrik. You will love it! But for now, we wait. Not all of my pieces have fallen into place just yet."

I felt sick to my stomach, unable to take my eyes off Goren. The massive chunk of meat with a rattle-snake tail was the one who'd led the charge against the Red Tribe. He was the one responsible for all the death and destruction, for killing Hansa and Anjani's sisters. My stomach churned as I pictured the monster attacking the camp, slaying little succubi and laughing as he set the tents on fire.

My heart broke. The agony, the grief, and the anger made me want to leave. I couldn't stand the sight of him anymore. I was already looking forward to telling Hansa the name of the Destroyer whose hands were tainted with all that silvery blood.

I WAS able to shift to another vision swiftly. I was standing on the ridge of a mountain, the evening air cold against my skin. The sky darkened in shades of purple. The sun had already set. Judging by the last flickers of red beyond the horizon, I was able to tell that I was somewhere north.

My mind suddenly clicked as I looked to my right. I could see the burned down camp beyond the deep green forest that unfolded at the base of the mountain. The Red Tribe had lived here for millennia, up until a couple of days ago. I squinted my eyes, my inner-wolf beating the distance and helping me get a better look at the ashes of a massive funeral pyre and the charred remains of tents, swords, spears, and arrows poked out of the purple grass. It all resonated with Jovi's description of the Red Tribe camp.

I had moved from Azazel's castle to the northern mountains.
Well done, Aida!

I looked to my right, where the lush forest broke into a small clearing beneath the evening sky. A small fire burned in the middle, and I could see several figures moving around it. A glimmer of hope pulled strings in my heart, and my feet moved in that direction.

I climbed down the ridge and made my way through the thick dark forest, riddled with animals. What sounded like small furry creatures rushed beneath the bushes. Slender deer chewed on leaves, and numerous night birds sang to each other. If it weren't for all the impending doom, this would have made a great camping spot.

I made it into the clearing and found twelve young succubi gathered around a small fire. The smudges of red war paint and torn leather garments helped me identify them as survivors of the Red Tribe. My heart leapt with joy as I realized that there were indeed sisters of Hansa and Anjani who had survived the massacre.

Two of them were extremely young, most likely in their teens. They were cuddled up beneath a thick fur, warming up by the fire as they slept. The others were adults, probably the same age as Anjani, judging by the similar attire. From what Jovi had told me, the succubi tended to dress their age. The older they got, the more weapons and metals they wore on their bodies. Which made sense based on the two succubi I knew personally. Anjani had a few strips of leather wrapped around her body, while Hansa favored silver chest and shin plates, leather pants, and the red cape.

These creatures were dressed like Anjani in different shades of brown and black leather with silver knives dangling from their belts. They looked tired. Their eyes shimmered with tears, as they roasted small animals on the fire. Their expressions told of defeat and grief, and they slowly chewed their food and drank from their water bladders.

"Do you think anyone else survived?" one of the succubi asked, picking pieces of meat from her teeth with the tip of her blade.

"I have a hard time believing that, Olia," said another, poking the fire with a stick. "We barely made it out of there in one piece."

A third one sniffed and wiped tears away with the back of her hand.

"Perra, what about Hansa?" the third asked the second succubus.

"She's probably back by now. She's probably seen it all. She's feeling what we're all feeling, maybe worse, since she raised most of us," Perra replied.

"Should we go there?" Olia asked.

"It's too soon, too risky. We have the children with us. We have to be smart about this," Perra said. "Adisa, do we have any prayer dust left?"

The third succubus nodded and started digging through her satchel, while a fourth stood up, visibly angry with her hands at her sides, balled into tight fists. My heart bled for them, but I couldn't do anything. I was merely a formless viewer.

"We can't just stay here!" the fourth growled, pacing around the camp fire.

"We have no other choice, Striga!" Olia replied, barely holding it together.

"So, what do we do? Just wait here around the fire and enjoy the starry night sky while our sisters burn?" Striga shot back.

"Look at us!" Olia raised her voice. "This is all we have left! Us, Hansa, and Anjani! We have to be patient, we have to hold on, and we have to protect the children. They're all we have left! We are all we have left!"

Striga roared and shoved her sword into the ground, succumbing to fury. Then she fell to her knees, choked up, and let tears stream down her cheeks.

Perra stood up and moved toward Striga to comfort her. She

kneeled and took the grieving succubus in her arms, whispering in her ear.

Adisa pulled a small pouch from her satchel and handed it to Olia, who untied its string and motioned for the succubi to get closer to the fire. Perra managed to bring Striga back. They both sat down with glazed eyes and trembling lips.

"What will prayers do?" Striga moaned, rubbing her face.

"It's all we have right now," Olia replied. "Hansa may or may not be back, and we need to reach out to the Daughters. They need to see this. They need to feel what we feel. Maybe they'll show mercy and intervene."

"Oh, please, they've not cared for this world in a very long time! If they did, Azazel wouldn't be slaughtering our sisters like this!" Striga hissed.

"We have to pray! Now, shut up and join hands! We might as well try. It won't kill us!"

Olia sat with her back straight as the succubi grasped hands around the fire. She closed her eyes, pouch in her hands. The flames threw amber reflections against her shimmering skin, and I watched with fascination as they recited a prayer directed at the Daughters of Eritopia. I couldn't help but feel sorry for them, already aware of how cruel and careless the goddesses really were.

"Hear our prayer, Daughters of this world," Olia started. "We are your subjects, your faithful servants, your daughters of the Northern Mountain. Hear our prayer, as we ask for your mercy, your compassion, your love, and your wrath."

"We are dying, Daughters of this world," Adisa continued.

"The darkness is spreading, the poison is turning peaceful creatures into monsters."

"The blood of innocents flows in rivers as the monster laughs and kills everything good and kind," Perra added. "We beg you, Daughters..."

"Listen to our pleas," Striga mumbled. "We sit here, mourning our mothers, our sisters, and our daughters. Listen to our pleas..."

"The darkness forgives nothing. It hates. It kills. It destroys. It soils the pristine fields of Eritopia with misery and greed," another succubus chimed in.

"Eritopia is dying, Daughters... We are dying... Show mercy. Look down upon us and feel what we feel. See what we see..."

"Eritopia is yours, and you are of Eritopia... We beg you, show mercy and save us..."

"Eritopia is dying, this world is dying, we are all dying..."

"Our sisters are gone. Our numbers are weak. Our weapons are failing," one of the teen succubi said, her voice trembling.

"We beseech you, Daughters of Eritopia, to feel what we feel. This world is suffering. This world is dying," the tenth succubus added.

"Can you not feel it, Daughters of this world? Can you not feel us?" Olia finished the prayer and scattered the content of the pouch into the fire.

The dust burned in a flash of violet sparks, and the fire swelled and burst into a bright pink flame, throwing the succubi on their backs. I took a step forward, fascinated by the effect. The pink fire gradually died down.

The succubi got back up, shocked by the flame's reaction to the prayer dust.

"This doesn't usually happen," Striga said, confirming my suspicions.

I could tell from their baffled expressions that their prayers didn't usually end in massive pink flames and violet sparks from a mild campfire. Olia got closer, looking down at the charred pieces of wood and incandescent embers. She picked up a stick and poked the remains, revealing a large diamond shaped like a tear.

I leaned forward to get a better look.

Olia used a leather cloth to pick the diamond up. We all gathered around her as she held the gemstone up. It was perfect, with a pristine cut and flawless polish, except for the small violet fire burning inside, suspended in crystal.

"That wasn't there before, was it?" Striga asked, her voice barely a whisper.

"I don't think so. I would have seen it," Olia replied.

"What do we do with it?"

Olia shrugged and put it in her travel pouch, looking up at the giant moon.

"I don't know, but I will keep it safe until we figure out what it does or where it's from," she said.

A thought bloomed in the back of my head. Had the Daughters heard the succubi's prayer? Were they responding with that diamond? Were they finally reaching out and giving us a hand in this dark mess?

"Do you think the Daughters sent it?" Adisa asked.

"I don't know... Maybe?" Olia was as clueless as the rest of us.

"Maybe they're finally feeling our grief," Perra said. "Maybe they're reacting."

"I guess we will find out sooner or later," Olia replied. "Let's sleep now. Tomorrow we return to the camp and look for survivors... Or at least wait for Hansa."

The succubi nodded and disappeared beneath their fur covers, while Olia and Adisa took the first watch. The sky above us stretched in deep shades of indigo. Billions of stars sprawled out. Some flickered yellow and red, while most were cold and white. A full pearly moon accompanied them.

My mind wandered again as I thought about Anjani, then my brother and Bijarki. I wanted to see them and make sure they were okay.

MUCH TO MY SURPRISE, I swiftly transitioned from the northern mountain to a lush jungle. Something told me I'd see my brother soon enough, judging by how well I'd learned to control my direction in these visions. The Druid's advice had certainly helped, as focusing on something in particular made it easier for my Oracle mind to narrow its search.

I was a few hours away from my previous location, as the sunset was still vividly pink and orange in the west, casting its warm light on the wax leaves and dusty road. I looked around, unable to figure out which way I was supposed to go next. All I could see was the straight road, flanked by dark woods.

I heard noises behind me. I turned and watched three figures emerge from the horizon. I stood and waited as they got closer. The sound of hooves and horses neighing reached me first. Before I could think, three gorgeous white stallions galloped past me, their long red manes fluttering in the wind.

My brother, Anjani, and Bijarki were riding them, their expressions grave. Their hands clutched the reins and their crossbows as they darted forward down the road. Thick rolls of dust were raised behind them. I sighed, aware that I was unable to keep up with that speed, even with my inner-wolf. Those horses were faster than any other creature I'd ever seen.

I heard whispers, swishing and crackling through the jungle on both sides of the road. I looked around and saw shadows moving swiftly through the trees. Several of them stopped, hissed, and moved even faster.

I focused and looked deeper into the woods fearing I'd see a pack of shape-shifters or worse, Destroyers. I caught a glimpse of the creatures. They were females, beautiful and athletic, jumping over the thick, gnarly roots as they gradually closed the distance between themselves and my brother's group.

Bright green and yellow scales adorned their arms, backs, and shoulders. Their eyes were the color of lemons with slim black pupils, and their forked tongues occasionally flicked, sniffing the air. Based on what I'd recognized at that point, those were Lamias.

But I couldn't say the same for all the shadows I'd seen running through the jungle after Jovi, Anjani, and Bijarki. Some were incubi, clad in camouflage uniforms, knives held between their teeth as they ran ahead of the Lamias.

My heart jumped at the thought of hostiles going after my brother. There were too many of them, and they were getting closer with each minute.

I ran, but darkness engulfed me, and I lost contact with the vision. I cursed as I sat up and found myself sitting in the attic, awake and unable to help Jovi.

20

SERENA

We mounted our satchels on our backs, strapping them over our shoulders and around our waists for the sake of mobility. With the invisibility spell completed, we were ready to go. The magic formula itself was a rather interesting shimmering gray paste—not something I would have instinctively ingested, since it looked more like makeup than an edible substance.

The Dearghs stood around us, watching quietly as Draven passed the bowl around, and we each shoved a handful of the paste into our mouths, washing it down with water. It tasted horrible.

We waited patiently on the edge of the clearing at the base of Mount Zur, as nightfall glazed everything in shades of black and indigo.

Draven pulled out the Daughter's notes and recited the spell.

"In darkness and light, we will not be seen. Shapeless creatures we shall become, foreign to the eyes of anything that moves. Between leaves and against stones, through water and dirt, we shall be like air. Unseen, obscured, concealed. We shall be cloaked in light, reflecting light, exuding light."

A few minutes passed as we looked at each other, waiting for the invisibility spell to kick in. By then, we'd already learned that the swamp witches' magic took a little bit longer than Draven's potions to take effect, triggered only by their specific chemical reactions and words.

"Stay in the shadows, even if you cannot be seen." Inon continued to give us little snippets of wisdom, ever the gentle giant that he was. "Follow the moon. Make sure it's always in the middle of the sky for you to find Azazel's castle."

I felt a familiar heat spread through me as Draven's hand took mine, gently squeezing it and sending me wave upon wave of his golden energy. I took it all in, even though I didn't really need to syphon off him right then. I looked at him, and he gave me a brief smile before letting go, his eyes saying more than his words.

"We'll have to run fast in order to reach the dungeons before sunrise. You need all the energy you can fit in your body right now," he said.

"Thank you." I nodded and stilled.

I watched as his skin began to glimmer slightly, as if diamond dust was suddenly seeping out of each pore. His eyes grew wide, and Hansa gasped as we looked at each other, watching ourselves slowly fade out and disappear as the spell took effect.

"Good to know it's actually working," I heard Draven say in front of me.

The Dearghs nodded and turned their heads to one side and then the other, unable to see us anymore.

"What do you know! I'm but a ghost in the jungles of Eritopia!" Hansa chuckled and kicked one of the stone giants in the knee.

The Deargh bent forward, smiling and swatting away at the air, unable to capture the fast and invisible succubus. I heard her laugh.

"This is fantastic! Make sure you leave me a copy of that spell, Druid! What we had left over from the swamp witches was nothing compared to this!" she said, having moved further down toward the edge of the clearing.

"Do we know how long it lasts?" I asked.

"Several hours for sure, but there's no precise figure." His voice tickled my ear as he closed the distance between us.

My spine tingled as I felt his body mold against mine. My cheeks burned, but I couldn't help the grin slitting my face at the thought that we were invisible and so deliciously close to each other.

"You should leave now," Inon said. "Use the spell to your advantage. Run like the wind. Don't stop unless it serves your mission. Otherwise, time is precious."

"Thank you, Inon. Thank you, Zur, for your help and kindness," Draven said. "This gesture will never be forgotten, and you have my word that I will repay you in full for this."

"It's not over yet, young Druid," Zur replied. "Fulfill your mission, and we shall rise against Azazel with you. The time for war is near."

"Indeed, it is. We're leaving now," Draven announced, taking my hand again.

"Draven, Serena, we cannot see each other, but we can follow each other's voices," Hansa said, walking alongside us as we entered the dark forest. She mimicked the sound of a snake, a brief succession of three hisses.

Draven responded with the same hissing sound.

"That's right," Hansa replied. "We'll use this when we cannot speak, should there be hostiles around."

I reproduced the triple hiss surprisingly well, prompting Hansa to clap her hands. Although, since I was unable to see her facial expression, I wasn't sure whether she was being sincere or sarcastic.

"Well done, Serena," she eventually said. "You're blending into Eritopia better and better with each passing day. If I didn't know better, I'd say you were born and belong here!"

I chuckled as I followed Draven through the woods. A part of me registered that statement—the notion of me belonging here, in Eritopia, sounded like a snippet of absolute fantasy, and yet, something tugged at my heart whenever I replayed the sentence in my mind.

I missed my home. I missed The Shade and my parents and our way of life. I carried the weight of that every day, heavy in my heart while looking for a way out of Eritopia. But as Draven's and my relationship developed, this whole world was growing on me. I liked the pink and orange sunsets, the taste of the food, and the weird creatures who called Eritopia home.

Draven was a pillar for me in my darkest hours, and he was slowly becoming more important than I'd ever expected. He challenged me in ways I'd never thought possible, and so did Eritopia. Nothing could replace The Shade, but I was feeling closer to this strange land now than I could have ever fathomed —and I couldn't completely deny the possibility that we might not make it back home.

I pushed the thought to the back of my mind as we followed the moon, a giant marble always in the center of the sky. The wilderness was quiet around us, the leaves and twigs crackling beneath our feet almost the only sound.

I heard Hansa up ahead, occasionally whistling just to make sure we knew where she was headed. Draven held my hand as we followed her, sending constant waves of warmth through my body. He'd opened himself up to me entirely, teasing my sentry senses with all the emotions that he was experiencing in that moment—tension, determination, an undertone of fear and anger, and a hefty amount of something I'd decided to call desire, although it felt like much more to me. It was aimed at me, and I took it all in, feeding off it and sending it back with my own emotions.

We didn't speak for a while, as we sprinted through the woods, following the moon. Feeling Draven's hand wrapped around mine kept my feet light as we treaded over the tall grass.

My heart pounded—with fear, and also with something beautiful yet dangerous; even though I knew, deep inside, that he felt the same, I was still wary of the many ways in which everything could go wrong.

I understood then that I was just as afraid of losing him as he was of losing me. If I even considered that thought, it was amplified into a true horror story filled with unimaginable pain. I couldn't stand it. It clawed at my heart.

I was falling for the Druid so hard and fast and deep that I'd grown too tired to try to fight it. There was no point in resisting anymore anyway. He'd burrowed his way into my heart.

A group of twinkling lights, about fifty yards away, paused my train of thought.

"Serena, can you see that far ahead?" Hansa whispered as we stopped.

I used my True Sight to discover a camp of about fifty incubi in military attire, most of them sleeping around several fires. Some were still eating and talking. They were all beautiful specimens, with symmetrical features, smooth silvery skin, deep set eyes, and short black hair, as if they had been sculpted by the same artist tortured by his desire to achieve aesthetic perfection.

"There's an incubus camp there. Four fires, about ten to fifteen gathered around each fire," I replied. They're soldiers, judging by the attire. Most of them are sleeping, but some are still awake eating. Their weapons are put away, except for two incubi keeping watch on the northern and southern side of the camp."

"We'll have to be quiet and move around them," Draven said.

"I think we should pass through," Hansa replied. "We might pick up some information on the way. They can't see us."

Draven pondered the issue for a minute, then whispered, "I agree with Hansa. Let's meet on the other side of the camp by the giant purple tree." He tugged my arm, and we moved ahead, straight into the camp.

I looked ahead and saw exactly which tree he meant. An incubus slept there, his head resting on one of the thick but smaller roots. It was the only purple tree around. Hansa hissed thrice as she swiftly moved into the camp.

We followed her closely, careful not to make any noise. The spell that Draven had spoken implied that we would be soundless, but we couldn't take any chances. After all, we could hear each other.

Most of the incubi were submerged in deep slumber, the occasional snore rising from the sea of bodies in military attire. We stopped in front of one of the camp fires, where five incubi were still eating from their rations of dried meat and bread. One was sharpening his sword with a black stone. The whistle of the metal cut through the peaceful night like a reminder that more blood would be spilled.

"I don't like this, Mal," one incubus said to another, his mouth full. "We're stuck here looking out for nothing in particular, while Sverik's stuck in a cage. It's not right."

"There's nothing we can do about it, Yaron," Mal replied while running the black stone down the blade again.

"We could go get him," a third one interjected.

"How do you suggest we do that, Capheus?" Mal asked sarcastically. "Do we just walk in and ask one of those grotesque

Destroyers to kindly escort us to Captain Sverik? Do you think they'll offer us sweet water as a courtesy, too?"

Capheus rolled his eyes and chewed another piece of dry meat, visibly displeased with its taste but hungry enough to eat it anyway.

"That's what I thought," Mal added. "We sit here and wait for orders, like we were told. Until then, we figure out what to do next and how to handle our new commander. Goren's a prickly bastard."

"Prickly? I would've gone for fat oversized snake with a brain the size of a pea!" Yaron replied. "I can't believe we have to listen to him."

I heard Hansa hiss three times from behind Yaron, who sat across the fire from where Draven and I were standing. We didn't move, but Draven hissed back. The incubi looked around, frowning.

"Snakes? See anything?" asked Mal, checking the ground behind him.

They all shook their heads, unable to see anything.

"They might be lurking in the grass nearby," said Yaron. "They won't come any closer. Like most creatures out there, they don't fare well with fire."

"My point is," Mal continued, "it's either obey or die with these creeps. It's bad enough we have sworn fealty to them. Let's keep our garrison alive and fight for Sverik another day. His father's planning another assault with Goren anyway. They're looking further north now. They might take us with them."

"So we can spill our blood while the Destroyers prance

around on their winged horses throwing their poisonous spears?" Yaron was clearly displeased with the entire situation.

"What would you rather do then, Yaron?" Capheus snapped. "Curl up and die? They won't let you. They'll lock you up and torture you and chip away at your very soul until you beg them to kill you. That's worse than death, my friend. Snap out of it. We obey or we suffer the same fate as Sverik. At least we can still bear arms."

"I'm not sure death by Destroyer is any better," Yaron replied. "I heard the poison is so vicious, it takes a long time for it to kill you. It kills your muscles, but you still feel everything as the toxin burns through your body. They say it's beyond agonizing."

"Kristos and Bijarki must have suffered for hours before the poison finally killed them," Mal added. "I heard from one of the Destroyers who went after them that they got them both. Poked them full of spears to send a message."

"I heard Bijarki's still alive," Capheus said. "They saw him moving through the jungles up north."

The other incubi looked at him, surprise raising their eyebrows in unison. Mal's black stone stopped halfway down the blade.

"Where'd you hear that?" Mal frowned.

"One of Goren's aides. He said they spotted Bijarki around that succubi camp twice. You know, the one they burned down the other day."

Mal shook his head, staring at the fire.

"One by one, the resistance keeps falling," he said slowly.

"We keep saying we'll live to fight another day, but it doesn't look like that day is coming. If anything, it's rapidly fading away."

"Well, it's not like there's much skill left in the wild anyway," Yaron smirked. "Almost all of the incubi have sworn fealty, and it's not like the succubi are capable of taking on even one Destroyer, not to mention a whole garrison complete with Sluaghs."

I heard Hansa hiss from behind him.

He quickly looked over his shoulder. I suddenly had a feeling that he was about to say something to set her off, so I squeezed Draven's hand.

"Yeah, don't rely on the females to save the day," Capheus grinned.

"I heard they wiped them all out. Didn't stand a chance, that Red Tribe," Yaron chuckled. "A bunch of succubi who were too proud and lazy to live with the males of our species, and look at them. Centuries spent pretending they know how to fight to end up with spears and arrows in them. Pathetic!"

Draven seemed to read my mind. He jerked my hand, and we both moved swiftly toward the source of the second hiss, this one longer and more menacing. I wanted to catch Hansa before she did something that would reveal our presence there, but I wasn't sure how to find her in time.

The incubi were all chuckling around the fire, and I knew it was only a matter of seconds before their heads would start falling off.

I took a gamble and used my True Sight to look around me. Much to my relief and surprise, I saw a shimmering silhouette prowling behind Yaron, which I instantly recognized as Hansa. She was moving in for the kill, quiet and liquid in her movement.

I lunged forward and grabbed her arm, pulling her back. She tried to resist but gave in. We slowly moved away from the camp, leaving the incubi behind still looking around for snakes.

As soon as we were far enough to speak again, I let go of Hansa's arm. She groaned, and I heard her sheathe her sword.

"Hansa, your short temper might get us killed," Draven reprimanded her, his hand still clutching mine.

"I am sorry, Druid. Anger got the best of me," she mumbled. "They were talking trash about my tribe, my sisters. I saw red."

"Your irregular hissing gave you away," I replied. "I can't blame you, though. I can only imagine how his words must make you feel."

A moment passed before she spoke again.

Crickets chirped in the background.

"How did you find me?" she asked.

"I used my True Sight," I said. "It turns out swamp witches' magic isn't fully impervious to my sentry abilities. I can't see you clearly, but I can make out the silhouette, as if I can spot the light reflections when you move."

"That's an interesting development," Draven mused. "Nevertheless, worth studying further when we get the chance. We're using spells we know nothing about right now, but once all this blows over, I'll want to go through each of them thoroughly."

"Planning on teaching swamp witch magic, Druid?" Hansa asked jokingly.

"Not necessarily, but it's an art that should not die. It will only be a matter of deciding who would be entitled to receive such powerful knowledge."

A throng of sharp hisses pierced the natural silence as dozens of Destroyers flew overhead. We stilled, and my heart froze in my chest. Shivers ran down my spine. Their winged horses neighed as they cut through the night sky, foaming at the mouth and flapping their wings against the warm summer air.

I kept looking up, watching the monsters with giant snake tails ride their animals, hissing as they looked down, scanning the dense jungle with their bright yellow eyes. As soon as they moved in the direction from which we had come, I was able to breathe again.

"Stay strong, Serena," Draven whispered in my ear. "It will only get worse from here. There'll be more of them as we get closer to Azazel's castle."

"Well, that's reassuring," I replied and kept moving, this time pulling him after me.

We kept walking with the moon guiding us.

Soon enough, a swarm of green fireflies buzzed above us, flying chaotically. I stopped to look at them, fascinated by their appearance. They looked like little green sparks against the black night sky.

"They're so pretty," I gasped, mesmerized by the visual effect.

They resembled liquid drops of fire levitating above the dark forest.

"Don't talk," Draven whispered again. "They're not of nature's making."

I didn't move, my words stuck in my throat.

Instead, I continued to watch as they moved through the air, swarming after the Destroyers we'd seen earlier. When we saw the last of them disappear beyond the trees behind us, I was finally able to breathe again. I let a sigh roll out of my chest and leaned against Draven.

"What are they, then?" I asked.

"One of Azazel's most powerful and most dangerous spells," he explained. "They're spies. Tiny little flickers of green fire, Azazel's eyes and ears around these parts of Eritopia. He sees and hears everything through them in real time."

"The closer we get to his castle, the more of these we'll find," Hansa added.

I looked ahead, and the realization crashed into me like a wave of cold water. A few dozen feet ahead, beneath the big white moon, constantly surveyed by swarms of Destroyers and green fireflies, was Azazel's castle.

The castle rose quietly over the jungle, its black marble towers stabbing the sky, challenging the stars above. Green fires burned on its walls and above its windows. The thick forest unraveled below, black and quiet and filled with nothing but danger and death.

I tightened my grip on Draven's hand and felt gloom settle in the pit of my stomach.

Soon enough, we'd be sneaking into the monster's lair.

The jungle opened up as we made our way to the River Pyros. The road widened, and the woods scattered, leaving room for several square miles of smooth plains with tall red grass and the occasional orchard patch.

Our horses were indeed strong, darting like bullets, their hooves barely touching the ground. Evening was settling in, giving the sky a dizzying array of reds, oranges, and pinks as the sun disappeared beyond the western woods.

"The river is just a couple of miles ahead," Anjani said, clutching her crossbow.

The tension made the air around us solid. We knew we were being followed—we'd heard the hissing and the sound of footsteps and branches breaking in the jungle around us. My hand was sweaty as it held the crossbow against my right forearm.

"The open space might make us or break us," Bijarki added, looking over his shoulder.

I noticed his eyes grow wide and shifted my gaze to see what he was looking at. There were creatures running through the tall grass to our right, incubi wearing dark red and green uniforms, resembling military camouflage patterns. I looked over to my left and noticed the same—more incubi sprinting toward us with knife blades in their teeth.

"Get your weapons ready," Bijarki shouted and pointed his crossbow at one of the incubi.

One by one they emerged from the tall grass, keeping up with our horses. I heard a hiss and the swish of an arrow behind me. I looked over my shoulder and saw Anjani reloading her crossbow. An incubus had fallen back, writhing in pain on the ground.

There were eleven of them left and three of us.

I shot an arrow and caught one right in the chest. He collapsed, foaming at the mouth, his arms and legs twitching.

"We're simply defending ourselves, brothers. Stop attacking us. We mean no harm!" Bijarki barked at the soldiers.

One of them got close enough to try and slash Bijarki's horse with his sword.

"You're worth a lot of money, you traitor!" the incubus hissed.

Anjani's arrow shot him in the back of his neck, the tip protruding out of his throat, glazed in silver blood. He fell flat on his face, lifeless.

Nine left.

"I think there's a ransom on your head," Anjani said to Bijarki as we all kicked our heels, persuading our horses to go a little faster.

Unfortunately, the incubi were just as unnaturally fast. Two of them brought out their long-distance bows. Anjani and I quickly reloaded our crossbows and killed them just as they shot their arrows, missing both of us by a couple of inches. My instincts kicked in, and my inner-wolf growled, eager to tear them all apart.

"Bijarki's head on a plate is worth a fortune these days," another incubus shouted, approaching Bijarki.

I shot him and watched him fall and roll on the ground, a poisonous arrow sticking out of his neck. His suffering would end soon. I had aimed for the carotid artery. He would bleed out in less than a minute.

Six left. I loaded my crossbow again. They were getting closer. I had to move faster.

Anjani took another one down. *Five.*

An incubus wielding a sword was getting dangerously close to my horse. He eyed the animal's back legs.

Suddenly, three long arrows shot from behind us, hitting three of our attackers simultaneously. They fell, their bodies hitting the ground with a thud.

A loud hiss oozed from the tall grass as the remaining incubi froze, prompting us to stop our horses and look back. The animals neighed as we pulled the reigns and pointed our crossbows at the two incubi still standing.

Sweat glistened on their pale faces, their eyes wide with horror. They didn't move.

I took advantage of their stillness and jumped off my horse, keeping my crossbow aimed at them. Anjani followed suit, coming to my side.

"There are others here," Bijarki said, his eyes scanning the road behind us.

"Don't kill us," one of the surviving incubi croaked.

"Then don't move," Anjani hissed.

"What others?" I asked Bijarki.

"Not sure," was his reply.

A few moments later, my question was answered. Three females emerged from the tall grass, aiming their longbows at all of us. They were beautiful creatures with slender bodies, toned muscles, and tanned skin. Their bright yellow eyes had slim black pupils. They wore pale green silk dresses with shoulder straps and slits on the sides all the way up to their hips. Massive gold belts adorned their waspy waists.

Leather bands crossed their chests, holding their quivers in place on their backs. Their hair was long and pale blonde, nearly white, cascading over their shoulders in large curls. Golden earrings looped from their delicate ears. Green silk threads wove through their braids, reminding me a bit of Nordic women from the human world.

They grinned at us, their pink forked tongues flitting and gathering chemicals from the air like snakes. They were Lamias. Their arrows pointed at Anjani and me, while ours pointed at the incubi.

Bijarki's horse trotted up to us. Bijarki aimed his crossbow at the three Lamias. Everybody was ready to kill somebody.

"Who are you?" I asked, my nerves stretched to the very edge.

One of the creatures gave me a sultry smile. Anjani cleared her throat, her emerald-gold eyes promising to send millions of poisonous arrows her way.

"He asked you a question," she said.

"We're the ones who were gracious enough to save your asses," the smiling Lamia replied. "I'm Una, and these are my sisters, Mira and Lira."

"You're Lamias," I replied, my voice getting weaker as I noticed their distinctive features.

A multitude of black and lemon-yellow scales covered their legs. They moved closer. The scales spread up their necks from the back, and a few were sprinkled on their forearms as well. The Lamia named Una looked at me and inclined her head.

"You're quite observant," she quipped. "And not from around here, are you?"

"Seriously, am I so easy to spot?" I asked Anjani and Bijarki, my voice laced with sarcasm.

"Unfortunately, yes," Bijarki replied. "We can all smell the wolf in you."

"We saw you three in the marketplace asking about the River Pyros, so we decided to follow you," Mira said.

"We come in peace, I can assure you," Bijarki's voice was low and calm. "We were attacked by these incubi."

"We know," Lira smirked, looking down at the soldiers, her lips twisted with disgust. "We saw these rats run after you. We had a feeling you three must be worth something, the way they gave chase."

"We are worth nothing, believe me," Bijarki replied.

"It turns out there's quite a hefty bounty on your head, Bijarki of the Strandh Clan," Mira grinned. "Sixty thousand pieces of gold for whoever delivers your lifeless corpse to Azazel."

Bijarki, Anjani, and I glanced at each other, as the grim notion sank in. Azazel seemed to think of Bijarki as enough of an inconvenience to want him dead. That, despite its dangerous implications, sounded like quite the achievement.

Lira broke the silence. "Relax, Bijarki. We're not interested in that filthy snake's gold. He can choke on it, as far as the Lamias are concerned."

I let a heavy sigh roll out of my chest, Draven's words echoing in my head. The Lamias had a serious bone to pick with Azazel. They didn't have any interest in making his life or mission easier, not after he'd wiped out all their potential mates, thus dooming their species to extinction.

"I am forever grateful then," Bijarki replied with a polite nod, then glared at the incubi. "On your knees!"

The soldiers obeyed, looking over at me and frowning. I was a stranger in their eyes, from another world, and it didn't seem to take them long to notice that. Despite their calm demeanor, I could tell they were terrified. I could smell the sweaty fear on them.

"You would kill one of your own for gold, then?" Bijarki asked them, his tone sharp and heavy like an axe.

"Times are tough," one of the incubi replied with a smirk.

"You are soldiers of Eritopia. Have you no honor?"

"What honor? We've been left behind by our commander, stripped of our ranks and titles, and doomed to walk this world without any fortune or fame," the other incubus spat. "Your father considered us too weak to follow him into Azazel's army!"

Bijarki frowned and took a step forward, pointing the crossbow at the first incubus's forehead.

"You know my father?"

"We served under Boovar of the Strandh Clan for five hundred years. Five hundred years of loyal and flawless service. Yet he saw fit to toss us aside, as if we're worthless little worms!" the incubus said, gritting his teeth.

"You've been discharged, then," Bijarki concluded.

Both incubi nodded.

"And you need the gold."

They nodded again.

"I have no gold to give you, but I can offer you a second chance, if you're willing to fight like loyal soldiers for me," Bijarki replied, putting his crossbow away.

"We don't work for traitors!" the first incubus hissed.

Mira slapped him over the back of his head, making him slump forward.

"The only traitors here are you two worthless rats!" she barked, fury sparking in her eyes. "You, who seek to serve the monster that is tearing our world apart. Not Bijarki, not the one who stood up to Azazel's reign of terror!"

"Why are you wasting your time with these insects?" Una

asked Bijarki, aiming her arrow at the back of the second incubus's head.

The metallic tip poked his skull, making him squirm.

"We can finish them off quickly," she added.

"Please don't," Bijarki raised his arms in a peaceful gesture. "They have information we might need. You can kill them later. For now, they're still useful."

Una shook her head and took a step back, then nodded at both her sisters. They put their bows and arrows away, while Anjani and I kept our crossbows focused on the incubi. We glanced at each other, and I noticed the shadow of a smile passing over her face. We made a pretty good team.

"As you wish," Una replied. "Then let's move on to the next order of business. What business do you have at the river, Bijarki?"

"We're here on behalf of the last Druid standing against Azazel. We seek an alliance with the Lamias to end that monster once and for all," he said.

The Lamias' eyes flickered black for a second, their lips stretching into three smiles.

"You mean to tell us there is still one Druid out there who hasn't turned into a filthy and sterile Destroyer?" Lira asked, her voice sweet as honey.

"Sterile?" I asked.

"You think we'd be in this predicament of utter extinction had we been able to bear our offspring from Destroyers?" Una replied. "Whatever Azazel does to them, they can no longer seed new life. We've tried. They like our bodies, but they cannot help us conceive, so we keep our distance."

That was a very interesting development, one I was sure Draven would want to hear. It meant that he was the only real Druid left in Eritopia. I couldn't help but feel sorry for the guy, being one of the last of his kind.

"Where is this Druid?" Una asked with newfound interest.

"Right now, I believe he's about to rescue Sverik from Azazel's dungeons and gain tremendous tactical advantage in the upcoming war," Bijarki replied.

"I wouldn't rush into trusting that two-faced bastard," Una said with disgust. "He's as loyal as a snake, good as long as there's something in it for him."

"No one is rushing into anything, but he is our only hope to gain the support of rebel troops scattered across Eritopia," Anjani interjected.

A moment passed as the three Lamias nodded and looked at each other, as if communicating with no words.

"We'll take you to the River Pyros," Una eventually said. "Our mistress will want a word with you."

Bijarki took a bow, smiling at them.

"You are too kind. Thank you."

"You are quite famous around here, son of Boovar," Lira noted admiringly. "He sided with the enemy, but you chose to fight and defend these lands. We have a soft spot for rebels, you see."

"I'm flattered and grateful," he said, looking at Anjani and me.

"Don't be," Una cut in. "If our mistress is unhappy with the terms of your proposed alliance, if either of you makes the wrong move or tries something against us, we will slit your throats and bleed you dry, regardless of your rebel fame."

The chilling statement came out in a polite tone, accompanied by a dry smile that sent shivers down my spine. I took a deep breath and kept my guard up, my senses flaring and picking up the scents and heartbeats of both hostiles and potential allies.

"Rest assured, that will not be the case," Bijarki replied bluntly.

"We shall see," Una shot back, then pointed at the incubi. "Since you decided to keep these rats alive, you get to keep an eye on them till we get to the camp."

We looked at the incubi, who wore the most desperate of expressions on their faces, their wide gray eyes begging us for mercy. I groaned and fetched two lines of rope from my horse's saddle, handing one to Anjani. We both moved to tie the incubi's hands behind their backs.

Bijarki nodded. "Like I said, we'll spare them *for now*. They have information we may need."

22

PHOENIX

I was upstairs in the attic with a couple of pillows and the Daughter. I figured I'd keep her close and comfortable since she had a peculiar habit of passing out when I had a vision. I let her relax on the pillows, while I prepared myself.

I followed the Druid's advice and focused on specific snippets of the past during my visions. I wanted to find out more about what had driven Azazel over the edge, which inadvertently took me to a grandiose feast inside a massive dinner hall. Its domed ceiling was as tall as that of a Renaissance cathedral adorned with massive arches and sumptuous sculptures of Eritopian deities, hybrids of various animals carved into the white marble.

Seven enormous pillars supported the dome, sculpted in the form of the seven Daughters of Eritopia and painted in gold and lavish purple. They were accurate representations of the goddesses. They held their arms up, supporting the ceiling and the plethora of marble creatures of Eritopia's diverse fauna across all the planets.

Ample chandeliers made with fine brushed brass and crystals hung from above, with hundreds of pink and yellow flames flickering where candles were supposed to be mounted. I chalked it up to magic and moved forward into the banquet hall. Twenty doors were carved into the circular white marble wall. They were made from solid purple wood and decorated with delicate gold floral motifs.

In the middle was a thick gold disc, serving as a platform for a superb dining table. Dinner was set for twenty, with beautiful china plates, gold-plated cutlery, silk napkins, and crystal glasses. Pink and yellow flames flickered in triple candelabra emerging from rich floral arrangements. It was an arrangement designed for royalty.

One of the doors opened. The sound of thunder and strong winds echoed from beyond. A tall man walked in. Behind him I saw darkness with specks of stardust, as if the cosmos waited in the room from which he'd emerged. He closed the door behind him and locked it with a large key, beautifully crafted with gold and fine gems. He dropped it in the pocket of his black overcoat.

The man seemed familiar, so I stepped forward to get a better look, following him as he walked up to the table. Two silhouettes emerged from the walls, ethereal figures made of white smoke that moved toward the man, bowing before him. He smiled, removing his coat and handing it to one of the creatures, while the other pulled out his chair.

He sat down. The creatures moved across the room to hang

the coat behind a decorative panel made of colorful stained glass with a solid gold frame. Pitchers of water appeared on the table out of thin air, and the man poured himself a drink. The medium, sand-colored hair; his gray eyes and sharp features; and his Cupid's bow lips and broad shoulders instantly rang a bell. I was standing next to a much younger Almus, Draven's father.

He wore an elegant suit that reminded me of 18th century attire. He wore feather pants and a vest made of fine black velvet matched with red leather boots, a white cotton shirt, and a crimson bow tie. He went through two glasses of water in absolute silence before the sound of another door opening made us both turn our heads.

Another man walked in. Judging by his appearance, I assumed he was also a Druid. He was slightly shorter than Almus but still taller than average with a narrow waist and slender arms and legs. His sartorial tastes seemed to have a flair for the dramatic, fitting red leather trousers with lateral laces tied all the way down to his black knee-high boots. A loose white shirt and a matching red leather vest displayed a multitude of insignia mounted on his chest, and over the whole ensemble, he wore a red leather cape. He handed the cape to the smoky servants, now multiplied by two and quietly hovering around the dinner hall.

The Druid grinned at the sight of Almus. His amber eyes and long black hair were caught in a ponytail. A trimmed mustache and beard masked some of his features, contrasting with his white teeth.

"Almus! Long time, good friend!" the Druid exclaimed, walking up to Draven's father.

Almus stood to shake his hand, then resumed his seat. He didn't seem very happy to see Mr. Drama-Suit, but offered a polite smile nonetheless.

"It's a pleasure to see you again, Azazel."

My stomach dropped as I realized that I was in the presence of pre-Destroyer Azazel. He seemed friendly and chatty and certainly nothing like the dark monster he'd become. I balled my fists and gritted my teeth. I was barely holding it together. Then I remembered that I was nothing but a ghost there, unable to do anything to prevent all the horrors that Azazel would become famous for.

"When was the last time we saw each other, Almus? Your inauguration day?"

Almus nodded with a nostalgic smile, as Azazel took a seat next to him and poured himself a glass of water infused with red rose petals.

"It seems only yesterday, though," Azazel added. "You were so green and sweaty and nervous as they handed you the keys to the seventh kingdom of Eritopia!"

"I was lucky," Almus replied.

"No, my friend. You earned it!"

Azazel rolled his sleeves up, revealing dozens of thick rings tattooed on his forearms, from his wrists all the way to the elbows. He showed them to Almus, beaming with pride.

"You earned it, my friend. All one hundred rings adorn your arms as they do mine, symbols of the highest rank among the

Druids. You are the rightful ruler of the seventh kingdom. It had nothing to do with luck, and you know it. Stop being so modest! It will get you nowhere!"

Almus laughed.

"How have you been? How is your first year as one of us? Finding your little slice of Eritopia manageable?" Azazel grinned.

"It hasn't been easy, I have to admit. I may be in charge of the smallest of our twenty planets, but believe me when I say that Persea as a kingdom is quite the handful. I've been dealing with a lot of corruption. I've just cleaned out the agricultural department, demoting all the chiefs to field labor as they were practically holding the meat farms hostage for unnecessary fees." Almus sighed.

"I can't say mine has been any easier. But we've been making great progress. I look forward to sharing it with the council," Azazel replied.

Almus gave him a weary look. "I've heard you say this before, and it has always ended in heated discussions and you walking out filled with rage. Please tell me you've run everything through the council, as per the rules, and that you haven't made infrastructure and legislative changes without telling us first," he said.

Azazel's laughter sounded tense, with an undertone of contempt. "Oh, please, Almus, as if these old fools will ever accept anything that goes beyond camp fires and burning coal! Traditionalists will be the end of us if we don't take executive action, and you know it."

A third door opened, then a fourth, followed by the rest, until twenty Druids, both men and women, walked in from what I assumed were the twenty planets, or kingdoms, of Eritopia. The doors were probably magical portals through which they could all meet in this massive hall. I started wondering in which kingdom my friends and I had been stranded and which of these Druids had once been in charge of it. Cooped up in the mansion for so long, it was easy to forget that Eritopia was much bigger than the small piece I'd seen on a map – that it was an entire galaxy and that we'd only seen parts of the planet Calliope, our temporary home.

The Druids all gathered around the table, taking their seats and nodding at each other politely. They smiled stiffly and made empty compliments. One of them, a beautiful blonde with hazel green eyes, passed next to Almus, prompting both him and Azazel to spring to their feet and bow with reverence. She reminded me of someone, but I couldn't figure out who it was, until I saw the looks between her and Almus. It made sense then —her firm cheeks and the shape of her eyes, even her smile; they all echoed in Draven.

His mother.

I walked closer for a better look. She wore a pale blue dress. The silk poured down her perfect hourglass body. A large platinum belt framed her tiny waist, and a myriad of diamonds glistened around her neck and wrists. Her arms were covered in the same tattoos as Azazel, symbols of her high rank among the Druids. She sat next to Almus, but they didn't touch each other. I had a feeling they had yet to take that step.

And judging by Azazel's lovestruck look, she had captured the hearts of many before she married Almus.

I hung around for a while, listening in on their conversations. I successfully learned the names of all former rulers of Eritopia and the twenty Druids who controlled each of the galaxy's planets. I learned that Calliope with Mount Agrith, the birthplace of the Daughters, had once belonged to Genevieve, Draven's mother. It was the largest of all twenty and with the most fruitful soils, at a perfect distance from the In-Between's sun. Azazel's was the closest to the center of the constellation, and the third smallest based on descriptions I'd plucked from their conversations. It was called Purgaris, and it sounded a lot like a literal hell, hot and scorching. Almus's planet, called Persea, was the smallest but a haven for Druids. It held the Grand Temple, where all Druids were taught the ways of natural and dark magic and where they received their ceremonial ranking tattoo rings.

Eritopia suddenly seemed gargantuan in size, and I felt curious enough to visit all twenty of these planets—provided we survived the impending war with Azazel. I spent a hefty amount of time around him, Almus, and Genevieve. I started to understand that he'd always been ambitious and generally unhappy with the size of his kingdom. I'd landed in the early days with this vision, when he hadn't yet begun to dismantle the Druid society.

But he was stubborn and proud, always looking to gain more without bothering with the rules. His political and territorial greed seemed to hassle Almus and downright infuriate

Genevieve, who poured herself another glass of rose-infused water and sternly reprimanded him.

"You can't just change the military laws in your kingdom, Azazel. You don't own that planet. You're merely an elected official, tasked with its administration. You're not its king, even if it is called a kingdom! You're a Master Druid, like the rest of us!" she snapped.

"Genevieve, I meant no harm, and no harm was done!" Azazel defended himself. "I merely changed the enrollment age for the army! My incubi are all eager to train, to join my ranks and serve their land. What's the big deal?"

"You didn't run it by us, Azazel, and you know the council laws very well, since you're an expert at breaking them!" she replied bluntly.

A moment passed before Azazel spoke again, his gaze softening as he looked at her.

"By the Daughters, I swear, if you weren't so stunning I'd have a lot more to say about your council laws." He smiled.

Azazel really did have the hots for Draven's mother. I recognized the oafish look on his face as she ran her fingers through her hair, pulling it over one shoulder to reveal her long, delicate neck. Almus couldn't take his eyes off her either, but his poker face was good enough to keep suspicions at bay. She occasionally glanced his way, a faint smile passing over her face.

"I've known you since you were a little boy, Azazel. That beard won't fool me!" She grinned at him.

Azazel didn't take it well, his smile dropping as he was reminded that he was much younger than the woman he seemed to love, as if it made him unfit to be with her. Truth be told, he didn't look younger, but given Druid ages, a few centuries probably didn't make a difference in terms of wrinkles on their kind. Most of them looked to be in their mid-thirties, and I had no skill at guessing their real ages.

"Like that matters. I'm more than you give me credit for," Azazel mumbled, a muscle tightening in his jaw.

"You're an extraordinary Druid, Azazel. But you have to follow our rules. They're there for a reason," Genevieve replied. "I share your progressive views for the most part, as we all want what is best for all of Eritopia, but you cannot draft prepubescent incubi just because they're eager to serve you. They're far too inexperienced and have so much to learn before you hand them a sword. You should have run this by the council."

"Well, it's done now. Give me a slap on the wrist and let's be done with it." He smirked.

"It doesn't work like that," Almus said, loud enough for the whole table to hear. "The council is unhappy with your decision, and a motion has been filed to reverse your legislative changes regarding the draft of young incubi. Only those above the age of adolescence can serve in the armies of Eritopia."

Azazel shot Almus a glare, and shivers ran down my spine. He stood up, furiously glancing at all the Druids seated around the table.

"Is that true?" Azazel's voice echoed through the hall.

An elder Druid stood up, his fingers playing with a strange medallion, a snake made of gold twisted in the shape of the number eight with small ruby eyes. It moved slowly, endlessly in its double loop, as if the precious metal were liquid.

"Indeed, it is, Azazel of the Third Kingdom," he said. "Without proper law and order, there will be chaos. If you wish to change any law in your district, you must propose it to the council first. Otherwise, it will be declared null and voided."

"This is unbelievable!" Azazel roared and slapped a few plates off the table.

Everyone jumped at the sound of porcelain shattering on the floor. None seemed used to violent behavior. Azazel's rage seemed to make them nervous and uncomfortable. The elders, in particular, avoided eye contact with the furious Druid, their lips constricted into thin lines.

Almus frowned and stood to face him. "Please control yourself," he commanded, his voice cold and heavy.

"After you've all made me look like an absolute fool in front of my people by reversing a law I set myself? You must be joking!"

"We've gathered here in peace, and your anger is misguided. You shouldn't have changed the law without the council's approval in the first place. This is merely a repercussion."

Azazel squinted his eyes, his mouth crooked with fury and disgust as he glanced at the whole council. His expression changed as soon as his gaze met with Genevieve's. He took a deep breath, then looked at Almus.

"You've changed, my friend. You've become a paper-pusher like the rest of this bag of old bones you call a council. I'm disappointed. I thought you had more fire in you," he said, then glared at the elder Druid with the snake medallion. "I'll show you repercussions, Lorenz, the next time you ancient fools decide to embarrass me in front of my people!"

"They're not your people, Azazel. They're Eritopians, like the rest of us," Lorenz replied sternly.

Azazel chuckled with contempt and stormed out of the dining room, disappearing behind one of the doors before the smoky servant could fetch him his red leather cape. The creature hovered by the door, cape in hand, unsure of what to do next.

I had gained valuable insight into Azazel's life before he'd transitioned into a Destroyer. Most importantly, I'd uncovered a love triangle I was eager to explore further. I wondered whether Almus and Genevieve's relationship had any impact on Azazel's descent into madness. Draven didn't give me the impression of knowing anything about it.

MY SECOND VISION took me to another moment before Azazel became a Destroyer. I was on a spacious terrace overlooking a lush tropical rainforest beneath an azure sky. It was like nothing I'd ever seen before. A huge garden sprawled beyond the terrace, a puzzle of colorful flower patches, river stones, and crystalline streams flowing as red and yellow birds sang from bountiful plum trees.

Azazel stood next to me, watching two figures walking through the garden below. His jaw was tense, and his amber eyes flickered black. I'd learned from Serena that Druids, being genetically tied to serpents, had a haw, a black membrane that flittered when they experienced intense emotions such as anger. He clearly wasn't happy about what he was seeing.

I looked down and realized he was watching Almus and Genevieve as they walked together. They held hands, and Genevieve was laughing. They'd become a couple by then, and Azazel wasn't taking it very well.

I heard a soft voice behind me. "Excuse me,"

I turned around and saw a beautiful young woman with golden yellow eyes and long, platinum hair standing in front of me. Her pupils were black and dilated, reminding me of a cat. She wore a pale green silk dress, the fabric glazing her gorgeous body, amplifying her curves to the point where my throat went dry.

Judging by Azazel's stunned expression, she had the same effect on him.

"I'm a student of Lady Genevieve," the young woman said. "I've been asked to speak with you about organizing a council visit to your kingdom, Lord Azazel."

I moved around to get a good look at this creature and noticed her dress open in a wide V on her back, revealing her spine and shoulder blades. I caught a glimpse of greenish yellow scales on her lower back as well as on her slender arms, where they were displayed in a delicately scattered pattern, like decorative gems.

"Yes, I've been told the council will attend our military

parade for the summer solstice," Azazel replied, his voice weaker than usual.

He couldn't take his eyes off her, mesmerized by her fluid moves as she took a step forward. I recognized her as a Lamia, based on what I'd learned about these creatures from Draven and Bijarki. I wondered how long it would take for Azazel to figure out what she was, since Druids didn't take kindly to Lamias. After all, they had banished them for their taste in incubus flesh.

"Indeed." She smiled. "She's asked me to liaise with you about setting a date and time for the council to be greeted and escorted to their accommodations in the summer palace, your grace. Perhaps now would be a good time to discuss these details?"

He measured her from head to toe, a shadow passing over his face. There was lust in his eyes, and I couldn't blame him. She was superb, and her voice was sweet and mellow.

"Please, call me Azazel. I'm no king for you to call me *Your Grace.*" He smirked, then looked over his shoulder.

Genevieve and Almus had disappeared somewhere beyond the tall rose bushes on the western edge of the garden. Azazel shifted his focus back to the Lamia.

"I wouldn't dare to call you Azazel, milord," she replied gently. "You are a leader, and I am but a young Druid with barely a couple of ranks. It would be highly disrespectful."

I noticed the two slim circle tattoos on her right wrist and began to wonder how she'd been accepted as a Druid when everything about her screamed Lamia.

"You're too kind, young lady," he sighed. "What is your name?"

"Tamara, milord."

"Tell me, Tamara, why do you wear scales on your skin? Are you a Lamia, perhaps?"

Bingo!

She blushed as she looked away, visibly embarrassed. Her smile, however, had the power to tear down any man's defenses, including Azazel's. His gaze softened.

"I assure you I am but a young Druid, milord. I've simply decided to embrace my serpent nature and wear it with pride, even in my Druid form," she replied. "I have no taste for incubus flesh. I have passed all the tests that Lady Genevieve requested before I entered her service."

A moment passed before she spoke again. Azazel continued to gaze at her.

"I like plums, milord. And honey. And the northern breads of the seventh kingdom, where I hail from." She sighed, contemplating the garden.

"I believe you, Tamara."

Azazel was bewitched by this creature. This was all probably happening millennia after they'd already been banished but long before they found out that Lamias had infiltrated the Druid society. Bijarki had told me a little about the entire scandal, dating a few centuries back, when dozens of Lamias had been ousted from Eritopia's high society. Before it all went to hell, thanks to Azazel.

I stood there, watching as she spoke to him. He liked her a

lot, and I couldn't help but wonder if his sudden attachment to her was related to Almus and Genevieve's developing relationship. Perhaps he needed someone to help him get over Draven's mother. Perhaps Tamara was the one who could take his mind off Genevieve.

Judging by how it all seemed to end, with Azazel as the self-proclaimed Prince of the Destroyers, I figured it didn't go too well between him and Tamara. But it was nevertheless interesting to discover that the "Prince" had once had a heart.

THE THIRD VISION tore me away from those days long gone, bringing me closer to the present time disaster. I found myself on a black marble platform atop a castle. The wind whistled at that altitude, brushing against giant glass spheres suspended from standalone black marble arches.

Azazel slithered around one of those spheres, which was filled with water and held an Oracle captive, whom I didn't recognize. My stomach churned, and my heart twisted in my chest, as I realized where I was. This was Azazel's castle, at the very top where he kept his Oracles. Two more slept in their spheres, floating in what probably felt like an eternity.

The clouds gathered above in menacing charcoal rolls, ignited by lightning and the occasional bang of thunder nearby.

"Where is she?" Azazel hissed at the Oracle.

He'd become a Destroyer, his thick black tail twitching as he moved around the Oracle, who cried inside the sphere, desperately trying to keep her head above the water.

"Oh, stop your whining. You're not going to drown. It's not really water!" he barked at her. "Tell me where she is!"

Her eyes were white and swollen from all the crying. She'd at least been spared the misery of seeing where she'd been brought, where she would eventually wither away and die.

I wanted to punch the monster, break his bones, and throw him off the platform. But I couldn't. I could only watch and listen and learn and use every bit of information I could gather against him.

"I don't know who she is," the Oracle sniffed between hiccups.

Azazel banged on the glass, startling her. He was raging, his eyes yellow, the snake medallion I'd seen on Lorenz now hung around his neck. I put two and two together and felt sorry for the old Druid, who was one of the many casualties of Azazel's ascension to power.

"You know Tamara! Where is that snake?!" he roared.

"I don't know. I can't see her! Please, just let me be! I can't see anything! I'm in too much pain!" she screamed.

Azazel didn't give up. Instead, he kept knocking on the glass and pushing the sphere around, enough to make the Oracle tumble and take a huge amount of water into her lungs.

"Stop wailing over your husband, you pathetic little soul! He's gone! Done! Dead! You're wasting your tears on that self-righteous ass anyway," he growled. "Now, tell me where she is!"

She struggled to breathe as the liquid entered her bloodstream and gradually relaxed her muscles, to the point where she floated around, eyes wide open and white. She was having a vision.

"Where is Tamara?! She ran off, and she has something that belongs to me, that wretched Lamia!"

A moment passed before the Oracle's voice echoed from the glass sphere.

"The Lamia fooled you, Azazel. You welcomed her into your bed, your heart, and your soul. You gave her a daughter, and she abandoned you."

"Well, thank you, darling, for the obsolete news! Now tell me where she is!" he shouted, banging on the glass.

"She has given birth now. Her daughter lives, a beautiful baby girl with golden eyes and black hair like yours."

"Where is she?!"

"I do not know. She is deep in the jungle, surrounded by other Lamias."

Azazel paced around her as she regained her consciousness. He trembled with fury.

She faced his direction, her expression filled with all the hate she could muster.

"If only I'd listened to my instinct when she first crossed my path," he mumbled. "If only I'd kept my distance. She fooled me. She fooled us all. She reminded me of Genevieve so much that I refused to see the truth. Serves me right."

"You will never see her again, Azazel. You will never see your daughter again either," the Oracle spat. "I will die before I tell you where they are. You took my husband from me, and I will die a thousand deaths before I ever give you the chance to see your daughter!"

A chill ran through me.

The monster had a daughter somewhere in Eritopia, conceived with a Lamia. A daughter he desperately wanted to see. Tamara had betrayed him. I wouldn't have been surprised if that exact predicament had pushed Azazel over the edge, forcing the deadly serpent out of him.

I stepped away from the glass sphere, unable to look at this Oracle anymore. I couldn't bear the thought of her in there.

Most importantly, I had gotten all the information I needed from my visions. I'd seen Azazel before he'd morphed into a Destroyer, before he'd brought death and destruction over this world. I had seen him as a young Druid, strong and ambitious, with the misfortune of having fallen in love with Draven's mother. I'd seen him battling the bureaucracy of Eritopian leadership.

But perhaps the most interesting fact I'd uncovered was that somewhere in Eritopia was a young Lamia with golden eyes and black hair, the daughter of Azazel and a very cunning Lamia. That was, if she was still alive.

23

SERENA

Azazel's castle rose menacingly from the dark jungles surrounding it, a magnificent construction with structural pillars and arches that reminded me of gothic cathedrals. Thousands of black marble statues sprawled across the façade. Green flames flickered by the large, glassless windows. Four slim, sharp towers reached for the sky.

We snuck through the trees until we reached the main road leading to the front gates. Draven had yet to let go of my hand, and I didn't mind at all.

I looked up and saw dozens of Destroyers flying on their horses, hissing as they patrolled the skies above. Millions of green fireflies hovered over the jungle, silent and all-seeing. My skin tingled, and shivers ran down my spine as I stood a few yards away from the monster's lair. I needed a minute to gather the courage to move forward. I had never been so close to so much evil before.

Draven sensed my reluctance and brushed his shoulder against mine. Had it not been for the invisibility spell, we would've been seen and killed before we could reach the castle. The thought gave me comfort and energy to proceed.

"This is Azazel's home, then," I mumbled.

"One of them, actually." I heard Hansa next to us.

"How many are there?"

"One on each of Eritopia's planets," Draven replied. "At least on the ones he's conquered. He's been busy campaigning against the 19th over the last couple of years. He's killed the Druid in charge of it, but the local government and military have been strong in their resistance."

That made me shiver.

"Do you think they'll retain their independence?" I asked.

"I doubt it. Most of their resources come from here, so once he cuts all trade ties they will have no other option," Draven said.

"Look over there. East side," Hansa whispered.

A small incubi garrison moved from the main road into the castle. A side path led up to secondary entrances through the eastern and western walls. The garrison headed toward the east passage.

"Now's our chance," Draven said and pulled me after him.

We walked quietly toward the incubi, joining the back of their group as they entered the castle. Thousands of green fireflies flitted around us, but we could not be seen. The passageway was tall and wide, clad in black limestone with green-lit torches mounted on the walls. I had a feeling that all the green flames were part of Azazel's spy spell, his eyes seeing everywhere the emerald fire burned.

The incubi grumbled and cursed under their breaths. Their backs slumped beneath the military uniforms. Their eyes sank in their heads, and their skin looked paler than usual. They seemed exhausted, and I couldn't help but feel sorry for them. It hadn't really been their choice. One does what one can to survive, and they were no different.

I heard our signature triple hiss and noticed a corridor opening to my right. Draven and I followed Hansa through it, leading us into a large service kitchen with hundreds of pots and pans and massive oak tables.

Green fires burned on wall sconces. A few incubi were finishing up, wiping the tables and putting the dry meats away, their expressions as dim as their fellow soldiers' from the hall-way. Nobody wanted to be there, and I could certainly sympathize.

We waited until the servant soldiers left for their quarters, cursing at Azazel and his Destroyers.

"I can't wait for the day when they're all lined up against a wall for us to drive our swords through them in return for everything they've done," one of them muttered.

"Yeah, repayment for their selfless service, right?" another said.

"Deck the halls with their blood, indeed," the third one murmured as they left the kitchen.

A moment passed before any of us spoke.

"Is it safe?" I asked.

He shushed me, and I felt him let go of my hand. One by one, the green fires were blown away, submerging the kitchen in absolute darkness.

"The green fire is Azazel's," I heard Draven say from the other side of the room.

A few seconds passed before I felt Draven standing next to me in the dark, his breath tickling the back of my neck.

"I'm guessing I'm not the only one with night vision in here, am I?" I said.

"I eat all my vegetables and don't read by candlelight," Draven quipped, making me fawn over him for a brief moment.

I pulled Aida's notes from my satchel and placed them on the table. I was surprised to see them visible as soon as I took my hand off them. I realized then how the spell worked. Everything I had on me was included in the spell until it left my body. Draven picked them up and looked through them, flipping the pages a couple of times to reveal the dungeon sketches Aida had scribbled. I used my True Sight to read them as he held them.

"If I'm reading this correctly, we need to go further below ground," he muttered.

I looked around and noticed a narrow black door at the far end of the kitchen, opposite from where we'd come in. I took the notes from Draven and stuffed them back in my satchel as I made my way toward the door. I reached it in a few rushed steps and turned the knob, opening it slowly. There was a set of stone steps descending underground.

"I think I found a way," I said.

Hansa and Draven joined me. We went down the stairs,

heading for the dim light at the end. It opened onto a wider staircase that ended in what looked like a sprawling basement. We kept ourselves closer to the left wall, taking one step at a time.

Green torches led the way, so we moved quietly.

Sudden hissing and shuffling behind us froze me in place. Draven's hand clutched my wrist, and we stilled as four massive Destroyers rushed down the stairs. I felt him let go of me as one of the monsters bumped into him, knocking him off his feet.

I inadvertently gasped, then immediately covered my mouth, moving so my back was against the cold black wall. My heart thudded as the Destroyers stopped and looked around, sniffing the air with confused expressions on their once humanoid faces.

Their tails were long and thick with black scales, while their upper bodies were well built with bulky muscles beneath their leather tunics. They'd once been handsome young Druids with short black hair, but their yellow snake eyes and the scales on their temples and cheeks were a sign that those days were long gone.

One of the beasts came back, slithering up the stairs and looking around, as if sensing there was someone there.

"What is it?" another asked from farther down.

"I hit something, but I can't see what I hit," the curious Destroyer replied.

"Why do we all have to stop for you to pretend you're not the clumsy oaf we all know you to be?" a third one said.

"You've got quite the mouth on you, you know that? Maybe

you should serve Goren for a while. You seem to be doing too well under Patrik," the Destroyer replied with a snarl.

He came dangerously close, his face barely a few inches from mine. I couldn't move even if I wanted to. My blood froze, and I held my breath, praying to all possible deities, including the Daughters, to not let this beast discover our presence there.

The creature eventually scoffed and followed his mates down the stairs.

"Come on. We need to fetch those two loyalists of Mermid for Azazel," the third one barked. "You know he likes them early in the morning!"

"I'll never understand why he enjoys tormenting the incubi he captures from the other districts. He just starves them in their cages, and when he gets bored, he starts slicing away at them just for kicks," the curious Destroyer grumbled.

"Does he ever get any information out of them?"

"I don't think so," he replied. "I think he does it mostly for the fun."

"You call that fun?"

"I don't! He does!"

"He finds more pleasure in torturing and tormenting the creatures he keeps in his cages than he does in ruling Eritopia with the iron fist he's always boasted about," another Destroyer chimed in.

Their voices dimmed as they reached the bottom level and advanced through the basement.

"All flash, no bang," the curious Destroyer chuckled as they disappeared from my field of vision.

I was able to breathe again. A wave of relief washed over me as I heard Draven scramble to his feet.

"Are you okay, Serena? Hansa?" he whispered.

We both hissed thrice. I used my True Sight to find his shimmering silhouette and took his hand. There was no time for me to digest the horror I'd experienced thinking of all the worst-case scenarios in which the Destroyers discovered our invisible presence there. I was grateful to have Draven in one piece next to me.

24

SERENA

As soon as we reached the bottom of the stairs we stopped, swallowing back the urge to scream with frustration. There were twelve corridors opening from where we stood, each leading in a different direction, and each riddled with danger and green fires.

Draven pulled me to the side, out of sight and reach of anyone who might pass by, and quickly retrieved the notes from my pack and glanced over them again before he shoved them into his pocket.

"If I'm not mistaken, three of these corridors will lead north, where Sverik is most likely to be held captive, based on what Aida saw during her vision," he whispered.

"Which one do we pick?" Hansa whispered from behind us.

"Might as well try the first one," he replied. "If not, we come back and go through another."

"I'm not sure there's enough time for this. The spell might wear off," I said.

"I made enough to have a second dose just in case." He ended the conversation there, and we followed him through the first corridor.

A few yards into the green-lit tunnel, we stepped into a basement chamber, an enormous hall with wet, black walls and a heavy dampness in the air. Hundreds of iron cages were stacked, two by two, one on top of the other with enough walking space between them to make the entire space look like a massive animal shelter—except everybody was doomed to die in here.

All kinds of creatures lay limp behind bars, most of them shackled, the black metal biting into their wrists and ankles. My stomach churned at the sight of so much misery, blood, and pain. They were literally sitting in there waiting to die.

We went straight ahead, walking slowly between the rows, hoping to recognize Sverik. A few minutes in, I heard Hansa gasp and looked over to my right. My heart leapt at the sight of a succubus lying on her side, badly bruised and severely injured with eyes half-open. I got closer to get a better look. Her leather garments and traces of blue war paint made me think she belonged to a tribe similar to Hansa's.

"Can you hear me?" Hansa whispered to her.

The young succubus was far too weak to even lift her head. She moaned softly and moved her eyes around, unable to see us. My heart broke for her, but deep down I knew we could do nothing for her in that moment. Our mission was clear—retrieve Sverik and run out of here as fast as we could.

"I'll get you out of here, sister. I promise." Hansa's voice trembled.

"I'm sorry, Hansa, but we don't have time for this," Draven hissed. "The spell might wear off, and dawn is near. We need to find Sverik, and this is just one of the many chambers where they might be keeping him."

I looked around and stilled. Heat ran through my body, followed by a peculiar coolness. The spell was already wearing off. Draven and Hansa first emerged as shimmering figures, then their full selves. I looked down and saw my own body and trembling hands.

"Oh, dear," I murmured.

"Well, that didn't last too long," Hansa groaned.

Draven looked at me, his gray eyes flickering black.

"I don't mean to make this moment any less grave, but it's good to see you again," he said to me, a smile tugging at the corner of his mouth.

I couldn't help smiling back. Hansa punched him in the shoulder, visibly aggravated. "There isn't any time for this sweet stuff, Druid! Whip out the rest of that spell before someone sees us!" she whispered, gritting her teeth.

Draven searched his satchel, then his pockets and then his satchel again. Shadows passed over his face before he looked at both Hansa and me with a stunned expression. A moment passed before his low voice broke through the silence.

"I think I lost the pouch with the rest of that paste," he said.

His words crashed into me, and the back of my neck caught fire. We were suddenly visible and very much vulnerable to Destroyer attacks from any possible angle. My instincts kicked in so fast, I didn't have time to consider panic. Judging by the way Hansa and Draven's eyes moved around, neither did they.

"It must have fallen off me earlier on the stairs with those Destroyers," he added with a frown.

One by one, the caged creatures caught glimpses of us in their half-sleeping states. One by one, they sat up, their bony fingers clutching the iron bars, begging us to release them. Incubi, succubi, Lamias, and many other species held down by shackles and locks—they all pleaded and offered us their services, their lands, and their fortunes if we could get them out.

One by one, we were forced to let them down, to lie to them and promise we'd come back for them. And yet, they persisted, their voices getting louder as more of them asked for help.

"Please, let us out."

"I beg of you, my children are out there. I need to find them..."

"Please, send a message to my father..."

"Please, I won't last much longer. Help me!"

It went on and on while we advanced through the chamber, shushing them and asking them to not give away our position. Some listened, keeping quiet while glimmers of hope bloomed in their eyes. My heart twisted in pain. How many of them would still be alive by the time we could return for them?

"Can't we do anything to help these people?" I asked Draven, who walked ahead of me.

"Not unless you want a horde of Destroyers to descend upon us and make us join them. I'm sorry, Serena. We can't risk it. We need to find Sverik."

I sighed as a fae caught my eye. She was beautiful, even beneath the layers of dried blood and dirt. Her once platinum hair was matted. Her eyes were the color of lilacs, and her lower lip was swollen and bruised. She must have been here when Azazel overthrew the government and forcibly took control of this planet.

"Excuse me," I asked her with a trembling voice. "You're a fae, aren't you?"

She looked at me and nodded, a frown pulling her eyebrows closer, informing me that she was leery of strangers. But she was sharp enough to recognize that I was as out of this world as she was.

"Do you know if there's an incubus named Sverik around here?"

"You're not from around here, are you?" she replied, her tone flat and dry.

I shook my head.

"Figures. If you were, you would've known not to walk into this miserable hellhole." She grimaced, bitterness lifting her upper lip.

"We need to find Sverik," I insisted, certain that she would be willing to help if I gave her good reasons. "He's the one who will help us free everyone from these cages, including you."

"I don't know of any Sverik. And there is no way out of here. But it's refreshing to see all that hope coming from you. I'm sorry, but you will lose it all. We all do in the end."

She'd succumbed to her captivity, hopeless and lightless. The shackles around her wrists had symbols engraved on them.

Judging by how sad she seemed every time she looked down at them, I figured they were the reason why she couldn't use her fae powers to get herself out of there.

"Let's go, Serena," Draven whispered.

I looked at him, then at the fae.

"I'm sorry," I told her. "I wish I could set you free."

"I'm sorrier for you than you are for me. You will never make it out of here alive. But there's a spare cage behind me. We might become neighbors," she replied dryly.

A husky voice caught our attention. "Are you looking for Sverik?"

We turned our heads and found an incubus locked in a cage on the other side. He looked young and had fewer injuries compared to the other captives. His military tunic was coated with dried mud, and a deep cut had formed a dark gray crust on his left cheek, but his bright green eyes were alert, beaming with the will to survive and fight his way out of there.

"Indeed, we are," Draven replied, stepping toward the incubus. "Do you know him?"

"I know where he is." He said, hope straining his voice. "But you have to let me out of here. They will kill me soon."

"You will slow us down," Hansa shot back. "We cannot fail on this mission. All our lives depend on it, not just yours."

"I won't! I promise! I'm not injured. I am strong. I can help you! I've only been here for two days! They captured me near Mount Agrith. I'd left my garrison when they were forced to join Azazel's troops! I couldn't! I can't die in here! I will take you to Sverik. I know where they're keeping him!"

Draven thought about it, but my nerves were too stretched for me to be patient. Our time was running out. Destroyers lurked. We could be discovered at any moment, especially with all the prisoners still moaning and begging us for help.

I made the decision. I looked around and found a heavy chunk of black stone discarded on the wet, dirty floor. I picked it up and smashed the lock that held the incubus's cage shut. It took a couple of hits for the metal to break free.

The incubus jumped out of the cage and stretched, beaming with relief and sheer joy. I noticed Draven's frown aimed specifically at me and shrugged.

"Executive decision." I smiled, then looked at the incubus. "What's your name?"

"Grindel," the young soldier replied.

"Grindel, you're free now. Take us to Sverik, please. Keep your end of the bargain," I told him.

He nodded enthusiastically and swiftly ran down the narrow lane between cages. Hansa, Draven, and I followed. We took several turns before we found Sverik. He was tucked away between two other incubi by the wall. Sverik was as handsome as Aida had described him, with beautiful features and light blond hair. His crude green eyes moved around, constantly scanning his surroundings, until they settled on our approaching figures and widened with surprise.

He sat up from his slumped position, gripping the bars and measuring us from head to toe. The bruises on his cheeks and temples were nearly black, as were the circles around his eyes.

He'd been there for a while, stuck in darkness and misery. Our presence seemed to bring him back to life.

"Sverik?" Draven asked as he reached his cage first.

"Indeed. Who's asking?" he replied bluntly.

"I am Draven, and these are my associates," he nodded toward Hansa and me. "We're here to help you."

"You're a Druid," Sverik squinted, pursing his lips. "Thought your kind was extinct, fully degraded into those snake-tailed abominations."

"As you can see, I'm still here. You can consider us critically endangered but not gone yet. We need your help, Sverik."

"How could I possibly help you? You might have noticed I'm in a cage."

"Bijarki and Kristos were allies of mine. We have a plan to defeat Azazel, but with Kristos gone, we need your help to rally the remaining troops left on Calliope against the Destroyers," Draven replied.

"So, you're the one responsible for my brother's death, then, along with that bastard Bijarki?" Sverik muttered with disgust.

"Kristos chose his own path. He rebelled. He couldn't swear fealty to a monster who only wishes to burn everything down, and you know it. Help us. Avenge him."

A moment passed before Sverik spoke again, giving me enough time to look around and make sure there weren't any Destroyers coming. We were clear for the moment.

He sighed. "What do you need from me?"

"Your presence. Your voice. You can help us gather the rogue incubi left hiding in the jungles. We've formed an alliance with the Dearghs, we've reached out to the Lamias and other succubi, and there are plenty of us out there who can fight and bring this bastard down," Draven replied. "We need to come together."

"Fine. Just get me out of here. My father betrayed me, allowing Azazel to throw me in this cage. I owe that old fool nothing. He wouldn't listen anyway."

Draven nodded then muttered something under his breath, his finger on the lock. Sparks flew from the keyhole, and the mechanism clicked. He pulled the lock apart, throwing it on the floor, and opened Sverik's cage.

The incubus climbed out and stretched, his bones cracking. Grindel saluted him, and Sverik smiled, shaking his hand. He then looked at the Druid, Hansa, and me.

"It's strange enough to see a Druid still standing, and of succubi and incubi I've seen enough, but you, my dear, you are something else entirely." He gave me a lascivious smile, unleashing his incubus nature over me.

My spine tingled, and my head felt light. I was unable to resist his naturally twisted charms. My body betrayed me, while my mind screamed and pounded against my skull. I felt horrible stuck in between and gripped Draven's hand in response.

"Stop it, or I will leave you here to rot," Draven spat, gritting his teeth.

Sverik paled, and I immediately regained my senses. He bowed and put on an innocent face, complete with puppy dog eyes.

"My apologies. I didn't realize," he said sheepishly. "I've been in here for too long."

Draven ignored his apology. "Where do we go from here?"

Sverik nodded, putting on his more serious face. He reminded me of Bijarki just a little, just as playful and nonchalant, despite the grim circumstances. Before he opened his mouth to give us an answer, a swish startled me.

Three spears shot past us, missing my shoulder by inches. They all pierced Grindel's chest. The incubus yelped and fell backward, writhing in pain and foaming at the mouth.

My blood froze, and my inner-sentry was instantly turned on. Our fight for survival and escape had just begun. We all ducked, looking around to find the source of those spears. My stomach shrank into a tiny ball as I saw three Destroyers hissing and slithering toward us, swords in their hands.

They were massive and bloodthirsty, but nevertheless I stood up and channeled the energy I'd previously syphoned from Draven to push out the strongest barrier I'd ever been able to conjure.

The pulse shot outward, knocking them on their backs. It gave Draven and Hansa enough seconds to pull out their crossbows, load them, and shoot poisoned arrows at the monsters. They hit their shoulders and chests.

The creatures groaned and seemed to be in pain, but it wasn't enough to kill them. Instead, they continued their advance, closing the distance between us.

I took another step forward and latched on to one of the beasts' minds, taking a deep breath and pushing for control. The golden fire coursing through my veins gave me surprising strength as I subdued the Destroyer and forced him to his knees. He dropped his sword on the floor with a loud clang.

Draven muttered something under his breath again, presumably one of his spells, putting his palms forward and launching spheres of blue fire at another Destroyer. The flames bit into its thick skin, sizzling through the flesh. It was enough to bring it down but not enough to kill it.

Hansa pulled her sword out and charged the third one, eager to exact some of the revenge she'd been planning against the Destroyers for what they had done to her sisters.

His sword cut through the air.

She dodged his hits and moved swiftly around him, slashing at the monster. With a lunge, she jumped up with a twist and beheaded him.

The Destroyer's head rolled on the floor.

She landed on her feet, breathing heavily. A smirk stretched her lips. Dark splatters of blood smeared across her face and chest.

My Destroyer was slowly inching toward me, despite my strong mind control.

"Wow. You do not give up, do you?" I snarled, incredibly frustrated as I channeled more of my energy into my grip on his movements.

I caught a glimpse of Sverik from the corner of my eye as he snatched Draven's sword from his belt. The incubus launched himself at my Destroyer and cut off its head with one swift move.

Draven shot out another series of blue flames that engulfed the remaining Destroyer just as it stood up to charge us.

It hissed and wailed in agony, giving Sverik the opening he needed to behead it. The head tumbled onto the floor, engulfed in blue flames.

Sverik then looked at us and smiled.

"You can play with your Druid spells all you want. I'm keeping the sword for now," Sverik said.

I had a hard time disagreeing with his logic, merely out of gratitude for the efficient way in which he'd spared me the trouble of depleting my energy on that Destroyer.

"I take it beheading them works?" Draven replied.

"Indeed," the incubus nodded. "We've tried everything before. It's just damned nearly impossible to get close enough to the snakes to do it."

I looked around again. My limbs shook, and my lungs were greedy for more humid, dirty air.

"We need to go," Sverik added. "The others must have heard the noise by now, and they'll be here shortly."

We nodded and followed him down the path toward another corridor which opened up onto a set of stairs leading back up to the surface. We entered another hallway, the fourth from the left.

"There's a passage way at the end of this tunnel," Sverik explained. "It will take us back up. The green flames have already spotted us back there. We need another way out."

"Do you know where we need to go next?" I asked, looking over my shoulder.

A wave of hisses and barked orders echoed through the corridor, as Draven blew out any green-lit torches along the wall.

"I can't believe we actually killed Destroyers." I couldn't help but grin. "I thought they were impossible to kill."

"They usually are. Don't let this little victory embolden you, young lady," Sverik replied. "Azazel keeps the weaker Destroyers in the dungeons to look after his prisoners. It's not the same as fighting one of his lieutenants."

"Why's that?" I asked.

"Because the weaker Destroyers would not be effective in battle. Azazel is quite specific about this, requesting only the strongest to fight for him. The ones in the dungeons aren't as skilled and have lower stamina, but they're big and heavy enough to keep the prisoners in their cages. Besides, there's not much for them to fight with. Most of these prisoners are too weak to put up a fight, and the ones with magic, such as the fae, are kept under control with warded cuffs."

It made sense, reminding me of the fae we'd met earlier. My assumption had been correct – Azazel had found a way to keep their powers under control.

We ran fast across another chamber filled with cages, not giving any of the prisoners time to notice us or call out for help. Nevertheless, their misery and hopelessness ate away at me, amplifying my growing hate for Azazel. I would make him pay for each and every single life he'd taken or ruined, including those of my brother and friends, stuck in an old and moldy plantation house in the middle of nowhere.

25

JOVI

We reached the River Pyros as night fell over the region, turning the sky a vibrant shade of indigo, riddled with billions of stars. The moon shone brightly and full, casting its milky light over the woods.

Anjani, Bijarki, and I were first, followed closely by the three Lamias, two of whom seemed to really enjoy dragging the prisoner incubi down the road. The Lamias' settlement sprawled across both sides of the river, which ran hot and steamy—something I'd never seen before.

"The River Pyros runs hot," Anjani explained, noticing the surprised look on my face. "It stems from Mount Asid, a volcano in the west. You can see it rising over the horizon during the day."

I nodded as I got a better look at the Lamias' settlement. It wasn't exactly a city, as I'd heard it described. It was about the size of a small town with hundreds of homes carved into giant purple trees on a wide radius, perhaps a couple of miles. Torches and candles flickered yellow all over, and colorful paper lanterns hung from the branches.

"What will you do with the incubi?" I asked the Lamias over my shoulder.

I didn't like the idea of seeing them killed, but I had a hard time trusting them.

"We'll kill them later," Una replied in a casual tone. "After Bijarki debriefs them. Or we'll enslave them. Either way, they're not getting out of here."

The closer we got, the better I could see how the Lamias had turned the hot river banks into baths, with hammocks suspended above the water and stone tubs. We entered the settlement, stopping in the middle of a square, where a fire burned bright and red on a pile of green marbles.

Five Lamias emerged from the gathering crowd, as beautiful as the three who had guided us there, clad in fine white silks with large emerald bracelets and necklaces complementing the green scales on their bare arms and their yellow snake eyes. They wore their hair loose in soft shades of ginger and platinum, and bright smiles stretched across their luscious lips. I couldn't help but gawk at their timeless beauty. All five struck me as well into their forties, and they were absolutely stunning. In Lamia years, I had a feeling they'd racked up a couple of millennia.

"Welcome, travelers," the one in the middle said. "My name is Tamara, Mother of the Lamias, and these are my sisters."

Bijarki got off his horse and was the first to bow in front of them. Anjani and I followed suit. The Mother and sisters bowed in return.

The triplets who'd brought us in took the incubi away.

Three young Lamias appeared almost out of nowhere, offering to take our horses and give them food and water. Bijarki gave Anjani and me an approving nod, and we let our stallions go.

"What brings you here?" Tamara asked, measuring us carefully.

"I'm Bijarki, of the Strandh clan. These are my companions and allies, Anjani of the Red Tribe and Jovi," he waved in my direction.

I felt awkward again with a sea of yellow eyes focused on me. I was the odd one out, after all. Tamara sniffed the air, her forked tongue flitting over her lips.

"Jovi of the wolves, I believe?" She smiled.

I nodded.

"You're not from around here."

"I'm not."

"Where are you from?" Tamara lifted an eyebrow.

"Jovi was visiting with a delegation from another planet outside this galaxy, many light years away, when Azazel attacked," Bijarki answered on my behalf. "He's been stranded here ever since but is extremely valuable to our cause. He's one of the most skilled fighters I've ever been honored to meet."

I wasn't sure whether Bijarki was just making all this stuff up to validate my presence here, but I didn't mind the whiff of pride gleaming through me at his description of me. I put on a confident smile to further validate his statement, and the Lamias seemed to appreciate it. I gave Anjani a sideways glance and noticed her frowning, tension pulsating in her jaw. I figured she wasn't a fan of so many creatures gazing at me with such interest.

"And yet you haven't answered my question, Bijarki. What brings you here?" Tamara replied.

"We're here to discuss an alliance with the Lamias," he answered. "Draven, son of Almus and the last Druid of Eritopia, wishes to arrange a discourse with you, Tamara. We are gathering forces all over the planet and beyond to rise against Azazel and put an end to his tyranny. Draven has faith in you as potential allies in the upcoming war."

Tamara cocked her head, looking at Bijarki with newfound interest.

"You mean to tell me that the Druids are not all dead or decayed into those filthy, useless Destroyers?"

By useless I figured she meant sterile, as the triplets had already confirmed. I noticed Anjani slowly moving closer to my side, inch by inch, until the back of her hand brushed against mine.

"Draven is the only survivor, from what we know," Bijarki replied. "Azazel never knew he was born. Chances are he still doesn't know."

Tamara nodded, looking at her sisters before shifting her attention back on us with a warm smile and arms wide open.

"We'd certainly be pleased to meet with the Druid and negotiate an alliance, as you say. But first, let us feast. We will look after your horses and offer you a place to rest for the night, along with our finest dishes and company," she said.

A moment passed, during which we looked at each other, distrust hanging loosely in the air. We were willing to initiate a dialogue against a common enemy. That didn't mean knives couldn't be thrust into our backs if we weren't careful. Most importantly, I still felt some degree of concern for the incubi we'd captured. Every able-bodied soldier counted in our war, even the ones hungry for Azazel's bounties.

"What about the incubi?" I asked.

"What about them, little wolf?" one of the sisters replied with a smirk.

"We captured them with the help of your sisters. However, we could use their help in this war, should they be willing to cooperate. Will you keep them alive, at least until we can decide whether they can be trusted or not?"

"We do not kill so easily," the sister said, her chin up and proud. "We will ask them questions, as they were far too close to the river to begin with, and will leave them in your care afterward, if that is what you wish."

I nodded in appreciation.

Tamara smiled. "But in the meantime, let us feast!"

"Why should we trust you?" Anjani interjected, her brow furrowed. "Your reputation doesn't exactly speak of peaceful demeanors and trustworthiness."

"Neither does yours, succubus, and yet we have a common enemy—one who is cruel and evil enough to put our troubled history aside for the moment. Wouldn't you agree?" Tamara's voice was laced with ice and contempt.

Heavy silence fell between us for a few long seconds.

"Besides, we would never think of harming the friends of a Druid," she added. "After all, nothing makes us happier than the thought of there still being one Druid alive in this wretched world."

26

FIELD

The day had been calm and sunny, but I still wasn't comfortable with just waiting around the mansion while Aida, Phoenix, and Vita were busy with their visions. I felt like I could do more to keep my friends—particularly Aida—safe, so I decided to fly out beyond the mansion's protective shield and do a wider perimeter check.

I was careful, flying low and soundlessly. I wasn't comfortable leaving the safety of the mansion, but I had to check the surroundings and see whether the Destroyers we'd seen in previous nights were getting any closer to our location.

Best to be prepared for anything.

I glided over the trees, my eyes scanning the areas both below and above me for anything out of the ordinary. I saw shifters running around through the occasional clearing, and other animals grazing by the dark waters. I saw giant lizards grab the water grazers by their throats and drown them. Eritopia was beautiful and cruel.

Eat or be eaten.

I widened my search perimeter until I heard hissing noises echoing from several miles away to the east. I saw flocks of Destroyers flying in the opposite direction, away from our perimeter. I was too far away for them to even notice me, and I watched as they disappeared beyond the horizon.

My stomach churned as I flapped my wings and moved upward to check the distant skies better. Black dots moved here and there, but none close enough to constitute an immediate threat. Something caught my eye, however, several yards in front of me—a swarm of tiny green fireflies moving around chaotically.

I wondered what they were doing out there during the day. I slowly descended and turned to head back to the mansion, when the little green buggers flew right into me. They buzzed and glowed as they frantically flew around me to the point where they became a nuisance. I swatted them away and increased my speed to get rid of them.

I left them behind and moved farther down, till I felt the tree tips brushing against me.

My mind drifted to Aida. She'd managed to set me on fire, and I was still recovering from our kiss. How had I not seen her in this way before? Had I been that blind, so hung up on Maura that I hadn't even been able to look around me?

I'd watched Aida grow from a rowdy little wolf-girl to the gorgeous young woman I'd been fortunate to feel in my arms the other day. Her curves ignited my every instinct. Her lips begged for my attention and utter devotion. How had I not seen it before?

I'd always found her fascinating, ever the brave and fearless fighter, standing up to GASP boys just so she could prove that she was as strong and capable as any of them. And she'd certainly proven herself over and over again during training. I'd been around for long enough to know a good fighter when I saw one, and Aida had the potential to become one of GASP's most valuable assets.

I could only imagine what she'd been going through with her Oracle transformation, and I'd spent plenty of nights thinking about how it could possibly affect her. As our days at the mansion went by, I found myself unable to take my eyes off her. Something pulled me closer to her. I drifted toward Aida, watching as she cried, frowned, fought, and laughed her way through each Eritopian sunrise.

Her determination gave me strength when I felt the pressure of doubt, when all seemed lost or heading toward disaster and death. She was ahead of her years. I'd seen glimpses of that in the past, back in The Shade.

When Jovi and Phoenix told me about her feelings for me, my stomach had dropped. I'd seen the looks, but I'd never paid attention. It wasn't until Maura walked out of my life that I was able to truly see Aida. When I first got injured in my scuffle with the shape-shifter, she was raw and trembling as she touched me, forcing me to open my eyes. I was floored and felt utterly stupid for not having seen it sooner. I'd been missing out on the most extraordinary creature I'd ever laid eyes upon.

It took me hours to stop reprimanding myself for being such a fool.

And then I kissed her, and something clicked inside of me. Suddenly it all made sense. She made sense. We made sense together. I had to be near her. I had to feel her and smell her and kiss her. I had to tell her that everything would be okay. That I'd never leave her. I couldn't leave her.

The moment I felt her lips on mine, I knew I had to find out more, to discover every facet of Aida and let it flow through me and fuel me higher into the sky.

Her insecurities had once been adorable, like when she was younger, unsure whether she'd ever fit in with her wolf hair and boyish demeanor. Little did she know that it was that very nature that had set her apart and made her special. These insecurities were becoming a nuisance. She was beautiful, strong, and resourceful, no matter what the Oracle transition threw at her. I didn't care. I just wanted to see her safe and happy.

I'd made it my mission to brush her doubts away. She'd been so frightened, so candid, so sweet and hot against my body. How could I not do my best to see her smile?

Aida had become extremely important to me very quickly. But with all that was going on around us, with our lives on the line as a mad monster wreaked havoc and death throughout Eritopia, there wasn't enough time to worry about how fast things were evolving between Aida and me. There was only time to make the most of it.

A fluttering sound broke my train of thought, and I looked over my shoulder to find a few green fireflies flying behind me. They looked pretty cool, their flames flickering in a vibrant emerald color.

I moved slightly to the right, watching as they followed me around.

A smile tugged at the corners of my mouth. I wondered if she'd like to see these little buggers up close. I was willing to bet they looked beautiful in the dark—the perfect ambient enhancement for what I was already planning for her.

27

SERENA

We could hear Destroyers and incubi soldiers roaming through the halls and corridors that we'd left behind. Sverik led us through the underground maze of dozens of interlinked tunnels carved into the black limestone. Each tunnel was riddled with green fires.

Someone was clearly watching us through the flames, because the hostiles were permanently hot on our trail. I'd lost track of where we were, turning left and right over and over again. Draven, Hansa, and I were compelled to trust Sverik's knowledge of Azazel's castle.

"Our best chance is to sneak out through one of the water canals leading to the river," Sverik said as we ran up a set of narrow stairs. "We can swim up to get as close as we can to Mount Zur before we continue the rest of the way on foot. If we take the old-fashioned way out, they will capture us before we reach the castle gates."

"Where are the water canals?" Draven asked as we reached the top of the stairs.

"Right here," Sverik replied.

We found ourselves inside a massive bath hall with black marble tubs carved into the floor and connected through a network of canals. Water poured slowly through them, filling the tubs before following a stream leading out through a narrow archway.

"This is one of the baths used by Azazel's soldiers," Sverik said, catching his breath as we walked toward the archway.

I looked around. Even the baths were creepy and dark and slimy. This place had all the attributes of an evil monster's lair, down to the amenities. I couldn't shake the feeling that something was bound to go wrong. Making it up here in the first place had been too easy.

"We might get lucky and get out of here alive," Sverik said. "It's too early in the morning. It will take a little while to—"

A hiss interrupted him, and before I could look behind me, I was viciously pulled back and thrown onto the wet floor. I hit the stone hard, the air instantly knocked out of my lungs.

I choked. Stars erupted. My vision cleared.

A Destroyer stood above me, spear in his hand ready to kill me. He lifted his spear to get the job done.

My heart stilled.

A sword slashed through the air, severing his head. His body dropped, head rolling to the side. Blood spurted all over me.

I saw Draven standing next to where the Destroyer had been, his fingers clutching the sword and his eyes flickering black. He pulled me up and held me close, one arm coiled around my waist firmly. He looked at me carefully, concern etched into his beautiful features, his eyes switching between gray and black.

I leaned into him.

Before we could say anything else, more hissing emerged from the staircase, along with more Destroyers with spears and swords eager to kill.

"Run!" Sverik shouted and darted toward the archway.

We followed, sprinting through one of the canals. Water splashed beneath our feet.

The monsters growled. Spears and arrows flew past us. We dodged them effectively, though some missed me by mere inches.

"Nowhere to run!" I heard one Destroyer shout after us.

I saw Sverik pass through the archway, enveloped in darkness. Hansa went in second, followed by me and Draven. Spears and arrows hit the wall around it.

We ran as fast as we could. The sound of our footsteps through the water echoed around us as we headed for the light at the end of the tunnel.

The closer we got, the more my heart shrank and my stomach tightened.

I could see the distant treetops outside. We'd made it well above ground level without even noticing. The sun was rising, casting amber and pale pink light across the sky. We'd gone up a significant number of stairs and through many corridors. I'd clearly lost track of where we were headed.

I looked over my shoulder and saw the bulky Destroyers slithering through the tunnel like massive black shadows.

"We have to jump," Sverik shouted.

He stood on the edge, where the water poured outward.

Hansa reached him first and glanced down. She gave me a wary expression.

"What?" I asked, my nerves stretched and patience running thin.

"We have to jump," she said, visibly unhappy with the decision.

Arrows swished through the air.

We dodged them. One grazed my shoulder.

I gasped.

"Run!" Draven pushed me.

I did as he said.

We ran. We had no other choice.

Whatever waited beyond the end of the tunnel was likely better than what was moving toward us. I heard swords whistling as they were pulled out of their sheaths. They got closer.

Sverik jumped.

Hansa followed with a roar that split the air and echoed through the tunnel.

It was too late to turn back or do anything else.

Three more steps, and it would be over, or worse. It didn't matter.

I ran.

I jumped.

The world opened up as I left the tunnel, flailing in midair.

The jungle sprawled below. A river flowed through it, thick and foamy. Water from the castle cascaded into it.

My mind instantly took me to Draven.

I fell.

28

JOVI

The feast was impressive to say the least. The Lamias had us seated at a large wooden table covered with a plethora of hot dishes, stews, fruits, vegetables and a multitude of nuts and dark breads. Pitchers of sweet tea and cool water with rose petals were being passed around, filling crystal chalices to the brims.

A bright red fire burned in the middle of the table, mounted on a marble plate filled with oil and supported by dozens of raw, unpolished emeralds. Young Lamias moved around, helping with food service. Two harps played nearby.

The sky was black above, sprinkled with stars. The moon was nowhere to be seen.

Anjani sat to my right, and Bijarki sat to my left. Both made me feel comfortable enough to relax, despite the Lamias' lascivious smiles, winks, and air kisses. I was beginning to feel like prey during open season but also mildly flattered, as I had rarely been in the company of so many beautiful creatures. I remembered my night at the Red Tribe and the succubi and their advances. The memory of Anjani's glowing reaction warmed my stomach.

Tamara sat across from us, listening to Bijarki as he told her about our mission, about the Oracles, and about our plan to defeat Azazel. Surprise lifted her eyebrows upon hearing about the existence of my sister and the rest of our group.

"I didn't think there were any Oracles left alive. Or at least free." She smiled, cutting a slice out of an apple and popping it in her mouth.

"We didn't either," Bijarki replied. "The last Oracle Azazel captured was careful to pass on her gift outside of Eritopia. They were raised in a different world, not knowing their true nature."

My eyes drifted around the table, occasionally meeting the glances of Tamara's sisters and the other Lamias seated with us. I felt Anjani's hip pressing into mine, as she pulled herself closer to my side. I couldn't help but smirk as I wrapped my arm around her waist and drew her in.

I looked down at her and found her shooting daggers at me.

"I'm only doing this to protect you," she mumbled. "I'm not sure whether they're all looking at you like that because they want to mate with you or eat you."

I tightened my grip on her, a chill running down my spine as the realization sank in. Perhaps what I'd considered to be salacious gestures were nothing more than the signs of predators eager to drive their fangs into me.

My ego deflated at the thought of becoming someone's dinner. I held Anjani close, thankful to have her with me.

"Tell you what, Bijarki," Tamara said after a while. "I will meet with your Druid and discuss an alliance with him under one condition."

Bijarki nodded, sipping his tea. "Name it. As long as it doesn't involve anyone here eating me."

The Lamias chuckled. Their forked tongues flitted through the air, and their eyes glowed with humor. Tamara grinned, her finger running along the rim of her glass.

"Nothing like that, I can assure you." She sighed. "You mentioned a safe space where the Druid lives. I wish to meet him there."

"That can be arranged." Bijarki looked at Anjani and me.

"Are you sure?" I asked him, wary of the prospect of Lamias discovering our mansion.

"We need to show these fearsome ladies that we are willing to trust them in order for this alliance to work," he replied, then turned his attention on Tamara. "Will that be all?"

She shook her head and snapped her fingers twice in the air. A young Lamia emerged from another table, where she'd been eating with her sisters. She was stunning, with long black hair and amber—almost yellow—eyes with narrow pupils. Her skin was white, adorned with charcoal scales growing up her arms and neck. A single large emerald clasped her red silk dress above her chest.

"My daughter, Eva, will come with us," Tamara said as the young Lamia walked over to our table and sat next to her.

Both Bijarki and I were in awe of the girl's beauty. I could feel the crisp night air filling my gaping mouth, which I instantly shut tight as Anjani's fingers painfully dug into my hip. It took a while for the incubus to speak again. His eyes were fixed on Eva.

"Fine. She may come with us," he reluctantly agreed. "But absolute secrecy must be maintained. No one can ever know where the Druid lives."

Tamara nodded, a satisfied smile slitting her face.

"That's perfectly understandable, Bijarki. Please rest assured that we do not kiss and tell," she replied, then clapped her hands twice, addressing the Lamias. "We leave at dawn. Please have everything ready!"

A few servants shuffled around our table, disappearing into the nearby massive purple trees. I figured they were packing bags for Tamara and Eva. I nudged Bijarki, unable to smooth the frown on my face.

"Are you sure that's a good idea?" I asked.

"It's not like we have much of a choice." He shrugged. "We need their support. If she wants to take her daughter sightseeing, it's fine, as long as we get our alliance."

I sighed and gulped down my water. My throat felt dry. There were plenty of risks to trusting a Lamia with our safe location but none spelled doom better than the prospect of their species refusing to help against Azazel. With the Red Tribe nearly extinct and only a handful of Dearghs to support us, it felt like we had no chance of defeating the monster.

LATER THAT EVENING, we were escorted to one of the purple

trees a few yards away from the town square where we'd been greeted upon arrival. It was a beautiful giant with violet lanterns hanging from its branches. The interior seemed spacious, carved in two separate levels connected by a set of narrow stairs and lit with dozens of small candles. Fine organza was hung across the walls, ruffled at the top and flowing down in wide creases.

Tamara walked in first, and we followed. Two beds had been prepared on the ground floor, along with pitchers of water and a bowl of fruits. She waved around with a smile.

"You fellows will sleep down here. I've made sure that no one disturbs you throughout the night. The succubus can sleep upstairs," she said, looking at Anjani. "We've left a few things for your consideration. Hopefully you will like them. Like I said, we do not make a habit of carelessly killing and eating your kind. Not anymore."

Anjani's eyebrows were raised in genuine surprise. She blinked fast as she processed the Lamia's gesture of goodwill—a historically improbable event.

She left us there, waving at us without bothering to look over her shoulder.

"I shall see you three in the morning. Get plenty of sleep. The air is heavy with dark omens," she said and disappeared into the night.

Bijarki was the first to fall asleep. I'd wanted to ask him a few questions about the Lamias, but by the time I put my head down and relaxed, I could hear him snoring. Anjani had already vanished upstairs. I couldn't help wondering whether she'd drifted off as well.

Several thuds from above made me sit up. I looked over to see Bijarki still sleeping, his chest moving slowly, his breathing steady. I got out of bed and climbed the stairs, quietly looking around.

I reached the top floor and found Anjani standing in the middle of the room. A mirror leaned against the tree wall in front of her. She wore a long black dress with a deep V-neck that took my breath away. The smooth fabric poured down her body, outlining her curves beautifully. Her black hair flowed carelessly down her bare back. She saw me and stilled.

"What are you doing here?" she asked, her skin glowing.

My heart twisted. Heat expanded through my body and filled my muscles. I felt my cheeks burning, and my throat dried up.

"Sorry. I heard noises. I wanted to make sure you were okay," I replied sheepishly.

Neither of us said anything for a while. My eyes wandered down her body to a pile of colorful silk dresses on the floor next to her feet.

"I take it they left those for you?" I asked, clearing my throat.

She nodded. Her wide, emerald-gold eyes darted from the dresses to me and back.

"Their way of making amends for eating succubi?"

"Pretty much," she replied. "Not that they can fix anything with silk garments."

I shook my head. "I didn't think so," I said.

"But the dresses are beautiful." She shrugged, clearly conflicted.

I stood there, gawking and unable to move. I needed another moment to put my foot down the first step, but my gaze was fixed on her.

"I'll leave you, then." My voice was weak.

"You can stay," she replied.

Her expression puzzled me. Judging by our previous interactions, I knew she felt attracted to me as much as I was to her. Perhaps it was time to use a little bit of reverse psychology.

"It's okay. I'd like to be polite and let you sleep. We have a long day ahead of us tomorrow."

She took a deep breath, drawing my focus back to her cleavage. This had a devastating effect on my senses. Tension gathered in my jaw. My stomach clenched.

"Please stay," she said. "I'm really not comfortable with you out of my sight, especially with all the Lamias hanging around."

"What about Bijarki?" I asked with a smirk.

"He's a big incubus. He can take care of himself."

"Take it you're jealous they're all into me, then?"

I had a hard time containing myself. She was such an easy target when it came to other creatures paying attention to me. Her inability to hide her discomfort was downright endearing and brought out the joker in me. I loved playing with her even when I knew I'd get scratched—like playing with a tigress.

A shadow passed over Anjani's face. She raised her arms to her side in a gesture of exasperation. "Yes! Okay? Yes, I'm jealous!"

Her raised voice stunned me. My heart stopped.

"I can't bear the thought of other creatures touching you or even getting close to you, okay? Is that what you want to hear? Well, there you have it! I don't want you looking at them. I can't get you out of my head, and I'm still shaking from your kiss! There! Happy?"

Her confession floored me. My mind suddenly put two and two together. The glances, the frowns, the way she got so defensive around me. Her whole play about influencing me with her succubus nature had been her way to prove herself strong. Whether she'd wanted to prove it to me or herself was still unclear. Nevertheless, it ignited something inside of me.

Silence fell between us as we looked at each other. My heart raced, frantically struggling against the constraints of my ribcage. She was so beautiful and fierce, and yet, in that moment, her vulnerability made my spine tingle. It must have taken great strength for her to tell me the truth about how she felt.

Anjani took a deep breath, then crossed the room in several wide steps. The closer she got, the faster my heart throbbed. She pushed me against the wall, and the next thing I knew, her mouth was on mine. Her lips beckoned mine to open, and I took her with everything I had.

My arms wrapped around her body. My fingers slid over the silk as our tongues met. My hands found her bare back, and I felt her quiver as my skin touched hers. She pushed her chest forward. Her arms coiled around my neck as I pulled her closer to me.

We were hungry and unable to stop devouring each other. I deepened the kiss, my fingers pressing into her flesh. She ran her fingers through my hair, building more tension in my lower body.

I felt her relax as her succubus nature unfolded, streaming through me like white fire and making my head light. I welcomed it all, everything she had to give, including everything she'd struggled to hide. I kissed her face and made my way to her ear, my teeth nipping the lobe. She trembled in my arms, and I instinctively pushed my hips forward, eager to make her feel everything that she was doing to me.

Our lips found each other again, molding perfectly into a kiss that nearly threw me off the edge. I ran my hands up her back and gently scratched my way back down. She moaned and abandoned herself in my arms, her heart echoing into mine.

There was no turning back from here. There was no way of pretending this kiss didn't happen. Something had shifted between us, and it could no longer be ignored. Our bodies reacted to one another like strings plucked in unison.

And I couldn't get enough of her.

29

JOVI

It felt as though it took us forever to regain control of ourselves. Anjani eventually pushed herself back, taking deep breaths as we looked at each other. Our eyes said what our mouths couldn't.

I took her hand and guided her to the bed, on which I lay and took her in my arms. We were both exhausted, as the events of the day finally started to kick in. She fell asleep first, her body perfectly molded against mine. I drifted off slowly, listening to the sound of her breathing. Her hair tickled my nose.

As dawn cast its warm light into the tree, I ran my fingers through those seemingly endless curls, patiently waiting for Anjani to wake up on her own. I didn't have the heart to trouble her dreams. I leaned forward, breathing her scent in. Meadows and sunshine flickered in my mind, along with the image of her dancing across the tall grass. Sunlight made her glow like a diamond.

She'd gotten me hooked without even trying. On the contrary, she'd done her best to keep me at bay. Unfortunately, her best was no match for the mind-blowing chemistry between us. It was as absolute as the sun rising in the east. The effect she had on me was undeniable. All I had left to do was ride that wave and prove myself worthy of her attention.

I knew, deep in my heart, that this was a creature who required someone as strong and fearless as she was. She was barely beginning her life as a succubus, and I wanted to show her that I was someone she could be proud of, someone she'd be thrilled to have near her.

I reached for the pendant in my pocket, pulling it out of its little pouch. I stared at the wolf's head, its fangs clasping the strange diamond, the little flame still flickering inside. The old fae's words echoed in my mind, making me wonder whether I'd already found someone to give this pendant to. She'd spoken of true love, a soulmate who would reveal what the pendant could do.

I lay on my back, Anjani's body warm next to me. She'd fallen asleep in her black silk dress. The fabric glazed her hips and thighs. The pendant dangled on its delicate silver chain, loose between my fingers.

Should I give it to her?

My eyes wandered up and down her side. Despite my usually carefree attitude as far as people and emotions went, I seemed to take Anjani very seriously. I wanted to give her the pendant, but I feared it was too early, as I had yet to fully grasp the weight of everything she meant to me.

Was she my soulmate, or was she a passing challenge, someone who would leave her mark on me and make me stronger? Would she stay with me? And if she did, would she come with me back to The Shade?

I somehow didn't see the latter happening. She was Anjani of the Red Tribe, after all. A silver-blooded Eritopian tasked with one day leading her sisters. I was but a wolf-boy who'd stumbled upon her, unable to walk away at the sight of her in danger. I was a stranger, an outsider who missed his home and old way of life and yet found himself fascinated and even thrilled by this new world.

There was a conflict brewing inside of me. How could I give her such an important gift, a pendant for which one day I'd have to repay an old fae with a favor, when I wasn't even sure whether we'd last?

Would I be the one to stay here? Or would she be the one to be persuaded to follow me?

I decided to hold on to the pendant for a little while longer until I'd figured it all out. I needed to have a better picture of what lay ahead, of what she truly felt for me, beyond the explosive physical attraction. I needed more.

30

SERENA

We landed in the river, the water thankfully deep enough for us not to break our bones on the bottom.

I quickly swam up to the surface.

The stream flowed away from the castle. My survival instincts were strong. My eyes darted around.

I saw Sverik and Hansa swimming ahead. I kept myself afloat, moving my arms for some kind of direction. Draven popped out from beneath, wheezing and spitting out water as he shook his head, regaining his senses.

"Are you okay?" I asked, and he nodded briefly.

We looked up. The black castle towered over us. Water poured out from where we'd jumped. Destroyers had slithered to the edge of the opening. They threw spears and shot arrows, but the projectiles failed to hit us. They flailed as they hit nearby trees and rocks on the river bank.

We weren't out of danger yet. Soon enough, more Destroyers and incubi soldiers would swarm along the river with no intention of capturing us alive.

Draven looked up and stilled, his muscles freezing. His eyes went wide and rolled back in his head.

"Draven!" I called out, but he didn't respond.

I followed his line of sight and saw a dark figure atop a terrace a few levels below where we'd jumped. I used my True Sight to get a better look, and my body instantly stiffened. Horror coursed through my veins like thick blocks of ice. Azazel stood there, massive and grinning, his eyes fixed on Draven's.

I recognized the serpent medallion that Aida had told us about, gold with ruby eyes, moving endlessly on the chain. I saw Azazel's lips move, as Draven broke into a seizure, sinking into the water.

"Serena! Draven! What's happening? We need to move!" Hansa shouted after us, several yards up the river.

"Something's happening! Azazel's doing something to him!" I yelped.

I grabbed Draven and pulled him above the water, wrapping my arms around his chest from behind. He was heavy, and I didn't know how long I'd be able to keep him afloat. My own body caved under the pressure.

"Draven, please!" I begged him, my eyes stinging with tears, as he trembled against me, choking.

I had to do something. I was losing him. I syphoned as much energy as I could from him, his golden warmth filling me, sating my inner sentry. I felt a ribbon of deep red pain slither into my chest. He was in so much pain and unable to control himself.

I channeled everything inside of me into a barrier. I let the power build in me and thrust it all out with a roar, throwing the pulse outward with all the force I could muster.

I switched on my True Sight again and watched as the barrier hit Azazel with enough strength to knock him off balance.

My whole body trembled from the insane amount of energy I'd just expelled, combined with the sheer terror of confronting the biggest threat to our lives. My mind went blank for a second, shocked at how I'd managed to find the strength to respond to his attack on Draven.

Azazel shook his head, blinking as he lost visual contact with Draven. I felt myself capable of doing even more if he tried to hurt Draven or anyone close to me again. I blamed my sudden jolt of courage on the adrenaline, which was beginning to wear off, leaving me in the river with a chilled spine.

I felt Draven relax in my arms, and I shook him a couple of times, enough for him to regain consciousness. We had to hurry —before Azazel tried to take hold of him again.

Draven looked at me, his body suddenly filled with tension as he pushed me forward up the river.

"I'm okay. Swim!" he shouted after me.

I followed Hansa and Sverik along the stream. Draven followed closely behind me. Fate was on our side, as the river flowed fast and heavy, tumbling into a thick patch of willows.

More barked orders emerged from the castle we'd left behind.

They'd soon be on our tails, but we moved with the water and disappeared beneath the trees, thankful for the cover.

I sought shelter beneath the Daughter's magnolia tree. I wanted peace and quiet, to feel close to nature, as I prepared to dig into my Oracle abilities. I closed my eyes and decided to try Draven's suggestion to pinpoint a specific topic, but I wasn't sure what to think of. I figured I'd try to relax into it…

As I slipped into my vision, my mind wandered to Marchosi, Azazel's newest disciple. Aida had told me about his struggle, his reluctance to join the dark side, so I wanted to see where his seemingly futile resistance would lead.

I was taken into what seemed like a near future, a possible outcome of our actions so far. I was inside Azazel's castle, its walls glistening black with a massive overhead chandelier burning green. Wails and moans echoed through the chamber as three Destroyers stood around a wooden table with a map sprawled on top.

Two of them were focused on the map, while the third fell

over with a thump, his thick black tail flailing. He pulled himself back up, his hands gripping the table as he broke into a sweat. His eyes were yellow, flickering black as scales emerged from beneath his skin, breaking it and drawing blood.

They spread up his arms and back, making him groan from the pain.

"Give into it, Marchosi," one of the two Destroyers mumbled, visibly bored with the sight of Marchosi in agony.

"Easy for you to say, Goren," he replied, gritting his teeth. "It was so easy for you to abandon yourself and become this abomination!"

Goren threw his head backward with a malicious cackle.

"The more you fight it, the more it hurts," the other Destroyer said, leaning on his forearms over the map. "Believe me, I tried. We all succumb to it, sooner or later."

"I can't," Marchosi sobbed, palms covering his face. "I can't… This isn't who I am… This isn't who I'm meant to become, Patrik. If I let it take over, there will be no turning back."

Patrik shook his head, sadness in his eyes.

"You don't understand, Marchosi," he said. "He's already won. The moment you started changing, he won. There's no way back. No way to fix it. His spells are permanent, the damage impossible to fix."

"Give it a rest, you crybabies!" Goren smirked. "Let's get back to work. Azazel has assigned us new territories on the west coast. I've got another raid to undertake tonight, and you're wasting my time with your incessant weeping. Just let it go already, and the pain will stop!"

Marchosi gasped, collapsing once more. I noticed Patrik's expression, a mixture of sadness and grief. He didn't seem to want to be there either, making me think that Azazel's effect on his Destroyers ran deeper than we'd originally thought.

IN A SECOND VISION, the world seemed different and still. The sky was red, a massive sun setting in the west, heatwaves rising above the horizon. Black clouds gathered above a citadel, an enormous construction made entirely out of obsidian. Its smooth, polished surface reflected the sunset.

I seemed to be on another planet. I heard roars and swords clashing below. I looked down to find a war unravelling at the base of the citadel, thousands of incubi and Destroyers fighting against a small army of creatures scattered around the black walls. There were no jungles here, just miles and miles of barren red and black stone.

I caught a glimpse of Hansa and Anjani on horseback, leading a charge against one of the incubi's flanks. Different species had joined the fight, including Lamias and creatures I'd never seen before, strangely beautiful but vicious. Dearghs had made it as well, ignited and casting massive fireballs that swallowed the Destroyers whole.

My heart leapt as I saw the power in a handful of our allies decimating Azazel's armies. Destroyers fell, one by one. There was hope.

It all came to a halt as a bright pink flash burst at the top of the citadel, splitting the top in half and spreading outward like a nuclear bomb, obliterating everything in its path. It swallowed everything with a horrifying, spine-chilling bang. Fire and brimstone rained from above.

Smoke, ash, and rubble poured over the land.

The fighting stopped.

They all looked up, as the entire citadel was engulfed in the same pink light. The ground shook beneath, and the structure crumbled as it caved in. It was all coming down, falling over the dry land, rumbling like summertime thunder.

I heard Anjani scream Jovi's name, and I saw her kick her horse to a gallop toward the source of the explosion. She was swiftly pulled off the stallion by her sister, who dragged her away from the unfolding disaster.

Anjani kept kicking and screaming Jovi's name, her voice cutting through the sky.

The realization crashed into me, tearing me apart. Jovi had been up there.

The potential future of Jovi dying from a Destroyer's spear had been changed. It now seemed like Jovi would die in a massive explosion. We'd managed to change something in the outcome of things.

But there would be war, and the result would be the same. It would all splinter. Jovi would still die.

I OPENED MY EYES, feeling myself wrapped in warmth. I

looked around and realized I was in a familiar space. One of the rooms in the mansion. The same large windows through which moonlight poured. Bijarki's body naked next to mine.

I couldn't move, but my heart froze. I'd seen this before in a dream. It all unraveled like a carefully crafted nightmare, except that it felt more real than the previous time I'd seen it. I heard Bijarki's voice whispering sweet words in my ear. His fingers moved lazily up and down my skin. His lips caressed my neck. I would've melted. But I knew what was coming next.

Without any delay, the windows crashed. Destroyers flooded the room, hissing and cackling, dragging me away from Bijarki. I screamed, but I couldn't hear myself anymore, as if the movie had gone silent. I tried to fight them off, my hands shooting out flames. But I was knocked out.

That outcome had not changed. They would come.

32

JOVI

We rode back to the mansion, joined by Tamara and Eva, each carried gracefully by a gorgeous white steed with gold plated reins. They certainly knew how to style up their royalty. I had to give them credit.

The sun was up as we took one of the side roads around the Sarang Marketplace. Our crossbows were loaded and ready to shoot. Anjani and I exchanged glances. She was trying not to smile but couldn't help it each time our eyes met.

I had a hard time containing my grin, constantly replaying the memory of her melting in my arms the previous night. The sound she made when I kissed her echoed in my head, stirring me to the point where I had to shift in my saddle, prompting my horse to neigh with irritation. I'd been doing that a lot, it seemed.

We heard movement through the trees around us as we went deeper into the woods. I looked around, my eyes scanning the shadows and spotting silhouettes running along, keeping up with our horses.

"We're not alone," I said, my fingers clutching the crossbow.

"Of course, we aren't," Tamara replied. "My guards are here, keeping their distance, protecting us from any hostility. These woods are filled with danger."

"That wasn't the deal," Anjani retorted.

"There's nothing wrong with protection, is there?" Tamara's smile seemed forced, her voice pure ice.

"That. Wasn't. The. Deal." My succubus didn't let go, boldly pronouncing each word. "We agreed to bring you and your daughter to the mansion and no one else. We're protected there, unseen by anyone. We are trusting you and you alone with that location. They have to stay back. Nobody else can know where the Druid and the Oracles are. I'm sure you understand the imperative here."

I wanted to jump off my horse, take Anjani into my arms, and smother her with kisses. Her authoritarian demeanor sparked a fire inside me. Who would have known I'd be so turned on by a succubus with that much spunk?

A moment passed in awkward silence, as I willed myself back to a cooler state. I took deep breaths while smothering a smirk of satisfaction at the sight of Tamara's irritated expression.

"She has a point," Bijarki finally replied. "Only you and Eva can know where the mansion is. It's what you agreed to."

Tamara shook her head, pursing her lips, then snapped her fingers.

I felt the hidden Lamias' sudden departure. The silhouettes

moved back, and the woods went almost silent. Once again, we were on our own, trotting through the jungle with our eyes peeled open, listening for any strange sound.

A while later, Tamara broke the quietude, her gaze fixed on me.

"You know, I have never seen a wolf-boy before," she smiled. "Are there many like you where you come from, Jovi?"

I shrugged, noncommittally. I didn't want to talk about my world with this woman.

"You're quite a joy to look at," Tamara said. "Not that you'd make a good mate, given our species' difficulty to procreate, but I would certainly take you for a spin. You're far too attractive to waste yourself on an inexperienced succubus."

Anjani's eyes grew wide, watching Tamara in disbelief.

I was stunned.

Bijarki and Eva tried hard to contain their smirks.

"Excuse me?" I managed to ask, feeling strangely insulted.

I could only imagine what Anjani was going through and the amount of strength it took for her not to rip Tamara's throat out right then and there.

"I'm just saying, and don't take this the wrong way," Tamara kept a friendly tone, "you are far too young and green to be with such a fierce wolf, darling. You can barely control your succubus nature, and, by the looks of you, you've barely got a couple of centuries in this world. You're simply too inexperienced to handle him, whereas I or Eva, on the other hand, would know exactly how to make Jovi tick. Over. And. Over. Again."

The tension was rising as Tamara had seen fit to retaliate for

Anjani's earlier statements. She'd spotted her weak point—her age—and had gone straight for the kill. On the one hand, I resented her and was eager to tell her that I wouldn't touch her or her daughter with a ten-foot pole but, at the same time, I couldn't help but applaud internally at how swiftly she'd managed to rattle Anjani.

Tamara was wrong, though. I wasn't all that fierce. I couldn't even turn. But that was not for Tamara to know.

"Perhaps you should mind your own business," Anjani shot back. "Which includes killing and eating innocent incubi and succubi. Let's not forget that. I can assure you that your diet alone cancels any interest a wolf-man like Jovi would ever show toward your species."

The fact that she'd acknowledged me as a wolf-man and not a wolf-boy like Tamara had called me earned Anjani some massive brownie points with me. I instantly made it my mission to take this succubus into my arms the first chance I got and thank her for that.

But, yet again, I was also amused by the exchange, watching it like a heated tennis match. So far, it was one to one between two very strong and intelligent creatures. I waited for round three.

Tamara laughed lightly, an undertone of mockery oozing forth.

"You're still fixated on that, aren't you?" she replied. "Lamias have come a long way from stealing incubi from their mothers' arms to feed. Those were cruel and ancient times. We only resort to eating a little bit of incubus and succubus flesh when we are young and still growing, and our mothers fetch this for us from the recently deceased only. We do not kill them ourselves. It's the same when we are pregnant. Our babies need the nutrients. Otherwise they cannot survive outside the womb. We don't snatch incubi, darling. Those are old folk tales."

Anjani scoffed, kicking her heels enough to give her horse a few yards' advance on our group.

"Besides, succubus flesh is far too stringy for our tastes. We'd rather chew the bark off a tree," Tamara added with a smirk.

And so, the score settled at an unpleasant 1 to 2 in the Lamia's favor. I'd have to do something to lift Anjani's spirits later. My mind tingled with ideas. I looked forward to being alone with her again.

At the same time, I'd completely lost any interest in Lamias. As gorgeous as they were, I just couldn't wrap my head around their diet tendencies. Eating incubus flesh simply didn't sound okay, no matter the context.

I moved forward, bringing my horse closer to Anjani and giving her a gentle sideways glance. She smiled and looked ahead. Despite Tamara's burns, Anjani seemed focused on other, more positive things. Like me.

33

SERENA

We made it out of the river and ran the rest of the distance to Mount Zur on foot. We kept a low profile, sprinting through the jungle and jumping over thick roots, occasionally looking over our shoulders.

We ran fast, as the shouts of Destroyers and their horses neighing was never too far behind. We reached the ridge of Mount Zur in record time, stopping for a minute to catch our breath.

My lungs burned. My hair and clothes still dripped. My whole body hurt, but we weren't done yet. Draven and I looked at each other, our eyes doing the talking. He nodded briefly with a half-smile and looked up at the mountain.

"Come on, we're almost there," he said.

"I'll need a hot bath after all this is over," Sverik said. "I can't live with this much filth on me." He smirked, looking at himself.

His uniform was tattered, wet, dirty, and riddled with smudges of silver blood. A wail pierced through the sky above us as ten Destroyers flew in from behind.

"Run!" Draven shouted.

We climbed up the ridge with surprising strength and speed. The prospect of death energized us. Only one thought crowded our minds: survival. We ran up, jumping from boulder to boulder like mountain goats as the Destroyers descended upon us, shooting their poisonous spears.

We dodged their attacks and finally reached the plateau leading into the volcano. We stumbled to our feet as the monsters came down. The Destroyers jumped off their winged horses, landing with a thud, and slithered through the grass toward us, their swords and sharp fangs out.

I shot another barrier out, enough to push them back a few yards as we ran back toward the limestone wall, where the Dearghs stood still like statues.

"Help us!" I screamed at them as the Destroyers quickly gained on us again.

My barrier had been weak. I was losing energy.

The monsters hissed, lifting their swords as they charged us.

The stone behind us crackled, and, one by one, the Dearghs rose from the mountain, massive and with flames in their eyes. Zur stepped forward, grumbling like an avalanche as he moved in front of us.

One of the Destroyers cursed. They all stilled, their tails twitching and rattling.

"They're still alive," he shouted. "Fall back!"

It was too late for them. The Dearghs, as big and bulky as they were, moved quickly across the tall grass. As they engaged the Destroyers, they lit up from the inside, turning into massive fire creatures, blazing with rage.

There were five Dearghs against ten Destroyers, but judging by the horrified looks on their faces, the stone and fire giants had all the odds in their favor.

Draven pulled me back.

Hansa and Sverik joined us as we watched the fight unfold.

Each Deargh grabbed whichever Destroyer was closest, pulling them by the tails and setting them on fire before they snapped their necks. The Destroyers were big, but the Dearghs were three times bigger.

It was over fast, with just one monster managing to slither away, hissing and cursing as he vanished into the jungle below.

We stood there, our mouths gaping, our eyes wide open, as the lifeless bodies of Destroyers burned. Black smoke rose into the sky. I'd never imagined witnessing such a scene.

The Dearghs were such gentle creatures. I'd had a hard time imagining they'd be capable of such carnage. And yet they stood before us, flames blazing from within, looking down at the handful of monsters they'd so easily vanquished. I wondered why they hadn't stood up sooner. Why had Azazel been allowed to do so much damage in the first place?

"That was surprisingly efficient," Draven quipped, his tone dry.

The Dearghs dimmed their flames, returning to their original form. Zur looked down at us, giving us a gentle smile, his eyes still flickering. Charred Destroyers lay at his giant limestone feet.

"Fire kills everything, young Druid, even snakes."

34

SERENA

We made it to Mount Inon in one piece. We used the swamp witches' spell again and struggled with Sverik as we flowed through the lava. He'd given in to the temptation to open his eyes during the transition.

It took us a while to calm him down after Zur pushed us to the surface and took us to one of the outer chambers of the volcano, where Inon waited with food and water.

A few minutes later, Sverik was down on all fours, heaving and gasping for air as the spell wore off. Sweat beads covered his face. His shimmering skin was paler than usual.

"I'm never doing this again," he groaned. "Next time, just leave me in the cage!"

Hansa smirked as she ate, tearing the meat off the bone and washing it down with cool spring water. She kept an eye on Sverik as he recovered.

Draven and I sat next to each other.

"We told you not to open your eyes," Hansa said dryly.

Inon watched us quietly, his eyes moving from one to the other with childlike interest.

"Yeah, well, that's the one thing my brother and I always had in common. No means yes." Sverik grinned.

A long minute passed before Inon spoke. We were far too hungry and thirsty to fill that time with chatter. I was just grateful to still be alive with Draven by my side. He occasionally leaned into me, giving me a sideways glance that was strangely reassuring. We'd made it this far.

"I've prepared four new horses for you and your friends," Inon said.

"I must admit, I'm surprised by your faith in us, to have four of them ready," Draven replied, smiling. "It means you knew for a fact we'd come back with Sverik."

"Indeed, I have all the faith in the world in the son of Almus and Genevieve," Inon nodded, prompting us all to look up at him in awe.

"You knew my parents?" Draven asked.

"Of course, I did. We all knew your parents. Two of the most noble and most powerful Druids to ever walk this world."

"I thought the Dearghs kept mostly to themselves, hidden in their mountains away from the others," Hansa said with a smirk.

"We do, but we make it our business to know who leads us. This planet once belonged to Draven's mother, after all," Inon replied.

I stilled, realizing what the Deargh had just said—something that Draven hadn't mentioned when he'd told me about

Genevieve. I knew she'd been in charge of one of these planets in Eritopia, but it didn't occur to me that it was precisely the one we'd been brought to.

I couldn't help but wonder what it must have been like with Genevieve ruling over this land. Based on what I knew from Draven, there must have been good times here with peace and progress.

"There is little time to comb through memories, I'm afraid," Inon added, standing up.

"Trouble coming this way?" Hansa asked.

I kept a close eye on Sverik for no particular reason, watching as he ate in silence, his gaze occasionally darting up to the Deargh. I felt sorry for him, for the loss of his brother and the treachery of his father.

"Swarms of green fireflies have been buzzing around the mountain," Inon replied. "You must ride back to the safety of your mansion before Destroyers come looking for you."

Draven stood up, taking a deep breath.

"Azazel has seen me, so it's only a matter of time before he sends out his troops to find me. My existence is a threat to his expansion, and he will stop at nothing to eliminate me sooner rather than later," he said.

Inon took us outside, where we jumped on our horses and bid him farewell. We were to see each other again soon enough. The Dearghs were ready to fight by our side.

"I am sorry," the Deargh said before we took off.

"Sorry about what?" Draven frowned.

"We should have risen sooner. We were comfortable in our

mountains, confident that our brothers dying was Eritopia's will. For that, I am sorry." Inon sighed.

I was touched by his candor and felt a tremendous amount of affection for the gentle stone giant. I smiled at him, and his eyes lit up.

"Better late than never, we say where I come from," I replied.

We rode out, thundering through the dark jungle, eager to return to the mansion.

35

AIDA

I sat on the front steps of the mansion, waiting for either of our groups to return. A couple of days had passed, and I'd woken with a very peculiar feeling that morning, as if something was about to go horribly wrong.

I watched the outer layer of grass before the swamps. Shadows darted through the jungle here and there. My mind wandered, worried about Jovi and Serena. It inadvertently slipped back to Field and our mind-numbing kiss.

Wings flapped above, and I looked up. My heart skipped a beat. Field descended from the sky, bare chested and as handsome as ever. But this time, as opposed to the many other times back in The Shade, his eyes were on me and nothing else. It felt good.

He landed in front of me, wings lowering and something glimmering in his hands. I didn't get a better look as he instantly bent forward and kissed me, jolting my heart into a quick race around the sun. He tasted like heaven, if heaven was a midsummer night with blooming jasmine and night-queen flowers beneath the window.

"Hey, you." He gave me a beaming smile, further demolishing my cool girl defenses.

"Anything out there?" I asked, wondering what he'd seen beyond the shield.

"Destroyers are still flying around, but they're not that close. Besides, we're underneath the protective shield. Even if they pass over the mansion they won't see us."

I nodded, losing myself in his turquoise gaze.

"I also found these little buggers and thought you might like them." He smiled, lifting a glass jar in front of me.

Five green fireflies buzzed around inside the glass receptacle, glimmering like emeralds. They were beautiful, making me wonder what the bedroom would look like with their gentle green light cast inside.

He'd caught them for me, and the thought made me giddy and giggly. I sprang to my feet and hugged him, giving him short kisses on both his cheeks, then his lips, thanking him repeatedly.

"Something tells me I should do this more often," he grinned.

I nodded. "You definitely should!"

He laughed lightly and caught my mouth in a long, gentle kiss, his lips soft against mine, his tongue searching as my temperature spiked. The effect he had on me was undeniably powerful.

But the sound of horses galloping in the distance tore us apart. We looked toward the source. To my relief, we saw Jovi, Bijarki, and Anjani accompanied by two other females on horseback.

My heart seemed to relax, and I could breathe again. A smile drew itself on my face.

"They're back!" I exclaimed.

"I knew they would be. I just can't believe they managed to bring Jovi back as well. I would've lost him somewhere on the way," Field said jokingly, prompting me to poke him with my elbow.

His hand slipped up my back. He laughed lightly.

Their horses trotted through the protective shield. The two females with them looked around, visibly confused, unable to see the mansion. Once they followed Jovi through the spell, however, it all became clear, and their eyebrows lifted with surprise.

I recognized the scales and yellow eyes identifying them as Lamias. Bijarki, Anjani, and my brother had been successful in reaching out to the Lamias. My vision of them being followed by the rogue incubi had kept me on edge for a while, until Field had managed to assure me that they were no match for my wolf-brother, a seasoned soldier, and a succubus warrior. Deep down, I knew he'd been right and was thankful once more to have him close in this world.

Jovi was the first to get off his horse and run straight to me, taking me up in his arms and laughing.

"There he is, my little trouble maker!" I laughed as he spun me around.

"I told you I'd be back!"

"I'm surprised they put up with you for that long." I grinned.

"Trust me, we got very close to dumping him." Anjani joined the joke, as she got off her horse with a playful smile on her face.

I noticed the change. Something had shifted between Jovi and Anjani. There was more there than before they'd left. I had a feeling they'd gotten closer. The looks they exchanged weren't difficult to recognize.

"See?" Field said to me, chuckling. "I told you he'd be trouble."

I shouted after Vita and Phoenix over my shoulder, positive they'd be as happy as I was to see half of our group back with what seemed like good news.

Bijarki stepped forward, his eyes darting around as if looking for someone. His expression brightened as he saw Vita emerge from the house to join us. He brought the two Lamias forward, introducing them to us.

"This is Tamara, Mother of the Lamias, and her Daughter, Eva," Bijarki said.

I looked at the two creatures, both incredibly beautiful, clearly related yet quite different. Unlike her mother's platinum hair and yellow-green scales, Eva's rich locks flowed black on her shoulders, her skin pale and scales black. They both wore soft silk dresses in shades of white and pale green, complemented by emerald collars and bracelets.

"They've come to speak with Draven regarding our alliance against Azazel," Bijarki added as we all gawked at them.

"It's an honor to meet you. I'm Aida," I said with a polite smile. "This is Vita and Field. Phoenix and the Daughter should be with us soon."

Tamara looked us over, measuring Vita and me from head to toe before she gave us a warm and charming smile. There was something about snakes that made me wary, even when they were nice and smiling. I had a hard time trusting anything that slithered, and my previous experiences with their distant Destroyer relatives had not exactly helped.

"You must be the Oracles," Tamara guessed with surprising accuracy. "And you, Field, you're just as strange as Jovi, yet different. What are you?"

Field smirked, running a hand through his long black hair. I didn't like Tamara much. She was far too confident in her own ability to seduce any living creature, and watching her set her sights on Field with her soft looks and sweet voice made me growl on the inside.

"It's kind of a long story," Field replied, giving me a sideways glance.

"Where's Draven?" Bijarki intervened, cutting the awkward exchange short, to my relief.

"He's not here yet," I replied.

But before any of us could say anything else the sound of thundering hooves and neighing horses made us look out toward the bridge again. Hope blossomed in my heart that I would get to see Serena, Draven, and Hansa next.

36

SERENA

We'd made it back with no major incident through the jungle. A few mindless shape-shifters had been brazen enough to try and jump at us, but Hansa swatted them away with a couple of poisoned arrows, leaving them writhing in the pain of death.

We darted through the woods, beckoning our horses to go as fast as they could, until we reached the protective shield.

"We're here," I gasped, as we passed through the barrier.

I nearly collapsed from my horse by the time we reached the front steps.

Vita, Aida, and Field waited with Jovi, Anjani, Bijarki, and two gorgeous creatures, briefly introduced as Tamara, Mother of the Lamias, and Eva, her daughter.

I sprang from the saddle right into Vita and Aida's arms, overwhelmed with joy and relief to be with them again.

"You made it back in one piece, you devil!" Aida grinned, kissing my cheeks.

Draven stepped forward, followed by Hansa, Bijarki, and Sverik. Aida's eyes glimmered with recognition at the sight of Kristos's brother.

"It's good to see you alive." She smiled at him.

"You know me?" Sverik asked, confused.

"I saw you in my visions," she replied.

"Ah, so you're one of the Oracles then!" He beamed and shook her hand.

We introduced them to each other, and I shouted after Phoenix and the Daughter, eager to hug him. The intensity of everything I'd been through was suddenly starting to weigh on me. The adrenaline still pumped through me.

We caught up with one another briefly.

Tamara and Eva watched quietly with fascination. We were the foreign ones in their eyes, creatures they'd never seen before.

Phoenix emerged from the mansion, followed by the Daughter. He came down the stairs, and I jumped in his arms. He laughed and held me tight, and the world seemed right again.

"I told you I wasn't going to accept any outcome other than you coming back to me in one piece," he whispered in my ear. "The universe listened."

The Daughter then jumped between us and hugged me, much to my surprise. I looked at Phoenix, and he shrugged, laughing lightly.

"I'm glad you're back," she said. "Phoenix has been worried sick about you!"

I loved seeing our group back together with a handful of new allies added to the mix. We'd had a successful mission, which gave me more hope. On top of that, after I'd launched that barrier at Azazel, I'd tapped into a previously undiscovered resource of courage. The initial gloom was slowly dissipating.

Draven cleared his throat and bowed before Tamara and Eva. Phoenix's eyes grew large at the sight of them, giving me the impression that he knew them.

"It's an honor to have you here, Tamara," Draven said. "I was hoping we'd get to discuss the terms of an alliance against Azazel."

"I've heard," Tamara replied politely. "Bijarki told me you're in possession of three Oracles and the support of the Dearghs and that you are hoping to rally all remaining species against Azazel. That is a most noble but dangerous pursuit."

Phoenix kept watching the exchange, frowning. I nudged him and gave him a questioning sideways glance, but he ignored me and kept watching Tamara. I could tell something was off, but Tamara's responses quickly recaptured my attention.

"Does that mean you'll join us?" Draven asked.

"It's why I came to see you myself. Your plan shows promise, and the Lamias would be willing to fight for you. Under one condition," she replied with an icy smile.

I had a feeling the conversation was about to turn bad fast. None of us said anything, waiting for Draven to respond.

"Tell me what the condition is, then, before I agree to anything," he said.

She pushed Eva forward. The younger Lamia looked at us

awkwardly. She hadn't said anything yet, and I wondered what her role was in this alliance. Her expression didn't give anything away either. She simply eyed Draven whenever she got a chance.

"You must mate with my daughter, Druid, and help her conceive a child," came Tamara's reply.

37

SERENA

"Only then will you have our full support against Azazel," Tamara added.

My jaw dropped, and I couldn't hold back an outraged gasp. My expression was mirrored by everyone else in the group, with the exception of Tamara and Eva, who seemed to have thought this through already. In fact, Eva seemed quite pleased with the idea, judging by her self-confident smirk.

Draven looked baffled, his eyes flickering black as he blinked rapidly, trying to digest the Lamias' request.

"You've got to be joking," he replied, his voice dim.

"Draven, I know her," Phoenix intervened with an alarmed expression. "I know Tamara. I've seen her in one of my visions of the past."

It then dawned on me why Phoenix had been so on edge over the last couple of minutes.

"You know me, Oracle?" Tamara looked at him curiously.

"Yes. You were a servant of Genevieve. You studied under Draven's mother," Phoenix replied. "You and Azazel got together, but you were revealed as a Lamia and ran off, pregnant with his child."

Silence fell between us, as all the pieces fit together neatly in a wider puzzle. My stomach churned. My heart sank. And Tamara smiled, further rattling my senses.

"You're Azazel's daughter," Draven murmured, looking at Eva.

The young Lamia seemed ashamed of that association but nodded in response, then proceeded to measure him from head to toe, as if sizing up a good steak. My blood simmered.

"And you're Genevieve's son," Tamara replied, a warm twinkle in her yellow eyes.

"Indeed I am. I'm just wondering how you managed to deceive her, pretending to be a Druid," he shot back, his face hardened.

"I never lied to Genevieve. She knew exactly what I was and accepted me. She kept my secret and helped me learn the way of the Druids. She understood that Lamias had the same abilities, the same potential as the Druids, and that our taste for incubus flesh should not have locked us out of the mystical circle. We deserve knowledge, and she agreed to teach me. Genevieve was the best thing to ever happen to me, Draven. Azazel was the worst, but then I had Eva, and my life gained new meaning. If it hadn't been for your mother, my child and I would have never survived in this world."

"Azazel looked for you," Phoenix said, his gaze fixed on

Tamara. "He tormented an Oracle to tell him where you were. He never found you, did he?"

Tamara shook her head, her brow furrowing.

"That was Raelle you saw. She was a good Oracle, and an even better being," she sighed. "I tried to get her out of there as soon as Azazel brought her in, but I was no match for him and his Destroyers. He beat me to a pulp, not knowing I was with child at the time. I nearly lost Eva, which was why I ran away. I'd witnessed his descent into madness, and I could no longer be a part of it. I never forgave him, and I never will."

"Why should we trust you?" Phoenix insisted, gritting his teeth.

"My kind is on the brink of extinction thanks to that monster!" Tamara burst out, overcome by anger. "I want to see him burn! We've been reduced to negotiating Draven's seed for my daughter just to help our species. Can you not see that?"

A moment passed before either of us could say anything. The gravity of the situation began to sink in. I looked at Draven, whose gaze moved between Tamara and Eva.

"You want me to give Eva a child," he repeated.

Tamara nodded. "You are the last Druid, Draven. It's you or nothing, as the nineteenth kingdom has fallen recently. You must help us produce offspring. Perhaps she will live long enough to find another way for our species to continue. Otherwise we'll all eventually die out."

"And you think me giving her a child will solve the problem?" he asked.

I was suddenly taken aback by the fact that he was actually

considering the option. My head spun. But I fought with myself for control, keeping my cool in front of a fragile alliance. I had to think of the bigger picture, no matter how furious it made me. A whole galaxy was at stake.

"It will delay the inevitable, at least," she replied.

Draven looked at me, his eyes flickering black. I stepped forward, closing the distance between us. No matter what happened, I had to support him. This wasn't about us anymore, and Tamara didn't seem like the kind of creature to soften at the sight of us suffering over this. She had the survival of her species in mind.

"Draven," I breathed.

"It's... It's not what I had in mind when she said she had a condition," he said hoarsely.

"I know, and I hate it. I'd love nothing more than to punch her in the face right now."

"I can hear you," Tamara smirked.

"I'm well aware, so listen carefully as we decide your fate, then!" I shot back with a hiss, prompting her to take a step back.

"What are you thinking?" Draven whispered.

My heart twisted at the sight of his tortured expression, and I closed my eyes, squeezing them tightly shut and breathing deeply.

"Neither of us is comfortable with this, obviously," I managed, almost whispering, "but I...I understand what's at stake here. If we could get the Lamias' support, then..."

I could barely finish my sentence. It hurt so bad just saying all of this. At the same time, as agonizing as this was, I couldn't let selfishness dictate the fate of billions of Eritopians. There was a universe far greater than myself out there. And for all we knew, the Lamias' alliance could make or break its future.

I inhaled. "Her Lamias and inherent magic would help level the playing field against Azazel," I said. "And that's what we need the most right now."

Draven looked at me, his gaze heart-wrenching as he gently brushed my cheek with his fingers.

"We need to talk about it," he managed, then looked at Tamara, his jaw clenched. "We can discuss this later."

Tamara nodded, then glanced at Eva, who rolled her eyes at me. The young Lamia continued giving Draven the same raunchy look.

I hated her.

"Well, this is awkward." Aida watched us with eyes wide and lips stretched into a thin line.

Draven sighed, then stilled, his eyes fixed on Aida's hand.

"What are those?" His voice was suddenly low and sharp.

"What, these? Fireflies." She lifted the jar she'd been holding with five green fireflies buzzing around in it.

My blood froze, and my breath hitched as a realization crashed into me. Those weren't regular fireflies. Draven snatched the jar from Aida's hand and muttered something under his breath before he smashed it into the ground. It burst into red flames, destroying the little bugs.

"What did you do that for?" Aida was shocked, as was Field. Both looked down at the broken jar.

"Where'd you get it from?" Draven asked through his teeth.

I felt the ground move beneath me. A million possibilities ran through my head, including the one in which Azazel had seen us through his fireflies.

"Th-they were flying around the mansion," Field said, his voice shaky.

"You shouldn't have brought them in," Draven snapped, running his fingers through his hair, then looking at me.

"I don't understand. What's going on here?" Aida asked, obviously confused.

She couldn't have known and neither could Field. They had no idea.

We were in so much trouble.

38

FIELD

"These green fireflies are part of Azazel's spying spell! He sees and hears everything through them. They fly wherever he sends them," Serena explained briefly, her face pale.

My stomach dropped, as I realized the gravity of my mistake. I had unknowingly brought Azazel's spies beyond the protective shield, revealing not just our location but our identities. My intentions had been pure, but the outcome was devastating.

My knees weakened. I crouched and groaned and hid my face in my palms. Shame and anger crashed into me, and I broke into a sweat. I'd just exposed my family, the people I loved most in the world, to Azazel.

"I'm so sorry," I managed. "I only wanted to show them to Aida. I thought they looked cool. I'm sorry. I was so stupid."

Aida and Serena crouched in front of me, and I felt Aida's hand on my shoulder. It seemed to relieve some of the pressure that had started building up in my muscles. I had never felt so bad. I'd become a liability when I was supposed to be protecting them.

"You couldn't have known, Field," Serena said to me, her voice soft. "I didn't know until Draven told me."

"Besides, they did look pretty cool," Aida mumbled.

"The only way Azazel's spell is able to get through the protective shield is if you were carrying the fireflies. You had some sort of contact," Draven explained. "It's like walking through the shield holding Azazel's hand."

I groaned again. The comparison knocked the air out of my lungs. The gravity of my mistake continued to sink in like an anvil in water.

"You're not helping!" Aida snapped at him.

"He's right. I've basically brought Azazel in here," I said.

"Don't beat yourself up," Draven said to me. "The worst part is that Azazel now knows our location, but the Oracles are beneath the protective shield, so he can't feel them. Technically speaking, he shouldn't know they're here, unless the Nevertide Oracle told him."

"But the fireflies were in here. They've seen us all," Serena frowned.

"True, but our Oracles don't look like regular Oracles, and, besides, the spies were in a jar. I don't think any sounds went through. I'm thinking that even if Azazel has seen our faces, he wouldn't be able to spot an Oracle without having heard something specific," Draven replied.

A moment passed before he spoke again.

"We should expect company soon, nonetheless."

"Draven, I've seen swarms of these green fireflies a couple of miles north of here," I said. "That's where I snatched the ones I brought in. They sort of tagged along."

He nodded slowly, then looked up. His eyes widened, prompting me to follow his gaze.

Soon enough, we were all staring at the same thing. A thick swarm of green fireflies hovered above the mansion, trying and failing to pass through the protective shield, which glimmered outward in ripples each time a little spy touched the Daughters' spell.

The Druid had been right. The fireflies I'd brought in had come with me. The swarm, on the other hand, could not get through the shield.

"They found us," Draven breathed.

39

VITA

My heart froze in my chest, my stomach reducing itself to the size of a walnut. Cold shivers ran down my spine. I stared up, watching thousands of green fireflies buzzing around, trying to get past the protective shield.

Bijarki stood next to me, the back of his hand brushing against mine. Our eyes met, and he seemed to understand the fear I exuded. Azazel's spies had found our safe space.

"I suggest going inside, away from this sight, to think things through. The Destroyers can't get past the protective shield and can't see inside either, so at least that gives us an advantage, still," Draven said.

I then remembered my vision of Bijarki and me in the upstairs bedroom and Destroyers crashing through the window. I'd kept it to myself at first, having considered it a bad dream, but the vision had been clear the second time around. The monsters were going to invade the mansion. It was a fact.

"I need to tell you something," I said to Draven, my voice trembling. "I had a few visions while you were away, and one, in particular, will be of concern."

He looked at me, his eyebrows drawn into a frown.

"I was in the upstairs bedroom, and Destroyers crashed through the windows, capturing me and dragging me away," I omitted the part about Bijarki in bed with me. I felt like I could keep that to myself for a little while longer.

"Destroyers will come in here at some point," I added. "I don't know how or when exactly, but they will."

Everyone looked at me in disbelief. I hated giving such horrible news, especially when our safety, our lives, were directly affected. But I had no other choice now. The only thing I could do was find a way to stop that from happening. If I could at least find out how the Destroyers would manage to get past the protective shield, we'd be able to take action and prevent it.

Hissing echoed through the sky from beyond the jungle.

We froze, our eyes up, watching as dozens of Destroyers emerged from all directions, riding their black-winged horses. They started circling the mansion, slowly descending. One tried to get through the protective shield, but the spell flickered and threw the monster back. It cursed and tried again but failed.

I gasped, my whole body trembling. Bijarki's arm reached around me, pulling me closer, enough to give me a small sense of security and prevent me from spiraling into a full-blown panic attack. Our mansion was surrounded by Destroyers.

Our worst nightmare was coming true.

We were all petrified, but none of us could speak.

Draven's eyes flickered black as he watched the Destroyers fly around.

The Mother of Lamias hissed, her tongue flitting in the air as she held her daughter's hand.

"You've exposed us to death, Druid! This wasn't part of the deal!" she snapped.

"There is no point in arguing now, Tamara." Draven was quick to politely dismiss her. "It's not like you've been great at negotiating an alliance anyway, so let's save our critique and alliance conditions for later. For now let's focus on the dozens of Destroyers circling the mansion."

My blood ran cold. Sweat beads dripped from my temples—I could feel them slipping down my skin. Bijarki's grip on me tightened, his eyes scanning the Destroyers' movements. We were all out of words.

"What do we do?" Serena asked, her voice faded.

"There isn't much we can do right now," Draven replied. "They can't see us, and they can't get in."

One by one, the winged horses landed around the mansion. The monsters slithered off and began circling the protective shield, occasionally slashing at it with their swords and generating shimmering ripples. They were stuck on the outside, indeed, but they had already figured out the size of our perimeter.

A Destroyer moved along the shield, looking in but unable to see anything. The tip of his sword scratched at the spell, leaving a trail of glimmering sparks behind. He was massive and stacked with muscles. His neck was thick, and his eyes were cold, while his smirk seemed to accurately describe how excited he was at the prospect of getting in and killing everyone in sight.

"I know him," Aida gasped. "Oh no, I've seen him."

Field took her in his arms and held her as we all watched the Destroyer slither along the shield.

"That's Goren, one of Azazel's top lieutenants," she added. "He's the one who led the charge against Hansa and Anjani's tribe!"

I saw the succubi's faces change, from frowns to smooth stillness, much like the tiger that has just identified its prey. Their skin glowed, and their emerald eyes darkened as they followed Goren around.

The Destroyer looked at no one in particular when he revealed his sharp fangs in a blood-curling grin. His forked tongue slipped out to get a whiff of whatever hid beneath the protective shield.

"You have nowhere to go, little mice!" he cackled.

40

SERENA

A few minutes passed as we all stood there, motionless, watching green fireflies swarm above and Destroyers circle the protective shield, unable to breach it. A thousand scenarios went through my head. I could think of multiple ways in which this could get worse and no ways to get us out of here. We were stuck.

"What do we do, Draven? What options do we have?" I asked, my voice trembling.

"They know there's something here, but they obviously don't know who's inside," Draven muttered, his eyes fixed on Goren, who kept sneering at us, though unable to see us.

"We're trapped in here," Hansa replied. "My passage stone went missing in the attack, but no one can use it unless they know exactly where Draven's stone is. I don't see anyone on their side willing to risk wandering from my stone to who knows where. The same goes for us, if we want to use Draven's stone to leave. Without knowing exactly where we're going, we're risking a full submersion in lava or water or who knows what else. We could pop out in the middle of a swarm of Destroyers. There's only so much we can avoid through what spells we have."

Sverik was paler than the rest of us, downright livid. His greenish eyes were wide, and his lips were nearly purple. His gaze was fixated on Goren. I could see the terror in him, as he unraveled and dropped to his knees, his breath erratic.

"This can't be happening," he gasped. "Out of one cage and stuck in another. This isn't fair."

Bijarki removed himself from Vita's side for a moment, crouched next to Sverik, and patted him gently on the back in an attempt to soothe him in the midst of his full-blown panic attack. "Tell you what, Sverik, look on the bright side. At least the food's much better here," he said.

As my mind raced through possible solutions, I found myself turning to the Daughter, who'd glued herself to Phoenix, her arms around his waist as her violet eyes watched the monsters outside. Fear was imprinted on her every feature, making me doubt whether she'd be able to help. She'd yet to recover her primordial knowledge, all that untapped power lying dormant and potentially deadly to all.

"Do you think you can help us?" I asked her gently.

She looked at me, her lips pursed and tears glazing her eyes. She shook her head. Her gaze darted from the Destroyers to me.

"I don't know. I don't think so." She sighed. "I'm not sure."

"Our predicament is pretty obvious." Draven's voice made me turn my head. "We're stuck here beneath the protective shield. If we go outside, we will most likely die. However, the

Destroyers can't get in. Our only chance of getting out is taking a gamble with the passage stone."

"Go wherever it takes us?" Bijarki frowned.

"I don't see any other choice, my friend. We need to reach out for help and start rallying the troops. We can't do anything from here."

"There's a remote incubi outpost on the western coast, five hundred miles from Mount Agrith," Sverik said, standing up. "They've yet to swear fealty to Azazel. They don't want to, either. If they know I'm alive, if I get a chance to speak to them, I can earn their support, and they can help spread the word and rally more rogues."

I looked at Draven, and his sideways glance told me what he was going to say before he said it.

"We'll have to try the passage stone, then."

Our options were limited, most ending in potential, if not certain death. The passage stone had a slightly higher probability of success. But, as Hansa said, there weren't enough spells in our arsenal to protect us from everything that could await us on the other side.

None of us knew what we'd be walking into and whether we'd survive. But we had to try. Billions of lives depended on it.

I sucked in a deep breath, closing my eyes and thinking of The Shade. Its moonlit beaches and swaying redwoods. Its regal mountains and glistening lake. The vision of home helped calm my racing mind—a calm I desperately needed. Now, more than ever, I had to stay strong.

I had to do my Novak lineage proud.

READY FOR THE NEXT PART OF THE NOVAK CLAN'S STORY?

Dear Shaddict,

I hope you enjoyed this latest adventure as much as I enjoyed writing it!

The next book, *ASOV 47: A Passage of Threats*, releases **July 30th, 2017.**

Visit **www.bellaforrest.net** for details.

I'll see you there.

Love,

Bella xxx

P.S. Join my VIP email list and I'll send you a personal reminder as soon as I have a new book out. Visit here to sign up: **www.forrestbooks.com**

(Your email will be kept 100% private and you can unsubscribe at any time.)

P.P.S. Follow The Shade on Instagram

and check out some of the beautiful graphics: @ashadeofvampire

You can also come say hi on Facebook: www.facebook.com/AShadeOfVampire

And Twitter: @ashadeofvampire

NOVAK FAMILY TREE

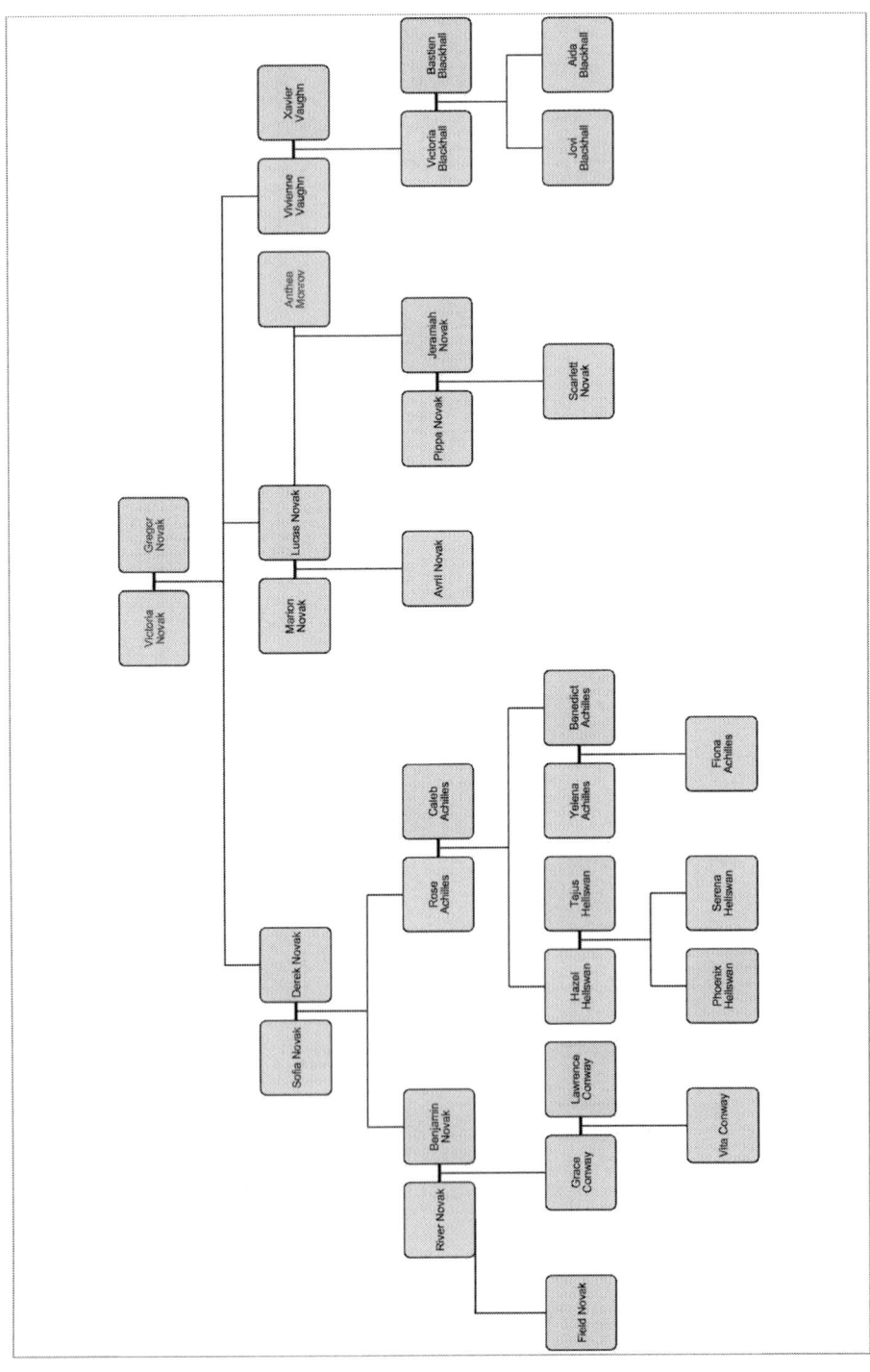

32235085R00194

Made in the USA
Middletown, DE
04 January 2019